D0034825

"Delightfully voice-y and atmospheric,
The Stars of Whistling Ridge is a gentle and magical story
about family and the true meaning of home."
—JASMINE WARGA,
Newbery Honor–winning author of *Other Words for Home*

Praise for BEGINNERS WELCOME

"As delicate and powerful as a sonata, Annie Lee's story
of music, magic, loss, and love should not be missed!"
—JESSICA DAY GEORGE,
New York Times bestselling author of *Tuesdays at the Castle*

"Baldwin's prose challenges [kids] to be the bravest and wisest
versions of themselves."—*School Library Journal* (starred review)

Praise for WHERE THE WATERMELONS GROW

An Indies Introduce Title • An Indie Next List Selection

"Della's story is a reminder that even under the toughest rinds
of troubles, we can find the cool, sustaining sweetness of friendship."
—KIRBY LARSON,
author of the Newbery Honor Book *Hattie Big Sky*

"This heartfelt story will stay with readers. A top choice."
—*School Library Journal* (starred review)

"Heartbreaking, yet heartening."—ALA *Booklist* (starred review)

"Hints of sweet magical realism touch *Where the
Watermelons Grow*, balancing this exquisite novel's
bittersweet authenticity."—Shelf Awareness (starred review)

"In her debut novel, Baldwin presents a realistic portrayal of life
with a mentally ill parent."—*Publishers Weekly* (starred review)

Also by Cindy Baldwin

Where the Watermelons Grow
Beginners Welcome

Baldwin, Cindy, author.
Stars of Whistling Ridge

2021
33305251373803
sa   07/01/21

the Stars of Whistling Ridge

Cindy Baldwin

Quill Tree Books
An Imprint of HarperCollinsPublishers

Quill Tree Books is an imprint of HarperCollins Publishers.

The Stars of Whistling Ridge
Copyright © 2021 by Cindy Baldwin
All rights reserved. Printed in the United States of America. No part of this
book may be used or reproduced in any manner whatsoever without written
permission except in the case of brief quotations embodied in critical articles
and reviews. For information address HarperCollins Children's Books,
a division of HarperCollins Publishers, 195 Broadway, New York, NY 10007.
www.harpercollinschildrens.com

ISBN 978-0-06-300641-6

Typography by Erin Fitzsimmons
21 22 23 24 25   PC/LSCH   10 9 8 7 6 5 4 3 2 1
❖
First Edition

For Mahon,
who will always be my forever home

1.

In stories, the number three is important.

Three princesses.

Three woodcutter's sons.

Three tasks.

My story is the same, I guess.

Three sisters.

Three fallen stars.

And three disasters.

Mama always says that disasters are like blessings—both of them come in threes. They follow on each other's heels, the way starlight follows moonrise, so that you can't untangle them even if you tried.

This is the story of how I proved her right.

* * *

Everywhere we travel, word about the wishes gets around. You'd think that for a family who lives on the road 100 percent of the time we'd have to advertise, but somehow we just show up to a town, park our Winnebago—we call her Martha—and by that night we've already had at least one knock on the door.

They're all different, the wish-seekers. Sometimes it will be a young mother with tired eyes. Others, a granddaddy with a cane and a tightness around the mouth. Every now and then it'll be a teenager, shifting from one foot to the other on the RV front step like his shoes are full of fire ants.

But they all want the same things:

Happiness. Peace. Resolution. And while Mama never barters a wish without first cautioning about how wishes have limits, and rules, and don't always work out the way you expect them to, the wish-seekers always leave with a lighter step, like the world is finally turning their way. Sometimes we see them again; sometimes we don't. Sometimes their wishes work out for the best; sometimes they don't.

But no matter where we go, they find us.

The evening we pulled up in Silverwood, Oklahoma, the visit came from a grandmotherly lady with short blond hair and a way of holding herself that made me think of the Queen of England. She wore a navy skirt and blazer without a speck of dust on them—the kind of outfit you could only get away with if you had a regular house with a regular closet, a laundry room, and a full-size ironing board.

We'd been wandering our way north from where we'd been staying in the Louisiana bayou country, where Mama had spent a whole week trying to calm a wellspring of swamp magic that was pouring enchantment into the water and creating some *very* unusual alligators. When we'd packed up our things and gotten back on the road, Daddy had asked where to go next, and Mama had pointed to a map. Even though none of us had ever heard of Silverwood before, Mama was never wrong about that kind of thing.

And once we reached Silverwood, we had barely plugged Martha's power cord into the campsite's adapter before the stranger showed up.

There was no actual knock on the door this time, on account of the fact that we were all already outside: Daddy and Sophie were down at the lake fishing for our dinner, Elena and I were putting a tablecloth and dishes on the campsite picnic table, and Mama was crouched by the firepit, laying logs with more precision than most people build houses.

The visitor paused at the edge of our campsite, her feet together in their tan pumps, and cleared her throat.

"Hello," said Mama, standing up and wiping char from her hands. Her hair swished and sparkled in the afternoon sunlight.

Mama's hair was long and white. Not stringy and white like an old lady's, and not white like people say when they're describing hair that's so light a blond it's nearly see-through. Mama's was bone-white, star-white, milk-white, shot through with glimmers of silver, so that sometimes when she moved it looked almost like water. Everywhere we went, people stopped to stare at Mama, at her golden-brown skin and white hair and eyes the clear gray-blue of moonlight on snow.

Nobody in the world looked quite like my mama and her sisters, Aunt Agatha and Aunt Ruth.

"Can I help you?" Mama asked, lifting a hand to shake the visitor's. "I'm Marianne Bloom. These are my daughters, Ivy and Elena."

Beside me, Elena shrank into herself, her shoulders curling in and her arms folding across her chest. Elena sometimes reminded me of a mouse—bright and cheerful and energetic when she was alone, or with people she trusted, but trembling and quiet around strangers. Sometimes it got so bad she could hardly talk when people we didn't know asked her a question.

The navy-blazer lady only darted nervous eyes at us and then looked back at Mama, like she didn't want to say whatever it was she'd come to say where me and Elena could hear her.

They were often like that, the wish-seekers, carrying their secrets in tight fingers.

"Ivy honey, come here and get this fire going while I take our guest inside a minute," Mama called, and even though curiosity burned through me hotter than any campfire, I obeyed. The regal lady followed Mama into the RV, Martha's door swinging shut behind them with a bang.

For as long as anybody could remember, people had been wishing on falling stars. And over time, those wishes had grown heavy and solid and real enough to weight down tiny pieces of that stardust, and give them hearts that beat and wings that could carry them through the warm night air. Because fireflies had come from stars once, it didn't take much for a fallen starwoman to breathe the wishes back into them, reminding the fireflies where they'd come from and how they'd come to be.

All you had to do after that was whisper your wish as you released the firefly, and as it drifted up into the darkness it would take your wish with it, wrapping that wish up in its glowing golden magic.

"What do you think it's about this time?" Elena asked, relaxed again now that the stranger was gone, as I stuffed some paper into the log cabin Mama had built in the firepit and lowered the lighter down after it. My charm bracelet jingled, the little silver RV on it catching the light and making my stomach twist unhappily. For something that used to make me smile every time I saw it, that bracelet was sure getting to be an annoying reminder.

"Shh," I hissed. "Maybe we can hear." Sometimes we knew what the wish-seekers wanted, sometimes we didn't, but Mama always respected their privacy if they requested it.

Two clicks and a burst of flame, and the paper caught. I sat back on my heels, straining my ears to catch the conversation from inside the camper. Mostly it was just murmuring, indistinguishable as the ocean, but every now and then I'd hear something from the wish-seeker: *"Husband . . . fire . . . job."*

A few minutes later the door opened again, and the visitor stood on the front step with her hands cupped around a glass jar, like it was maybe the most precious thing she'd ever held.

"Thank you," she said to my mama, in that trembly half-there-half-gone sort of voice people often had when they were leaving with a wish in their hands. "Truly. Thank you."

"May it bring you joy. And remember the rules," said Mama, the way she always did. Standing there in the gloom of the RV, she glowed just a little bit, silvery-gold light rolling from her hair and skin.

The visitor stepped down. Between her fingers I could see a glimmer of light, there and then gone: the firefly in her jar, blinking its golden glow on and then off quicker than a whisper. With one last grateful look at Mama, those fancy pumps carried her out of our campsite.

A minute later we heard the sound of a car engine turning over, and then she was gone.

Still in the shadow of the doorway, Mama sighed, rubbing her face with her hands. "I hope it helps."

"Won't it?" I asked. Mama was the only one of her sisters who bartered wishes. Aunt Agatha and Aunt Ruth both had forever homes—in North Carolina and Montana, respectively—and Mama always said it was too hard to trade in wishes if you never moved on from a place, because you'd get too invested in fixing your neighbors' problems, and maybe you'd end up giving out wishes that were never meant to be granted.

Mama stepped out of the RV now and shrugged, her hair sliding over her shoulders like starlight. "I hope. But wishes aren't always predictable."

Mama and Daddy had drilled that into my head over and over again, until it was all I could do not to roll my eyes as I heard those words coming out of Mama's mouth for the zillionth time. *Wishes are unpredictable. Wishes are powerful. Wishes don't always work out the way you think or hope they will. Wishes aren't to be treated lightly or taken for granted. Wishes are to be respected, honored, earned.*

"The fire looks good," said Mama, dumping ingredients for skillet cornbread into a bowl and beating them together until they were creamy and yellow. "Thanks, Ivy Mae."

"You're welcome," I said. My full name was Ivy Mae Bloom, which was only one letter away from being a sentence. *Ivy may bloom.* Mama and Daddy named me Ivy because they liked it, and Mae had been my Grandma Bloom's name before she died, but still. You'd think that they would have thought about the possible psychological damage before filling out the birth certificate. It's like before I was even an hour old, my parents knew I'd spend my whole life looking for a place to put down roots.

As the fire I'd built burned down to coals, the air filled with the smell of charcoal and wood and smoke— smells so familiar that I had to pay attention or I didn't even notice them. Once, when I was Sophie's age, we'd stayed for a while somewhere in Kansas, and I'd been playing at a park one morning and met a little girl wearing a plastic tiara that glittered and sparkled in the light. When we'd first shown up, me and Elena with Mama pushing baby Sophie in a stroller, the tiara girl had run over to her mom and whispered, *She smells weird*, loud enough that we could all hear it.

The girl's mom had scolded her, and the girl had shot a guilty look my way. But still, that afternoon, I'd gone home and scrubbed my hair and skin with shampoo three times in a row, afraid that I'd never smell like anything other than campfire and the scent of the road.

Back then, it had been a small thing, one hurtful moment in a lifetime made up of adventure and fun. But the older I got, the more those bad moments seemed to crowd out the good. Everywhere I went I carried with me a notebook—my writer's notebook, so I could always have it handy to jot down inspiration or collect the definitions of words that sounded cool, or work on stories or poems or plays as the inspiration struck. And in the back of that notebook there was one thing that never changed, no matter how many actual notebooks I might go through: a list called *Things I Wish*. When I was little, they were pretty dumb, like wishing for ice cream for dinner or my parents to stop making me take showers. (Ew.)

But these days, that list of wishes looked different. In my current notebook, the wishes were mostly the kinds of things that no family who lived on the road full-time could ever have. Like *my own bedroom*, or *a tree house*, or *a library card*, or *the chance to see a whole year of seasons in one place*. I didn't know exactly *when* living in Martha, traveling all the time, had stopped being fun and become frustrating, but I knew one thing—the closer I inched toward my thirteenth birthday, the more I envied Mama's clients, who had a chance of their wishes actually coming true.

I thought of the rows and rows of glass jars inside the camper, each one with its glinting firefly, each one holding within its little light the power of one wish.

Wishes may not have been predictable, but even so: those wish-seekers didn't know how lucky they were to walk away from our campsite with the thing they'd hoped for cradled in their arms.

2.

Martha smelled like campfire and the last vestiges of the trout Mama had cooked over the firepit when I woke up the next morning. Her windows were flung open, their screens in place to keep the bugs out but let the night air in. She had an AC, of course, but Mama and Daddy never ran it except when we were on the road.

Nights like these, in summer's last golden breath, were sweltering.

I sat up. The RV was quiet, but I wasn't the only one awake. Sophie was flopped on her stomach across her bunk—the one below mine in our stack of three bunk beds—arms wrapped around a four-inch-thick book.

"Did you know that not all stars become black holes

after they've run out of fuel?" she said, not looking up at me. Sophie was like that: she was *aware* of the world in a way most people aren't, especially people who are only eight. She could always tell where Elena and I were if we were close by, like she had special radar tuned only to us sisters. I sighed. "No."

"Only especially massive stars become black holes after their gravitational collapse," Sophie went on. "A smaller star would form a planetary nebula as it aged— losing the gravitational hold on its outer layers—and then become a white dwarf. The sun will never be a black hole, for instance. It's too small."

A pillow sailed down from the bunk above mine, ruffling the book's pages. Elena was the nicest, most patient person I'd ever met—*except* in the morning. And I could sympathize. Being woken up by one of Sophie's astronomy lectures was not exactly a delight.

To the rest of the world, there was nothing cuter than an eight-year-old whose angelic blond curls and China-blue eyes hide the kind of science prodigy morning talk shows dream about. When people first met Sophie, they'd inevitably make some comment about what a beautiful little girl she was—right up until she coolly told them that beauty was an inconsequential and ephemeral concept and less important than intellectual aptitude. (*Ephemeral* was one of the words in my note-book. It meant something that didn't last.) After the stranger had finished gaping, they'd beam even brighter, as though the chance to meet somebody like Sophie had reminded them how much life had to offer.

I loved Sophie. I really did.

But most days she made me want to tape her mouth shut so we could all get some peace and quiet.

Maybe it wouldn't have been so bad if we'd had a real house, a regular house that didn't move around and had actual rooms and windowsills and a front porch. If we'd had a regular house, the three of us girls wouldn't feel so much like we were mashed together, never able to take a breath without breathing somebody else's air. But inside Martha, Sophie got to be too much way too fast.

Now Sophie rolled off the bed, her book held up against her chest and a dignified tilt to her chin. "I won't stay where I'm not wanted," she said, and flounced out of the RV.

I followed a few minutes later, my latest notebook tucked under my arm with a pen pushed into its spiral binding. Mama and Daddy were already awake and outside, too. Daddy was lifting a Dutch oven out of the coals in the firepit.

Mama stood between the table and the firepit, her

gaze intent on a little burnished silver plate in front of her. White smoke swirled up from it, smelling like the sharp licorice of star anise. I knew better than to bother Mama when she was divining. Burning herbs on the star-metal plate, watching the way the smoke poured out for messages only she could see, was one of the tricks she had for finding the places in the world where things were going wrong and needed her attention.

Even though Daddy was a travel writer, Mama's work was the *real* reason we lived on the road. As a fallen star, it was her duty to tend to the magic that wove underneath the world, whispering to it when it was weak and scolding it when it became unruly. Without fallen stars, she had told me for as long as I could remember, the magic would all disappear, and with it would go all the things that made life worth living.

Long ago, when they had first fallen to earth, Mama and her sisters had lived together in a cottage in Whistling Ridge, North Carolina, a little apple-orchard town tucked into the Appalachian Mountains. But eventually, they'd realized that it was too hard for them to touch the magic of a whole country from one house, and so Aunt Agatha had stayed in Whistling Ridge to care for the East, and Aunt Ruth had moved to Montana to care for the West, and Mama had married Daddy and bought a

Winnebago camper so they could live on the road and tend to everything in between.

"Morning, honey," said Daddy, his Alabama accent like melting butter. No matter how old I got, I'd always love listening to my daddy speak. Mama's voice was clear and precise and rich, like an actress in a movie, and all of us girls had the kind of unspecific accents that came from being raised all over the country. But Daddy's voice was beautiful.

"Can I use the computer?" I asked.

"Sure," Daddy said. "Be quick, though. Breakfast is nearly ready."

I ducked back into Martha and found one of the laptops we used for school on the dinette table. It only took a minute to open the computer, wake it up, and log in to my email account. I'd had an email account for as long as I could remember. It was a necessity, when you never stayed in one place for more than a few weeks at a time; without email, I'd never have been able to stay in touch with extended family members or friends I met along the way. A cell phone would've been even better, so I could text or video-call, but Mama and Daddy had a firm no-phones-until-high-school policy.

A little frisson (another word from my collection: *a sudden strong feeling; a thrill*) of excitement zinged through me as the log-in screen disappeared and showed me my in-box.

But that thrill lasted only two seconds: exactly as long as it took to register the fact that my in-box was completely empty.

I clicked through to the *Sent Mail* tab, just to make doubly sure that the email I'd sent to Ada four days ago really *had* gone through. And the email I'd sent a week before that. And the one the week before *that*.

When the time stamps assured me with depressing accuracy that all my emails had been delivered just fine, I hit the *Compose* button.

Just in case.

I wasn't as fast at typing as Daddy was—his fingers flew over the keyboard so quickly that the click of keys sounded like the rat-tat of machine-gun fire. But I was getting pretty good for a kid my age. It only took me a minute to peck out the message I wanted to send.

Hey, Ada! Long time no talk, right? Did you get my email from last week? How did your birthday party go? We just stopped in Oklahoma, at this gorgeous lake. I really like it. Hopefully we can stay awhile. Write back soon!
xo, Ivy

I used to sign my emails to Ada a different way: *RV Girl*, or sometimes *Ivy Bloom, RV Girl*. Ada and I had met two years ago, when we were both ten-almost-eleven. Mama had taken me and Elena to a play at a children's theater in the North Dakota town we were camping in, and Ada and her dad had been sitting in the seats next to us. She overheard us talking about how much we loved the book the play was based on, which was *her* favorite book, too—and after the play finished, we all went out to get ice cream together.

We saw Ada and her dad and little brother six whole times before we left that town the next week, and the last time we were together, Ada gave me a goodbye present. When I opened the small box, there was a silver charm bracelet inside, with a shining fingernail-size RV on it.

"I saw this and it made me think of you," Ada had said shyly, "because you're the RV girl. So Dad said I could buy it with some of my birthday money. Isn't it so cute?"

I hadn't been able to say anything in response—I'd been too filled up with feelings I couldn't even name. Gratitude and excitement, but also a rush of happiness that Ada had seen exactly who I was and thought that it was cool enough to commemorate it with a bracelet.

But lately, that bracelet on my wrist had become itchy

and hot, reminding me of all the things that defined me that I wasn't sure I liked anymore.

I hit *Send* on the email, and a second later, the *Message Sent* notification popped up. I closed the computer and sat there at the dinette for a minute, listening to the whir of the computer motor go silent. When we were on the road, the dinette benches became seats for me and my sisters—my parents even took the padding off one of the benches so they could hook Sophie's booster seat in. I'd seen so many miles, so many states, so many different worlds pass by us from where I sat right now.

I liked that line, the way it felt full of mixed-up nostalgia and whimsy. I opened my notebook and jotted it down. Sometimes, when I was kind of in my feelings, the next-best thing to feeling better was to make the sadness sound poetic.

"You know that different climates aren't actually different *worlds*, right?"

I was so startled I choked, the air whistling in and out of my lungs like an out-of-shape accordion. Sophie had appeared behind my shoulder, quiet as a ghost. I hadn't even heard Martha's door open or close.

"Daddy says it's time for breakfast," Sophie said. Then, without moving from her place by my head, she hollered, "ELENA! Time for breakfast!"

For such a small girl, Sophie had a truly amazing gift for vocal projection. I winced, trying to cover my ears and close my precious writing notebook at the same time. This moment—sitting on the bench that did quadruple duty as a car seat, a dining room, a storage compartment, and sometimes even a fold-out bed, listening to Sophie screech at Elena from two inches away from my head—felt like a perfect encapsulation of all the things I was growing tired of. The lack of any privacy or personal space, no matter what. The way sound traveled in a 270-square-foot RV. The way, no matter where I went or what I did, my sisters were always right there with me.

"Sophie!" I said, unable to keep the irritation out of my voice. "Can you please *not*?"

"Sorry!" Sophie chirped, not sounding sorry at all, and bounded out of the RV.

From the other end of Martha, I could hear Elena stirring on her top bunk. We'd changed positions on those triple bunk beds more times than I could count—for a long time it went youngest to oldest, but last year, Mama and Daddy had decided that Elena should get the top bunk, because it gave her the most private place to retreat to when she was feeling overwhelmed because of her anxiety. What I'd *wanted* to say was that there was no such *thing* as privacy in an RV, but I'd bitten my tongue as hard as I could.

A minute later, a bleary-eyed Elena climbed down the bunk ladder, her wavy light-brown hair as tangled as a bird's nest. She shuffled zombielike past me and out of the RV, pausing only to grunt a garbled "good morning."

As Martha's door swung closed again, I took a deep breath, inhaling the feeling of silence and stillness, the way my sisters leaving made the RV into the kind of sanctuary it almost never was. A place where an almost-thirteen-year-old could think, breathe, *be*, without worrying about sisters yelling in your ears or somebody accidentally opening the door when you were mid-shower (something that Mama called an *occupational hazard* of five people sharing one tiny closet of a bathroom).

But the peace only lasted a moment, before I could hear Daddy's voice calling me from outside. "Ivy! Come to the table, please!"

By the time I got outside, Mama had finished reading the smoke for clues to the problem in Silverwood and packed the herbs and silver star-metal plate away. Everyone was sitting around the picnic table while Daddy dished up oatmeal. I snagged a berry from one of the wild blackberry brambles that ringed our campsite as I sat down; maybe if they were any good, I'd pick more and we could top our oatmeal with them.

But when I bit into it, the berry tasted like salt and ash, with none of the bright zing a blackberry should have. Without even meaning to, I gagged and spit it back out onto the packed dirt of the ground beside the table.

"Ivy!" Mama chided, while I gulped a big drink of water and then took a bite of sweet honey-and-milk oatmeal to try to get the taste from my tongue.

"Sorry," I said when I'd swallowed. "It tasted *horrible*."

"It probably wasn't ripe enough," said Sophie, in that maddening way she had of sounding like the arbiter ("a person who has ultimate authority") of all knowledge.

"No," I said, "it wasn't that. It tasted . . . wrong. Like something that got pulled out of the coals of an old fire. Not like a berry at all." I shuddered.

Mama sighed. "Things aren't doing well here," she said. "The magic that winds under Silverwood is damaged. I'm not surprised it stole the flavor from the berries. After breakfast, we'll drive around the lake and see if we can find the broken spot."

"Did the computer get back where it belongs, Ivy?" Daddy asked, passing a plate of orange slices around the table.

"Yeah," I said.

"Did you hear back from your friend?"

The frustration of that empty in-box slammed back into me. "Nope."

"I'm sorry, honey. I'm sure she's just busy, and you'll hear back soon."

"I hope so," I said, but *hope* wasn't how I'd have described the heavy weight that had settled into my stomach more deeply with every week that passed without Ada responding to my emails. She'd probably been the best friend I'd ever had, and now she'd disappeared on me more thoroughly than a cinder winks out when you bank a campfire. Before I could stop myself, the question that had been rising in me all morning tumbled out. "Why do we always have to be *moving on*?"

I didn't know if it was coming up on thirteen, or the fact that I'd started getting my period over the summer, or the way my body felt strange and unfamiliar half the time these days, but lately I found it more and more impossible to be pleasant and polite when I spent almost 100 percent of my waking *and* sleeping hours packed into a tiny space with the same four people.

"You know why," Daddy chided.

"Your daddy has his work," said Mama firmly. "And I have mine."

I knew that Mama's work was important. I did. The

taste of that ashy blackberry, the wrinkle in Mama's forehead when she'd been divining this morning, was proof of that.

But wasn't *I* important, too?

"Just think of all the people who are tethered to their homes," Daddy said, "who can't get up and go wandering whenever the mood strikes. We're lucky, Ivy Mae."

I thought of the wish list in the back of my notebook, with all the things I couldn't have if we stayed on the road forever. *A pet. A garden. A tub for bubble baths.*

Mama and Daddy may have felt lucky. *They* may have had important work. *They* may have chosen this life intentionally. But as far as I was concerned, lucky was the things on my list. Having a forever home, a place to sink your roots into.

And I didn't know exactly what I was going to do to fix all that. But a certainty had been growing in me, rising up like the tendrils of smoke from Mama's magic herbs, ever since I'd seen that empty email in-box. Whatever it took, whatever it cost, I was going to do *something* to make those wishes on my list come true.

I was going to find a place to bloom.

3.

Before we'd even finished breakfast, we had another visit—two wish-seekers this time, a middle-aged man and woman who wore grief etched into their faces like the veins on a leaf. Mama stood up from the table as soon as we'd seen them.

"Hi there," she said. "I'm Marianne Bloom."

"We heard . . . you might be able to help us," said the woman, squeezing her fingers together anxiously.

Mama nodded, her silvery hair twinkling in the morning light. "I can't make any promises, but I can certainly try. Would you like to go inside?"

They followed her into Martha, emerging a few minutes later with a wish jar, which the man held as carefully as though it were worth a whole life's savings. In reality,

Mama didn't charge all that much for the wishes— enough that, taken together with Daddy's income from travel writing, we had enough to live on, but not so much that people couldn't pay, and never more than a person could comfortably spare. Once, when I was little, I'd asked why she had to charge for them at all; wasn't it better just to give them freely, so that nothing would hold anyone back from getting the things they needed most?

It's not quite that simple, Ivy Mae, she'd said. *Wishes don't just work for the wanting. For a wish to come true, you have to be willing to give something of yourself—even if that's only five dollars, or twenty. The magic has to know you're serious, has to know you're ready to sacrifice. Because you can't achieve your dreams without being willing to sacrifice a little bit along the way.*

Daddy started clearing the dishes from the table as the wish-seekers left. Mama sank back onto the picnic bench, looking thoughtful.

"I think I know what needs to be done in Silverwood," she said. "Last night and today—all three of the people who came here were suffering because of a fire in a factory on the other side of the lake. I'd like to drive over there to see what's going on."

Daddy nodded. "Girls, help me get all this cleared up, and then Mama can go."

I'd asked once why we didn't have one of those RVs that was pulled by a truck, and Daddy had shrugged and said this way we only had to take care of one vehicle, not two, and that Martha had always served us well and met our needs. But still, there were times—like now—when it was annoying. Because Daddy had a deadline to meet that night, he elected to stay back at the campsite with us while Mama drove Martha to investigate the broken magic.

"I want you three to get started on schoolwork while I'm gone," Mama said. Even though some homeschoolers worked all year round, we always took the summers off because Mama believed that children *need time to play and be bored*; we'd started school barely three weeks ago, in mid-August. "Elena, help Sophie with her spelling words, okay? And Ivy, I'd like you to add an entry to your travel journal for Silverwood."

"Could I come with you?" I asked. I wasn't even sure *why*, except that it had been an awful long time since it was just Mama and me in Martha.

Mama hesitated for a moment, but then nodded. "Sure, as long as you get your work done later."

It wasn't a long drive—only a few minutes, once we'd left the campground and gotten onto the highway that led toward town. Silverwood Lake was long and

"Delightfully voice-y and atmospheric,
The Stars of Whistling Ridge is a gentle and magical story
about family and the true meaning of home."
—JASMINE WARGA,
Newbery Honor–winning author of *Other Words for Home*

Praise for BEGINNERS WELCOME

"As delicate and powerful as a sonata, Annie Lee's story
of music, magic, loss, and love should not be missed!"
—JESSICA DAY GEORGE,
New York Times bestselling author of *Tuesdays at the Castle*

"Baldwin's prose challenges [kids] to be the bravest and wisest
ersions of themselves."—*School Library Journal* (starred review)

Praise for WHERE THE WATERMELONS GROW

An Indies Introduce Title • An Indie Next List Selection

"Della's story is a reminder that even under the toughest rinds
of troubles, we can find the cool, sustaining sweetness of friendship."
—KIRBY LARSON,
author of the Newbery Honor Book *Hattie Big Sky*

"This heartfelt story will stay with readers. A top choice."
—*School Library Journal* (starred review)

"Heartbreaking, yet heartening."—ALA *Booklist* (starred review)

"Hints of sweet magical realism touch *Where the
Watermelons Grow,* balancing this exquisite novel's
bittersweet authenticity."—Shelf Awareness (starred review)

"In her debut novel, Baldwin presents a realistic portrayal of life
with a mentally ill parent."—*Publishers Weekly* (starred review)

Also by Cindy Baldwin

Where the Watermelons Grow
Beginners Welcome

snaking, with narrow fingers of little creeks that jutted out from it every so often. One of those creeks ran right through the town of Silverwood, weaving its way down the center of a place that could've been a postcard of Small-Town America. Except that nobody would've wanted Silverwood on a postcard right now, not with the big, burned-out building surrounded by blackened trees at the edge of the city limits.

As Mama parked and got out of the RV, I could feel that something was off in this place. Most people couldn't see or sense the magic that wove underneath the world—the bright, pulsing energy that held everything together, giving strawberries their sweetness in spring, creating the crimson sheen of a maple leaf in the autumn, folding richness and life into music and art. It wasn't that people weren't *capable* of seeing it; it was just such an ordinary thing, such a fundamental part of how the world worked, that most people didn't even notice it.

But when you're the daughter of a fallen star, even if you have no magical ability of your own, it's hard not to catch a glimpse every now and then of that magical web.

I breathed careful and slow as we walked toward the factory, doing the exercises Aunt Jenny had taught me to lessen the chances that the smoky, ashy air of the factory lot would kick off an asthma attack. We didn't talk as we picked our way around charred debris, but Mama hummed quietly to herself, a sound that was so familiar it felt like it was part of my own bones. Her hair shimmered brighter as she neared the factory entrance.

"How did the fire happen?" I asked, trailing after her.

Mama made an expansive gesture at the world around us. "It doesn't take much for the magic of the world to get out of sorts, Ivy Mae. Maybe the owner of this factory was harsh to his workers, and the magic woven through the earth here dwindled away. Or maybe this town has just been forgotten, and over time, the magic grew bare. Whatever happened, this spot lost enough of its magic to let the fire in. Without its magic, the earth turns on itself, breaking things that once were whole."

"What would've happened if we hadn't come along?"

Mama smiled. "We would've come along eventually. That's why there *are* star-women in this world, to find these places and fix them. Your aunts and me in the US, and other star-women elsewhere. It's been that way for as long as the earth and the heavens have existed, one star-woman following another, so no place is left untended."

"But what if we *hadn't*?" The burned-out lot was creepy, with its blackened brick walls and dead-looking trees.

"Then the magic would have weakened further, and

more places and people would have been hurt. Remember when we learned about Pompeii in world history last spring?"

I nodded. I'd had nightmares for days after we learned about the city in Italy that had been buried by a volcano thousands of years ago.

"Pompeii is one of the most famous examples of a magical failure we have," Mama said gravely. "In the stories that we pass from one star-woman to another, it stands as an example of the worst that can happen. Or the San Francisco fire of 1906. All through history, where magic fails, disaster and destruction aren't far behind."

I swallowed hard.

"But," Mama added, reaching over to give my shoulders a quick squeeze, "those times are rare, honey. For every Pompeii, there are hundreds of thousands of millions of other moments where star-women have found and fixed the world's magic exactly as we're meant to. Just like we'll do here."

Just outside the factory door was a weeping willow, its leaves singed off and its bark rough and black. The tree shivered in a breeze only it could feel.

"Hmm," Mama murmured. Without warning she dropped to her knees, her hands digging into the ashy soil near the tree, sending up a sharp, wild, living scent that mingled with the charcoal smell in the air—the earth reminding us that it was still alive, under the fine coat of ash and smoke. After a minute, the glimmer of Mama's hair brightened, and then brightened some more, until Mama shone so much I could hardly look at her anymore. Instead, I let my eyes follow the veins of gleaming gold that unfurled in the ashy dirt, stretching outward from Mama's fingers.

The starlight crept up the trunk of the willow tree, until the tree itself was glowing almost as bright as Mama. The willow shook its branches once, like a dog shaking off water, and when they stilled, there were tiny green leaf buds lining its ropy branches, and the dirt around the trunk was brown and healthy again, like Mama's magic had banished the char.

"There," she said. "That's much better, don't you think?"

"How does fixing the tree fix the factory?"

Mama smiled, briskly brushing the dirt from her hands. "Magic flows through living things. Plants, animals, people. The easiest way to connect my own magic to the magic woven under a place is through something living, like this tree." She laid a golden-brown hand across the bark, like it was an old friend. "Fixing the magic won't rebuild the factory. But it means that when people are ready to do the rebuilding, they'll all be safer and happier."

"Cool," I said, thinking of the citizens of Silverwood joining to clean up the ash, tear down the burned bricks, place bright new ones on the ground. It made little goose bumps pop out on my arms, imagining a whole town coming together that way, making their dreams come true with the work of their own hands, like each individual was part of something bigger.

What would it be like, to *belong* to a place in that way?

"Let's go back," Mama said. And even though it was a tiny word, *back*, it rang like a church bell in my ears. Wouldn't most moms have said *let's go home* in moments like these?

Most moms whose families actually *had* a home. A home that wasn't on wheels. A home where my list of wishes could've come true.

A home where I wouldn't have had to depend on Ada to answer my emails from faraway North Dakota in order to feel like I actually had a friend.

I knew that Mama's work was important. I did. But standing there surrounded by fire-scorched walls and the ghosts of burned trees, the knowledge of that importance sent a snag of pain through my middle. Because I knew that, no matter what else ever happened to the Bloom family, we would *never* stop traveling. Mama's work would always keep us moving on, and on, and on—never stopping long enough to put down roots, never even pausing to wait for one of the wishes on my list to come true. Mama's work would always, always be more important than anything else for our family.

And I knew it was selfish, wishing things were different.

But I couldn't stop myself from wishing.

And suddenly, I had an idea. An idea to change things. To *fix* things. To create the life I knew, deep down in my bones, I needed to thrive.

I was going to steal Mama's wishes. Not one wish. Not even two. But *all* of them, every single jar that she had collected over the last few days of travel.

And when I had stolen them, I was going to set every one of those fireflies free, and I was going to use the power of all those wishes together to find the one thing I wanted more than anything else in the world:

A real, true, *forever* home.

4.

My chance came that night. Darkness lay across the world as gently as a blanket, the stars bright and burning and the moon bathing the campsite in milky light. Elena and I had been sent to bed an hour before, and I could hear soft sleep-breathing from above me and below me in the bunk beds. Mama and Daddy were out at the campsite, but their voices drifted clearly in through the open windows.

"Let's take a walk," Mama murmured. "Down by the lake. It's so lovely here."

I heard the crunch of gravel as Mama and Daddy stood. There were a few pattering noises—putting away the camping things, I guessed—and then crunching again. I counted to three hundred, lying as still as I could well past the point that the sound of their footsteps had receded into the woods, barely breathing.

Then, as quiet as the night itself, I slid out of my bed, grabbed an empty backpack from my box of belongings, and tiptoed over to the wishes.

Mama kept them on a special shelf Daddy had built for the purpose—a shelf the exact depth of a quart-size canning jar, with a wooden bar across the front that sat snugly across the jars' middles and held them in when the RV was on the road. The shelf and the bar were both lined with soft felt, to muffle the clanking as we drove.

Inside the jars, the fireflies winked on and off. Mama never kept them in captivity for very long—they wouldn't have survived more than a few days. Most of this batch had been caught yesterday at dusk, though a few were from the day before in Louisiana. Places where extra magic spilled out of the earth, like it had in the bayous, were always full of firefly wishes, so thick Mama hardly had to work to catch them.

There were nine wish-filled jars today. The tips of my fingers tingled: *three times three.*

As quietly as I could, I packed them into my backpack, padding them with towels so they didn't make noise or break. I was hardly breathing as I slowly closed the zipper after the ninth jar had gone in; the navy canvas of my backpack was glowing now, pulsing softly with the green-gold light of the captive fireflies inside.

I took a deep breath, as much to steady my twitching, jumping nerves as to get air in my lungs. As an afterthought, I slid my inhaler from where it sat by my pillow and stuck it in my back pocket. The last thing I needed was for the wind to shift and bring with it some kind of pollen that would close my airways tighter than fists.

It was better to be careful.

Inside the jars, the fireflies winked on and off. Mama usually didn't keep them more than a few days. Whenever we went out west—where there *were* no fireflies—Mama had to be extra careful with her supply of wishes, putting sliced fruit or cotton balls soaked in sugar water in the jars to keep the fireflies healthy. Most of *this* batch had been caught yesterday at dusk, though a few were from the day before in Louisiana. Places where extra magic spilled out of the earth, like it had in the bayous, were always full of firefly wishes, so thick Mama hardly had to work to catch them.

"Ivy?"

The whisper made me startle. The backpack full of jars listed dangerously to one side. I straightened it.

Sophie was sitting up in bed, her yellow curls glinting in the filtered moonlight.

"What are you doing?"

"Nothing," I hissed. "Go back to sleep."

Sophie swung her legs over the side of the bed. "Are you going somewhere? What's in your backpack? Are those *wishes*? You can't, Ivy!"

"Go back to sleep." That itchy, almost-thirteen-years-old rage that always simmered just below my skin these days rose in me like an especially cranky dragon.

"How many are in there?" Sophie sounded genuinely panicked. I shoved down the teeny, tiny bit of guilt that twinged through me.

"Are you going outside?" Sophie asked. "It's so late!"

My teeth were clenched so hard a muscle in my jaw started to twitch. "I'm fine, okay? Now go back to sleep. And don't you dare tell Mama and Daddy!"

In the darkness, I could see the slump to Sophie's shoulders, the way her little body caved in on itself. But I didn't care. For eight years, Sophie had been *the special one*, the one who knew everything, the one adults fawned over and complimented and called things like *prodigy* and *incredible talent*. For as long as she'd known how to talk, she'd been the center of attention. For as long as she'd known how to talk, Sophie had had all the answers.

Even when it was factually *impossible* for her to have answers, like when it came to reconciling her precious astrophysics with Mama's star stories, Sophie found a way. And right now, I hated her for it. I hated how Sophie never seemed to feel lost and alone, the way I did all the time lately. I hated that she had a practical explanation for all the things that seemed maddening and mysterious to me.

And there was no way, *no way in the world*, that I was going to let her ruin the most important night of my life. I'd tried so hard to be the responsible big sister, to take care of Elena and Sophie ever since they were born, to make Mama and Daddy happy. I'd tried to respect Mama's magic and the way it healed the world, even if it meant she was only ever granting *other* people's wishes and never my own.

But it was *my* turn now. My turn for a little happiness. And if I had to take nine wishes to get it, I was going to do exactly that, no matter what Sophie said.

Without another word, I turned and left the RV.

Cicadas sang as I crept through the campsite and into the woods. Mama and Daddy had gone to the lake, but that didn't mean that I couldn't, too. That afternoon after we'd finished our schoolwork and chores, Elena and Sophie and I had found our way through the trees to a tiny, protected cove, a place where the lake dipped into the forest, licking at the tree roots and folding itself in between the trunks. There was a little crescent of beach, just enough for three sisters to stand side by side.

Or one sister and nine glass jars.

It was dark in the forest; I had to take care to avoid

smacking headfirst into a tree trunk. But it brightened up when I got to the cove. In front of me, the three-quarters-full moon hung like a prayer over the shining black water of the lake. *A gibbous moon*, Sophie would have said, and if I'd responded that *three-quarters-full* sounded more poetic, she'd have looked at me like I was a baby.

Almost without breathing, I moved forward and knelt on the soft, muddy sand of the beach and unzipped my backpack. Inside, the fireflies crawled and flitted around their jars, their lights winking on, off, on, off, on.

I took them out one by one, lining them up in a neat row with hands that shook only a little.

All my life, Mama had drilled into us the rules for wishes. Sometimes we'd use one for something small, like the time we were on the road in the middle of Kansas and Sophie needed a bathroom *really bad*, but Martha's toilet was broken and there was no rest stop in sight, and Soph had refused to go by the roadside because she said it was unsanitary. So Mama rolled down the window and released a firefly, and a few minutes later, we looked out and saw a gas station.

I smiled to myself, thinking about that.

But we never used wishes too often, even for small things, because Mama said that if you weren't careful you'd come to rely too much on wishes, and that over time using too many could *take* something from you.

"Take what?" I'd asked when I was younger.

"Take the things that make you who you are, Ivy," she'd answered. "If you use them too much, wishes will feed on the deepest parts of yourself. And the more you use wishes to solve your problems, the more you'll crave the easy solutions they can provide, until you're living a half-life. A dream-life. There was a star-woman once, a long time ago when fallen stars were new, who used wishes to mend the heartbreaks of being human—more and more wishes, every time a problem arose. Except the more wishes she used, the less happy she became, until her life was more a prison than a gift. All star-women since have been careful with wishes."

And Mama had told us over and over and over, just as she told each of her customers before she'd allow them to walk home with a wish in their hands, that wishes had rules. Three rules, specifically—rules so important Mama had made each of us girls memorize them.

Rule One: Never wish in anger.
Rule Two: Never use more than one wish at a time, because wishes are unpredictable when combined.
Rule Three: Never make a wish that's too big, because big wishes have disastrous consequences.

Carefully, so carefully, I moved down my line of jars, unscrewing the rings around the top but not taking the cheesecloth lids off yet. Then I sat back on my ankles and closed my eyes, breathing deep and slow, trying to let the calm of the gently lapping lake seep all the way through me. I couldn't do anything about the fact that I was breaking rules two and three. I knew, deep down in my bones, that my wish was bigger than one firefly, or two, or even three. I needed every bit of magic I could get.

But at least I could make sure not to wish in anger.

I opened my eyes again just in time to see a shooting star track its way across the sky, leaving a trail of light in its wake. Would that star fall to earth, too, and wake up tomorrow morning with fingers and toes and silver hair, like my mama?

In twelve or so years, would it have a daughter who was sneaking out and breaking the rules of wishing, too?

I took one last deep breath and slipped the RV Girl bracelet from my wrist. I'd stolen Mama's wishes, not bargained for them like the wish-seekers did. But maybe the bracelet I'd worn around my wrist for two whole years, the bracelet that had meant all the good things about my friendship with Ada, would be enough of a sacrifice. It felt fitting, giving up the proof that I was *RV Girl* in order to make my wishes come true. I raised my hand high over my head and then threw the silver charm bracelet as hard and as far as I could.

When it fell and slipped beneath the waters of the lake, I could hardly even tell.

I thought of the instructions Mama gave her clients: *Hold the wish close to your heart, so clearly you can see it with your eyes.*

All I wanted was a home. A real home with walls and a foundation, a home that didn't have wheels or a septic tank that had to be emptied every time we stopped. A home that could hold all the wishes on my list.

Before I could think twice about it, I pulled the cheesecloth from all nine jars.

It took the fireflies a minute to realize that they'd been released. Once they did, they swirled up in great gold spirals, their glow reflected in the lake, as if the sky itself had shaken nine bright stars down into the dark water.

"*I wish to have a forever home,*" I whispered as they rose higher and higher, farther and farther from the glass that had held them close. "*I wish to find my One True Place.*"

I watched the fireflies until they disappeared into the crushed-velvet sky. And then I wrapped the jars back up into their towels and zipped them into my backpack, and headed back through the trees to Martha.

Mama and Daddy were waiting, lips tight, as soon as my feet crunched onto the gravel of the campsite.

5.

"Ivy. Mae. Bloom." Daddy's words were clipped so sharp you almost couldn't hear the Alabama in them. "Care to explain yourself?"

Mama sat at the picnic table next to him, her arms crossed over her chest. Her skin glowed faintly in the darkness, an echo of the stars that spread out in the sky above.

My mouth wouldn't work. A hand crept to my backpack strap before I could stop it; behind me, the jars shifted.

"Sophie told us," Mama said.

"Everything?" I whispered, even though I already knew the answer.

"Everything. Did you use them all, Ivy?"

"Yes." There was no point in lying. If Sophie had told them, Mama surely would've checked the jar shelf before coming out to lie in wait.

Mama shook her head, like she couldn't believe my answer. "*Nine wishes*, Ivy? *Nine?* I don't even know what kind of havoc that could wreak. Do you have any *idea* how dangerous that was?"

"Yes."

Daddy sighed. "What on God's green earth was so important that you'd risk that much, honey?"

I smashed my lips together. Silence pressed like a blanket on all three of us, like we were each trying to out-stubborn the other.

"Well?" Mama said. I pushed my teeth together so hard my jaw ached.

Finally, she stood. "It doesn't matter right now. The horse is out of the barn. Put the jars back and get into bed. Daddy and I will decide what consequence you'll earn later."

I fled into the RV before either of them could say another word.

I dreamed that night, shivery, strange dreams with fire, and ice, and stars that fell and drowned in black-mirror lakes.

I woke up in the washed-out light of early morning to see Mama leaning against my bunk bed. She was holding a nebulizer mask to my face, misty medicine curling in wisps and whorls from the air holes on either side of the plastic.

I coughed.

And I coughed again.

And a third time.

My lungs felt like the silty mud of the beach last night—thick and sucking. When I breathed in, it was to a symphony of whistling and rattles. And I was cold, so cold I was shaking, even though Mama had dug my winter duvet out from who-knows-where and tucked me into it.

"Shhh, sweetheart," she said when she saw that my eyes were open. "It's all right. Go back to sleep."

Without even meaning to, I did.

The next time I woke up, the sun was brighter, and Mama and I weren't the only ones awake. Sophie and Elena sat next to each other on Sophie's bottom bunk. Sophie was scribbling away on a multiplication worksheet while Elena plucked at her ukulele, singing a sad, silly song about a man who told his best friend to pass a kiss on to his girl, and ended up pretty mad when the best friend married the girl for himself.

"Give my love to Nellie, Jack, and kiss her once for me . . . ," Elena sang, her voice as clear and sweet as a morning swim in Silverwood Lake. Daddy always said that Elena had been born with music on her tongue. Mama and Daddy had gotten Elena the ukulele for her tenth birthday a few months before, and if she could have, she would have slept with it, arms wrapped around the neck like it was a baby.

Elena's bangs were limp and sweaty. So was I, I realized: I'd sweated so much that the duvet Mama had wrapped me in earlier that morning was damp.

But I was still cold, a frosty coldness that went all the way to the center of my bones. And when I breathed, it felt like swimming through Jell-O. It was a wall-closing-in feeling, like I was claustrophobic in my own body. I squeezed my eyes shut again and wished I could fall back asleep.

Elena stopped singing and called softly up to me. "Are you okay?"

I wanted to say *I'm fine*, but breathing took too much effort.

Sophie's eyes narrowed. "I'm telling Mama you need more albuterol," she said, scooting off the bottom bunk. "It's been almost long enough since your last one. It can be taken every four hours."

"Want me to read to you?" Elena asked. The shadows under her eyes were bruise-like. She held up the book in her lap: *Little Women*. Mama had assigned it to us for a language arts novel study, and we'd been taking turns reading aloud to each other every day. Sophie, too, even though she was technically only in third grade and Mama didn't believe in overloading eight-year-olds with required reading, even if those eight-year-olds *were* geniuses.

Sophie would be mad as a bee's nest if Elena and I read without her.

I nodded, the same anger I'd felt last night bubbling through me. After the way she'd told on me to Mama and Daddy, Sophie deserved every bad thing she had coming.

Mama had had us all read aloud practically as soon as we could muddle through our first easy reader, so we were all good at it—but Elena was the best. The music in her voice came out when she read, too, and as she dove into the part of the book where Amy falls through the ice of the skating pond, I lay back and closed my eyes and focused on breathing. It was hard not to give in to the panic that clawed and clutched at me, but I breathed as deeply as I could, forcing my lungs to hold the air a little longer at the top of the breath, and exhale a little further than they thought they could.

Time slipped strangely. After what was either a few minutes or a few centuries, the thin mattress sank a little as Mama leaned on the bed next to me again, a nebulizer in her hand. I took it from her and put the mask over my mouth and nose, looping the elastic around the back of my head.

Mama put her hand on my forehead. I couldn't tell if my skin was cold as snow or burning up, but the pinch between Mama's eyebrows made me think it was the second one.

"Ivy Mae," Mama said, chewing on her lip the way Elena did when she was feeling anxious, "what on earth did you use those wishes for?"

I was so tired, I thought about telling her. But I kept the secret locked up tight in my chest, together with the sickness that squeezed the breath from my lungs.

The morning dragged on, a mess of albuterol treatments, and warm broth, and eucalyptus oil spread on my chest. At one point, I heard the RV door swing open and then closed as Daddy came inside, stomping dirt off his shoes.

"Have you texted Jenny?" he asked.

"Yes," said Mama quietly. I strained to hear. Even being sicker than I'd maybe ever been in my life didn't make me any less curious. Aunt Jenny was Daddy's sister, a pediatrician who lived in Daddy's hometown in Alabama. Since we never stayed in one place long enough for regular doctor's visits, Aunt Jenny doctored us all over texts and phone calls and sometimes Skype. "She says to keep an eye on her fever, and give her albuterol every four hours round the clock. She also strongly recommended we get to a town with a hospital. Says Ivy probably needs a steroid, and somewhere to stay put while she heals."

"Stay put? For how long?"

"A few weeks," Mama said. "I think we should go to Agatha's. Something happened last night—strong enough to wake me up from a dead sleep. I don't know what it was, but there's trouble in Whistling Ridge, and I think Agatha needs me."

"It's what, thirteen hours away? If we got on the road by tonight, we could be there in the morning. Early enough to schedule a doctor's visit, I bet. That girl," said Daddy, those two words twisted up with frustration and love and laughter. "Is this because of the wishing?"

"It's impossible to say," Mama said. "She still won't tell me what she wished for, and I don't have the heart to push her when she's this sick. But it seems like too big a coincidence to be otherwise."

"Could we use a wish to set things right? Make her better?"

"Too risky," said Mama. "There's no telling what layering wishes on wishes like that might do."

I was alone in the RV for a little while after that, though I could hear talking and laughter from the campsite outside my open window as Mama and Daddy and my sisters had lunch and broke camp. I fell asleep again while they were outside, and when I woke it was already time for dinner and another nebulizer treatment, and then we were all strapping ourselves into our seats—me and my sisters padding the dinette benches with pillows and blankets so we could fall asleep while Daddy drove. It wasn't the most comfortable way to sleep, all propped in funny positions, but Mama always said that seat belts laws were seat belt laws even when you were sleeping, and we'd all been doing it so long it was second nature.

I could feel the bench rumble a little as Martha's engine roared to life. After all that napping I wasn't sure I would be able to sleep again at all, but before long I was drifting off to the hum of the road streaming away below us.

6.

We pulled off the highway just as the sun was emerging from the tree-covered mountains, painting the indigo sky with dusky gray and shadow purple and thin brushstrokes of violet-pink.

The change in the roar of the RV engine woke me, that shift from the loud highway rumble to the small-town murmur, the sound as familiar to me as my own breath. When she'd seen I was awake, Mama had unbuckled from her seat long enough to come feel my forehead and pronounce that my fever was broken. Now I was pushing the blankets off me, hot as a July day, sweating so much it felt like all the liquid in me was being wrung out. I was more present, more real, more *me* than I had been since the morning before—but my lungs still sang with crackles and squeaks, and Mama still handed me the nebulizer before getting back into her seat.

On the bench across from me, Sophie stirred and rubbed her eyes. Elena was still sleeping, her head flopped onto my shoulder, her sandy hair tickling my cheek. In moments like this, it felt like me and Elena were two parts of one whole, like I couldn't tell where I ended and she began. Mama always told me that the very first thing I said when they brought Elena home from the hospital when I was two was *That is my baby!* Ten years later, that's still how Elena felt to me.

According to Mama, the first thing I'd done when *Sophie* came home from the hospital—when I was four—had been to pinch her to try to get her to stop crying all night and all day, which I figured said a lot about our relationship, too.

"Are we there yet?" Sophie asked now, which is the biggest cliché in the world but absolutely what she whined whenever we were on a long trip.

"Almost," Daddy said softly. "Just a few more minutes."

A little nervous flutter ticked in my chest, and I didn't think it was only because the albuterol made my head light and my heart fast. It had been more than two years since we were in Whistling Ridge, North Carolina, where

Mama's oldest sister had made her home. I'd been ten the last time we were there, the same age Elena was now. It had been so long that my memories of Aunt Agatha were fuzzy around the edges, like a photo that's gotten wet. I remembered being a little afraid of her last time we visited; she was one of those no-nonsense grown-ups who was so confident in the way she did things that she could be a little scary.

We knew Mama's family even less well than Daddy's— at least with Daddy's sister, Jenny, we kept in touch a whole lot because she was our doctor. What would Aunt Agatha say about all of us tumbling into her quiet life?

Across from me, Sophie was still awake, leaning against the window and looking out at the sunrise. "Did you know that the really bright star you can see in the morning isn't a star at all?" she asked, sounding annoyingly chipper for as early as it was. "It's the planet Venus. It's usually the first star you see in the evening and the last one you see in the morning. It's so bright at both times that the ancient Greeks thought it was two different stars."

I turned away, as much as I could on the dinette bench. It was hard not to be extra cranky. It felt like I was breathing underwater, and my whole body was heavy as lead. Sophie's astrology lectures were hard enough to deal with at the best of times, and doubly hard when it was barely seven in the morning. "Shouldn't you be going back to sleep?"

"I'm not tired!" Sophie grumped. "You're not the boss of me, anyway, Ivy Mae."

I bit my lip so I didn't spit out the retort that was on the tip of my tongue. I sort of wished I could pull a Jo March and lose Sophie in a frozen pond.

Through the window on the other side of Martha, I could see a green sign, its supports wrapped in kudzu vines: *Welcome to Whistling Ridge, North Carolina, Home of the World's Sweetest Apples!*

Three things happened as we passed that sign.

The first was that Martha jolted—a bumping, stuttering pause that made me drop the pillow I'd been propping myself up with and woke Elena up next to me.

Daddy pulled Martha to a halt at a stop sign, but when he put his foot back on the gas a moment later, she hardly moved. "Darn it all. If this thing gets stuck here—"

After an agonizingly long moment, he got the RV going again. It bounced and jangled with every foot.

"It's the transmission, Marianne," Daddy said. "I'm sure of it. I'll take a look inside when we get to Agatha's, but I'm positive what I'll find. I can't fix that myself. And I've got no idea where the closest mechanic who can work on an old RV like Martha is."

The second thing that happened was that Mama's voice drifted back to me from the front of the RV. "Something isn't right here, Daniel."

"What do you mean?" Daddy asked.

"I don't know." Mama hesitated. "I can't put my finger on it. But it's not just Agatha—something is wrong with *all* of Whistling Ridge."

"Like in Silverwood?"

"So much worse than Silverwood. I've never felt anything like it before."

A trickle of unease, as strong and uncomfortable as the fever flush had been earlier, slipped down my spine. I remembered what I'd overheard last night:

Is this because of the wishing?

It seems like too big a coincidence to be otherwise.

Practically since the moment I'd let those fireflies loose, things had gone wrong—me getting sick, Martha coming near to breaking down right in the middle of Whistling Ridge's sparse downtown.

And the third thing that happened as we entered Whistling Ridge?

I knew, from the top of my scalp to the tips of my

toes, that my wish had come true. I didn't know how to explain it, but it was like the town was a *part* of me, like the red soil and heavy-laden apple trees outside the window belonged to Ivy Mae Bloom as much as my fingernails or the little freckle on the end of my nose.

I'd wished for a forever home. A One True Place.

I knew, deep down in the part of me that had wanted that wish more than anything, that I'd found it.

And I had a strange, queasy kind of feeling that Mama was right. That it was my stolen wishes that had brought us to Whistling Ridge. That taking three-times-three fireflies out to the lake had changed all our lives forever, even if I didn't know how yet.

In stories, the number three is important. And when those three things happened as we crossed into town, I couldn't shake the idea that everything was for a reason. Maybe my wishes had caused all these things to go wrong—but maybe they'd led me toward something *right*, too. Maybe we'd been *meant* to come here. And not just for a visit.

All I had to do now was figure out a way for us to stay in Whistling Ridge for good.

7.

Aunt Agatha was waiting for us when we came, sitting on the front porch of her little white house, rocking back and forth in a porch swing that creaked and sang with each pass. Her hands were full of delicate blue yarn, her fingers dipping and diving like birds as she crocheted it into something unidentifiable. I stared out the window as Daddy maneuvered Martha into the long, curving driveway. It had been two and a half years since we'd visited Whistling Ridge, and that felt kind of long, but that wasn't so much time that I'd have expected Aunt Agatha to have gone from looking strong and middle-aged to positively *old*. She was stooped, her silver hair gone feathery and thin, her skin dry and fragile.

"Oh my heavens," said Mama, her voice outlined in

shock. "What's wrong with her, Daniel?" As soon as Daddy had finished parking, Mama tumbled out of the RV door.

When I caught up a few minutes later, Elena and Sophie trailing behind me, Mama and Aunt Agatha were both standing.

"Honestly, Marianne, you're enough to drive anyone to the grave," Aunt Agatha was saying waspishly. "I'm fine! Fit as a fiddle! I've never been better!"

I was starting to feel flushed and weak again. I let my legs fold up and sank onto the top step, resting my head against one of the supports that led to the porch roof.

"You are *not* just fine," Mama hissed. It was clear that she had seen us girls come up and didn't want us to hear whatever it was she and Aunt Agatha were arguing about. "I could tell something was wrong with you all the way from Oklahoma. And now! You look as though you've aged twenty years since I saw you last!"

Aunt Agatha craned around Mama to look at me with narrowed eyes. "You'd better bring these children inside, Marianne, before Ivy expires on my front porch step."

"Don't think I'm through with you," Mama said in her most no-nonsense voice, but she shooed me inside and then swept Elena and Sophie along with her to help Daddy unload our things from Martha.

"Come lie down on the couch, honey," Aunt Agatha said, following me inside.

Her house was just like I remembered it: spare and beautiful, a sweet old mountain cottage whose bones breathed memories. The wood floors shone in the reflections from the overhead lights, and the walls seemed to sigh with happiness as you came through them. On one wall in the living room was an enormous quilt, intricately pieced together with a hundred different colors, so that when you looked at it from one angle it reminded you of an apple orchard just when the fruit has begun to blush red, but if you turned your head a different way it seemed more like a sunset wreathed in cotton-candy clouds. Aunt Agatha had won first place in the North Carolina State Fair for it the year I turned six.

It was the kind of house I would've chosen to live in, if we had been the kind of family who lived in a house.

"Would you like some cider?" Aunt Agatha asked, flicking on a light as she passed into the kitchen. "Best you'll ever taste."

"Yes, thank you," I said, feeling shy and sick and spent. How could two and a half years make a relative feel like a stranger? Even though Mama had lived in this house until she'd met Daddy and decided to travel full-time, we only came every few years; Mama said that it was more important to go where the magic needed her, and what was the use of spending too much time someplace where Agatha or Ruth had things well under control? Besides, Mama always added, she and her sisters were always connected, no matter how far apart they were.

We came from the same sky, she would say, a smile in her voice. *No amount of space can divide us.*

Which left the rest of us—the ones who weren't made of star stuff—a little bit on the outside.

A minute after Aunt Agatha had disappeared into the kitchen, a little shadow curled around the doorframe that led out of the front room, and stalked toward where I lay on the couch. It was a tabby cat, all brown stripes and sleek fur, eyeing me with a very skeptical expression.

"I didn't know you had a cat," I said when Aunt Agatha returned with a cup filled to the brim with frothy amber liquid.

"I didn't," said Aunt Agatha. "He's a new arrival. Got conned into adopting him and his sister a few months back. His name is Coffee. Cream is around here some-where, probably hiding—she doesn't like people. Coffee, though, might let you pet him if you give him a minute."

Aunt Agatha's voice was grumpy, but her eyes were soft as we watched Coffee's tail swish slowly back and forth. I thought of the list in my notebook.

A pet.

"Drink your cider," she said abruptly. I lifted the cup to my lips and drank—Aunt Agatha was right. The juice tasted cold and deep, like sunshine and earth and happiness.

Coffee crept closer while I drank, until he was right up next to the couch. I reached a careful hand down and ran my fingers over his silky fur. He held very, very still for a moment, but then relaxed a little, like he was a king, deigning to accept my offering.

"Thanks for the cider," I said when I'd finished the cup. Aunt Agatha waved a hand.

"Don't mention it, Ivy. Makes me happy to see you enjoy it. Especially since I don't know when the next batch'll be ready for pressing, with the apples—"

Aunt Agatha stopped short, then shook her head. "Never mind about that. Now, I made some beds up for you and your sisters in one of the guest rooms. Your parents will be in the other. It's been a long, long time since this little house was so full, but we'll make do! There's a regular bed in your room, a trundle bed, and a mattress on the floor with some sheets on it. I figured you could take first pick, seeing as you're the oldest. I know how that goes."

"What's wrong with the apples?" I asked.

"Oh, nothing much. Don't you trouble yourself about that, Ivy—they've just got a spot of fungus. The orchards, they're having a bit of a rough go of it right now, but they'll be fine. You just focus on getting better while you're here."

Mama and Daddy and the girls came in then, and Mama made me do an albuterol treatment and then told us to take our things and get settled into the guest bedroom Aunt Agatha had marked for us to use, before getting started on school for the day.

I laid claim to the real bed, an old-fashioned twin with an intricately carved headboard and four knobbed bedposts, and when Elena was about to cave and give Sophie the trundle, I put my foot down. "You're the baby. You get the mattress."

Sophie shot me a look that was pure fire, but I didn't care. *Somebody* had to stick up for Elena, who went through life so worried of giving offense that she'd probably have apologized if you ran over her puppy in the road. Sometimes I worried that she would get so silent and shy that she'd disappear right into the walls, forgotten by everyone but me and Mama and Daddy and Sophie.

As we finished putting the things we'd need over the next few weeks—pajamas, clothes, notebooks, boxes of schoolwork—into the closet and dresser or tucked under our beds, a snatch of conversation from the kitchen floated in through the half-open bedroom door.

"We're going to be here for a while, Agatha," Mama said, her voice made of titanium and diamonds. "I may not know yet what's wrong with this town, or with you, but I swear: I *will* figure it out."

8.

Sunlight streamed through the windows of Aunt Agatha's kitchen the next morning when I came in for breakfast. Elena and Sophie were still sleeping, and Daddy was outside doing something with Martha's engine hatch open, but Mama and Aunt Agatha were at the kitchen table, deep in tense conversation.

They broke off and looked up when I came in.

"Good morning, honey," Mama said, standing up to give me a hug and feel my forehead. "You aren't too warm. How are you feeling?"

"Fine," I said, and then the rumble in my chest caught up with me and I coughed a few times. "I mean, better than yesterday."

"Good. Breakfast?"

I sat down and poured myself a bowl of cereal. Aunt Agatha only had adult cereals, the kind that had sheaves of wheat on the boxes and adjectives like *heart-healthy* and *high-protein* on the labels.

"Sleep well?" Aunt Agatha asked, passing me the milk. Her hands trembled as I took it, fluttering leaves in a breeze. "Was the bed comfortable?"

"Yes. Thank you." The brown tabby cat, Coffee, slunk into the kitchen and twined his way under Aunt Agatha's chair. When she thought Mama and I weren't looking, Aunt Agatha slipped the cat a little piece of the sliced cantaloupe on her breakfast plate. Thank goodness cats didn't set off my asthma; watching Aunt Agatha sneak the treat to Coffee filled my chest with a warm, tingly feeling. I thought again of my list of wishes. I'd always wanted a pet, for as long as I could remember, but Mama said pets were too hard to care for in the tiny RV and that most pets would've been stressed by a life of constant travel anyway.

"Good." Aunt Agatha smiled, though I couldn't tell if she was smiling because I'd liked her bed or because of Coffee, who had stalked away with his cantaloupe prize.

It was all I could do not to stare at that smile, wrapped in tired-looking wrinkles. How old was Aunt Agatha, exactly? I was fuzzy on how a star aged; Mama said that there were only ever as many star-women in the world as there needed to be, which wasn't a very large number, so it wasn't like I'd ever met any others besides my aunts. Mama's stories always began *Once upon a time, a star fell to earth* and then skipped through her time living in Whistling Ridge to when she met Daddy, who had traveled there to write an article about the apple orchards. I knew stars did get older, and eventually they kind-of-sort-of died—Mama called it "retiring," when a star grew weary of human existence and returned to the sky, becoming a star again instead of a star-person.

But even if I didn't know precisely how old the star sisters were, I knew that Aunt Agatha had never looked *twenty years older* than Mama until this visit.

"You've got a doctor's visit soon, Ivy," Mama said. "Hurry and eat."

I glanced between her and Aunt Agatha again as I ate my cereal. Mama was the youngest—there was Agatha, then Ruth, who lived far away in Montana, then Mama. Mama and her sisters had always seemed to get along perfectly, but if the ice-thick tension in this kitchen was anything to go by, maybe Sophie and I didn't fall so far from the tree.

It was funny, thinking of the star sisters as actual *sisters*, with arguments and irritations just like I had with my own sisters. Had Aunt Agatha ever craved her own space, the way I did? Was Aunt Ruth shy, like Elena? Had Mama ever driven her older sisters crazy the way Sophie did?

Both of them were silent as I ate. Sophie and Elena came in after a few minutes, and then Daddy, wiping grease from his hands.

"I was right," he said as he went to the sink and lathered all the way up to his elbows. "The transmission is kaput. I couldn't even get her to drive two feet this morning. I've got a list of mechanics to call, but they're all more than an hour away. We'll have to pay to get it towed."

"Of course," said Mama grimly. "It never rains but it pours."

"It'll be pricey. An RV tow isn't cheap. Even if we could get it fixed right off, we'll have to stick around here for a while to scrape together enough money to pay for the tow and the repair. I'll email my editor later this afternoon, see if we can come up with any pieces to do. I could do some driving on the Blue Ridge Parkway."

I squirmed. Had my wish really done all this?

Mama and I went alone to my doctor's visit, driving half an hour on winding roads to Asheville in the car Mama had borrowed from Aunt Agatha.

"We might need to get a rental while we're here,

Daniel," she'd said before we left, "so we're not inconveniencing Aggie so much."

"You're not inconveniencing me," Aunt Agatha had interjected.

Mama smiled thinly. "Oh?" she had asked, and I'd had a feeling she was referring to a lot more than just the car.

The clinic was in a tall hospital with an echoing parking garage. I had to do a bunch of different breathing tests, and then a doctor with a steel-wool beard and no-nonsense handshake announced that I had a touch of pneumonia and gave Mama prescriptions for an antibiotic and a steroid, along with instructions that we stay put for a while so I could heal.

"And Ivy," he added as we left, "try to take a gentle walk every day, all right? Don't overexert yourself, but your lungs will need exercise to get your airways clear and strong."

I thought of the apple orchards we'd driven through as we left Aunt Agatha's, red and gold apples shining in the September sun.

"I don't think that will be a problem," I said.

Aunt Agatha was tucked into an overstuffed armchair in the living room when Mama and I got back from the doctor. The blue crochet project she'd been working on yesterday morning when we'd arrived was spread out in her lap; her hands made a steady rhythm as she worked, looping the hook over and under and through, over and under and through. Coffee was curled at her feet, looking *almost* like he was asleep, except for the wary slit of golden eye peeping through one eyelid.

Daddy was in the kitchen, pacing back and forth with Aunt Agatha's landline held to his ear, saying something about *transmission* and *vintage* and *can be finicky*, which I figured meant he was trying to find somebody to fix Martha. My sisters were nowhere to be seen, but from the soft strains of ukulele music coming from the hall, I figured they must be in the bedroom we shared.

Mama kicked off her shoes and headed back into kitchen to get lunch started, but I found myself lingering in the living room, watching Aunt Agatha work. It was mesmerizing the way the thing in her lap grew slowly but surely bigger. A scarf? A blanket? I still couldn't tell.

"Did your mama ever teach you this, Ivy?" Aunt Agatha asked without looking up.

"I don't think so," I said. "She taught us all some sewing as part of school. But with the five of us, there's not much room for craft supplies in Martha."

"It's how I meditate," said Aunt Agatha with a little smile. "It keeps my hands busy and lets my mind go calm."

"It's beautiful," I said, eyeing the mystery thing in her lap. "What is it?"

Aunt Agatha held up the project and shook it out a little; it was bigger than I'd realized, cornflower blue with a delicate, lacy pattern. "It's a shawl. The weather's warm for it yet, but I figure in a few weeks when things start to cool down, it'll be perfect. Here. Come over and I'll show you how it's done."

She patted the fluffy arm of the chair she sat in, and I perched hesitantly on it. Aunt Agatha fished in a basket at her feet for a moment and emerged with a second crochet hook and a new ball of yarn, this one the color of fresh butter.

"You start everything with a chain stitch, like this," she said, putting her wrinkled hands gently over mine and showing me how to make a loop in the yarn and then pass the hook through it, catching the yarn on the other side and pulling it back out. It only took a few tries for my fingers to get the hang of it; a thin, snakelike rope emerged, inch by inch, as I practiced.

"Exactly," said Aunt Agatha, sounding satisfied. "You're a quick study, Ivy. Give it a few months of practice, and I bet you could make yourself a shawl of your own."

"Oh, I don't think so," I said, looking at the shawl spread across Aunt Agatha's lap. "It looks so complicated."

"Doesn't everything in life?" Aunt Agatha asked. "It's all a tremendous mess, until you find the right thread to pull and everything becomes clear."

"I guess so," I said, wondering what thread would explain everything that had happened in the last two days—the things Mama had felt when we crossed into Whistling Ridge, the way Aunt Agatha had aged decades since we'd seen her last.

Aunt Agatha picked her own crochet hook back up, her hands flying through the complicated stitching. It was like watching a painter or a sculptor—the way the shawl formed in real time under her hands was its own kind of magic. After a few more minutes, she pulled the thread tight and snipped it off with a pair of scissors from her workbasket.

"There," she said, holding the shawl up again to show me. It was lacy and triangular, the kind of thing the March sisters of *Little Women* would have worn for sure.

"You know," Aunt Agatha said with a sideways glance at me, "this pattern turned out smaller than I expected it to. I'm not sure it will fit me, after all. Would you like it, Ivy?"

"*Me?*"

Aunt Agatha wrapped the finished shawl around my shoulders. The yarn was as soft and light as the down on a baby bird, and feeling Aunt Agatha put it on me was better than a hug.

"It suits you," she said. "You should keep it, Ivy. Until you're ready to try making one yourself."

"Thank you," I said. I didn't know what else to say. How could I have gone for so many years without this—the chance to sit next to my aunt, to learn from her, to feel the solid walls of a real house holding us like an embrace? She was so much less scary than I'd thought when we'd first gotten to Whistling Ridge; already, the two and a half years since I'd seen her last were dissolving, and it felt like she'd always been a part of our lives.

"I'm glad you're here, Ivy," Aunt Agatha said. "You and your whole family. It feels right, having you here in Whistling Ridge."

"I'm glad, too," I said, hugging the shawl to me. Its warmth and weight around my shoulders felt like *home*.

9.

Later that afternoon—after Daddy informed us at lunch that he'd called six mechanics before finding one named Al who lived two hours away but figured he could work on a vintage Winnebago, and Sophie had told me sixteen hundred facts about galaxies that I didn't even really understand, and Mama had needled at Aunt Agatha three more times to try to get information about what was wrong with her and the magic of Whistling Ridge—Elena and I took the doctor's advice and decided to go for a walk.

"Are you sure it won't make you sicker?" Sophie stood in the middle of the doorway, her toothpick arms on her hips and her blue eyes round as quarters.

I didn't even bother to dignify that with a response,

just grabbed her arms and hauled her out of the way. I'd spoken to Sophie as few times as possible since she'd turned me in to Mama and Daddy on the wishing night. It was easier to hold on to being mad at her for snitching than to think about whether my wishes had given me pneumonia and killed Martha's transmission. And maybe, from the look of Aunt Agatha, made things in Whistling Ridge go from bad to worse.

"I'll take care of her, Soph," Elena said, hugging Sophie before following me outside. "Don't worry."

"She's not worried," I said, pulling Elena away from Sophie and down the front steps. "She's just a *pest*. And a busybody."

"She loves you a lot, you know, Ivy."

"Whatever." I knew I was being mean, but I wasn't ready to forgive Sophie. Not yet. Not while the anger simmered and burned inside me still. I didn't know when I *would* be ready.

The air outside was balmy, thick and wet but not too hot. Martha loomed in the gravel drive, the brown stripe down her middle looking faded all of a sudden, like she was only just now realizing how old she really was. Just as we walked past, a frantic cacophony of chirping erupted from somewhere near the RV's roof.

"What on earth?" Elena asked, just as startled as I

was. We craned our necks up but couldn't see anything.

"Hang on a sec," I said, hooking my hands into the rungs of the roof access ladder bolted beside the spare tire on the back of the RV.

Underneath one of the solar panels on Martha's roof, I could see a dark shape. It was a little cinnamon-colored house wren, thrashing wildly.

"It's a bird, I said. "Trapped under a solar panel."

"A *what*?" Elena asked. "Maybe I should get Mama."

"No, don't. I think it's just scared. Come on, little one. It's all right."

I breathed as steadily as I could, ignoring the crackling in my chest and trying to slow my heartbeat down as I inched my hand forward, one finger extended. As soon as I got close, the bird freaked out again, beating its wings against the confinement of the solar panel.

"Sing something," I called down to Elena as quietly as I could.

"Sing what? I can't sing out here! Anyone could hear me." Fear laced through Elena's voice.

"Nobody's anywhere near us. Please, Elena? I need something to calm this poor bird down, and *my* voice certainly won't do it."

I could hear Elena take a deep, nervous breath below me, but a minute later the clear notes of "Blackbird" rose into the air. I inched my hand back toward the little bird, slowly and carefully, trying to be as quiet as I could. By the time I was a finger's-length away, it had calmed most of the way down. It watched me with a sideways tilt to its head, chirping sharply every now and then like it wanted me to remember it was on its guard, but not flapping its wings like it had at the beginning.

Finally, I got my finger close enough to reach in and sweep the bird out from under the solar panel. It tumbled free, squawking again and pecking at where my hand had been just a minute before. It was all I could do to keep hold of the ladder and not tumble backward as the bird shook its wings hard and then zoomed screeching over my head and into the trees.

"And stay away," I hollered after the little wren. If I thought Martha made a lousy home for me, it was even worse to think of a bird taking up residence on the old RV.

Elena stopped singing as I climbed back down the ladder and pulled my inhaler from my pocket. The albuterol hissed as I pressed it down; it didn't take long for it to start working, untying some of the knots in my airways. In movies, people with asthma only carry inhalers to show that they're weak or nervous, and once they manage to find some confidence, they leave the inhalers at home or toss them in the trash. But really, that's stupid. You could be the bravest person in the world, and it wouldn't much matter if you were allergic to dogs or trees or dust mites and your body responded by cutting off your air supply.

As soon as I'd caught my breath, Elena and I headed away from Aunt Agatha's house, into the orchard that began where her property ended. It was early evening, the time of day when the sunlight was extra golden as it filtered through the leaves of the apple trees. I paused and wrote that line down in the notebook I was carrying tucked under my arm. I was between projects at the moment—I'd gone almost two whole weeks without thinking of something worth starting—but I couldn't ever bear to let a beautiful phrase go to waste. Plus, there was my word list. I only saved the very best ones, like *mellifluous* or *aubergine*, and I tried to work them into my stories as often as I could.

"I like it here," said Elena wistfully as we walked through the middle of the nearest orchard. The trees were laid out in rows, with long aisles of green grass between them, soft as a bed. Bees hummed around our heads, dipping in and out of the dandelions and flying up to examine the blushing apples where they hung. The whole orchard was filled with a scent of cider so strong I could smell it even with my nose still stuffed up.

"Me too," I said, and my sigh turned into a cough. "I would live here." The certainty of what I'd felt yesterday as we crossed into Whistling Ridge slithered back into me. This place was *meant* to be my forever home; I knew it. I just had to figure out how to show Mama and Daddy that. Maybe my wishes had caused my sickness and Martha's transmission problems—maybe they even had something to do with whatever was wrong with Aunt Agatha.

But still, I knew I'd do almost anything to stay in Whistling Ridge.

"Here, in the orchard?" Elena laughed.

"Right up there, in that exact tree. I'd build a tree house and leave a hole in the roof so I could see the moon and the stars while I fell asleep. And every night, I'd dream about applesauce and apple juice and apple pie."

"Maybe we should try one. An apple, I mean. I've got a pocketknife—we could cut one and share it between us. Would that be stealing, do you think?"

"Of course not," I said, even though I thought it might be, because Elena would never do anything that bent rules. I reached up and picked one of the apples that grew just over my head and examined it. "Aunt Agatha said the orchards were fighting some kind of fungus, but this looks completely fine."

I tossed the apple to Elena. She sliced carefully, making one smooth cut with the core at the center, so that when she was done it fell easily into two halves.

As soon as it did, Elena dropped the knife. Both of us stared.

Inside the apple, instead of seeds and a stem and white, juicy flesh, there was a dark cavity filled with swirling, undulating, charcoal-gray smoke.

Elena looked up at me, her eyes extra dark and scared-looking. When she spoke, it was a choked-sounding whisper. "What is that?"

"I don't know," I said back, my own voice sounding too loud in the suddenly silent orchard. "I've never seen anything like it before."

I took a deep breath, so distracted I hardly even noticed the rattle and buzz of congestion in my lungs. "But I'm pretty sure it's not a fungus."

"Ivy," said Elena, and even before she said anything else, I knew that she'd heard it, too, Mama fighting with her oldest sister. "What is Aunt Agatha not telling Mama?"

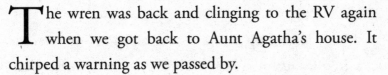

10.

The wren was back and clinging to the RV again when we got back to Aunt Agatha's house. It chirped a warning as we passed by.

"Shoo," I called, waving my hands in its general direction, but my heart wasn't in it. Over and over in my mind I could see the smoke inside that apple, swirling and curling and proving that Mama was right: something was very, *very* wrong in Whistling Ridge. In a whole lifetime of driving around the United States and watching Mama sniff out all the places where the world's magic was weakened, I'd never seen anything like that apple.

The screen door slammed behind us as we came inside. Daddy was on the living room couch, his laptop perched on his lap. Sophie lay next to him, reading something called *The Basics of Stellar Astrophysics, 4th Edition*. I didn't know how she could spend so much time poring over those textbooks when everything about our life called the star science inside them into question, but whenever I asked, Sophie serenely said that just because nobody had made the connections yet between science and magic, that didn't mean that both couldn't be true.

Mama and Aunt Agatha sat at the kitchen table, cutting new cheesecloth squares for Mama's wish jars.

The ones she'd have to spend half the night refilling, thanks to me.

Mama looked up as soon as we came in. Whatever she saw in our faces had her surging to her feet, cheesecloth and canning jars forgotten. "Girls, what happened?"

Elena shrank toward me. She'd dropped the apple halves in the orchard almost as soon as we'd seen them—and, I realized now, left her pocketknife there, too.

I took a deep breath. "We went walking in the orchard next door," I said, squeezing Elena's hand. Even if Elena hadn't been two years younger than me, she was the kind of person you couldn't help protecting, the sort who comes into the world a little more fragile and a lot more loving than everybody else. "And . . . everything smelled so good, and it was such a nice day, and the cider

Aunt Agatha gave me yesterday was so amazing, so . . . we decided to share an apple. We didn't think it would be stealing."

Aunt Agatha covered her mouth with one hand. I was pretty sure it wasn't because of my half-confessed theft.

"And?" Mama pressed.

"It wasn't normal. The apple, I mean. Instead of seeds and stuff, there was . . ."

I stopped. I didn't know how to describe what we'd seen.

"Smoke," Aunt Agatha said quietly, lowering her hand. "Swirling gray smoke. Is that what you saw, Ivy?"

"Yes."

With an anger so hot you could almost see sparks sizzling on her skin, Mama turned to Aunt Agatha—but before she could even open her mouth, Aunt Agatha reached for Mama's hand.

"I'm sorry, Marianne. I'm so sorry. I hoped that you and your girls wouldn't get wrapped up in this. I should have told you—I know I should have—but I was worried. Worried that involving you might put *you* in danger, too."

Aunt Agatha closed her eyes, like seeing Mama was too painful. "You have to understand. You and Ruth— you are the two sides of my heart, and it could not beat without either of you. Sometimes I love you so much it scalds. And you, Marianne. You're the best of all three of us, with your beautiful family, with the love that spills out of you wherever you go. Ruth and I, we've holed up in our mountain towns, never quite able to settle or commit to the kind of love you've created. But you—you've made a life out of loving strangers. You carry blessings with you wherever you go."

"Agatha," said Mama. "What. Is. Going. On?"

"It started—I don't even know when it started. Something's been wrong in Whistling Ridge for a long time now. Like a tiny hole in a basin, the magic has been seeping out of this town for years. I couldn't figure out a way to stop it, but for a long time, I've been able to patch it here and there. Until lately. Something happened this week. Like all the patches I'd put in place were ripped right out."

"That's what I felt that night in Silverwood," Mama murmured. "That's why I knew I needed to come here."

By now, Daddy and Sophie had come to stand in the kitchen doorway, identical expressions on their faces: Wide eyes, sucked-in cheeks, hardly breathing. I had a feeling that was what Elena and I looked like, too.

"Even before that," Aunt Agatha went on, "it was speeding up. Like the hole's gotten bigger, and the leak has grown faster. It's been so strong that nothing I do seems to have much of an effect. No matter what I try, the magic of Whistling Ridge continues to be siphoned off, faster and faster with every day that passes."

"And you?" Mama asked. "Is that what's happened to you, too?"

Aunt Agatha gave a half smile and turned one of her liver-spotted hands from back to front, looking at it. "Yes, I think so. I can't be sure, but I believe that I've lived in this town so long and given so much of myself to it that everything I am is tied into Whistling Ridge. It's my One True Place, you know. As the leak has sped up and taken more of the town, it—I suppose it's taken more from me, too."

"I'm so sorry, Aggie," Mama said. "Please. Let me help. Let me call Ruth, too."

Aunt Agatha nodded. "I think we have to. This is bigger than me. I'm afraid that if we can't stop this thing, it will swallow Whistling Ridge whole, and then go beyond the town lines to threaten other places, too. Who's to say where it would stop? This is like nothing we've ever seen before."

I thought of what Mama had said back in Silverwood. *Pompeii. The San Francisco Fire.*

Surely things in Whistling Ridge couldn't be as bad as that.

From the doorway, Daddy cleared his throat. "Marianne, do you think . . ."

Mama turned to him, and they shared one of those long, speaking kinds of looks that adult married people have, where it feels like they have a whole conversation even though nobody says anything.

When their silent conversation finished, Mama looked at me.

"Ivy, I think it's time you told us what you wished for in Silverwood."

The whole room contracted around me, like the walls were squeezing the breath from my lungs. Did we really have to do this in front of *everyone*?

"Your mama and Aunt Agatha are going to need every bit of information they can get," Daddy said gently.

I squirmed. When I finally answered, my voice was as quiet as I could make it. "I wished for a forever home."

"A what?" Mama asked. Apparently I'd been *too* quiet.

"I wished for a forever home," I said again, louder this time. I was surprised to find that the words came out strong and brave, not matching the trembly feeling in my stomach. It was like the words themselves knew how important they were, how much they could change my life.

"What do you mean?" Daddy asked, his forehead wrinkled.

"I don't want to move anymore," I said, the nervousness

fading away, replaced by stubborn surety. "I don't want to live in Martha. I want to live somewhere *permanently*. Like Aunt Agatha does."

Aunt Agatha looked away, like she was staying out of the whole thing, but not before giving me the tiniest hint of a wink.

"You know we can't do that, Ivy," said Daddy.

"Ivy's wishing wouldn't have caused this," said Aunt Agatha. "It was happening before. Like I told you, the magic has been leaving this town slowly but surely for years. And the further it's gone on, the stronger it's gotten."

"But you said something happened *this week*," Mama interjected.

"True," said Aunt Agatha.

"Could Ivy using the wishes have caused that?" Daddy asked.

Aunt Agatha shrugged, looking defeated. "I suppose we'll never know for sure, but it could've been a factor."

Guilt sat like a brick in my stomach.

"I'm sorry," I whispered, even though I wasn't 100 percent sure I was. Hadn't my wishes led us to Whistling Ridge, after all? Hadn't they given me a place I already felt I'd belonged the moment I crossed the town line? With Mama and Aunt Agatha working together, surely my wishes couldn't do too much permanent damage. And maybe, if I figured out a way to convince Mama and Daddy to stay in Whistling Ridge *before* the star sisters repaired the magic . . . I could finally make that list of wishes come true.

Mama stood up. "I need to call Ruth," she said, looking distracted and upset. Daddy handed her the cell phone they shared, and she disappeared with it into the bedroom they'd slept in the night before.

"Thank you, Ivy, for being honest," Aunt Agatha said when Mama had gone.

"You're welcome," I said, because I couldn't quite bring myself to say *I'm sorry.*

Mama returned to the kitchen a minute later.

"I got her," she announced, and Aunt Agatha looked torn between relief and sorrow. "She was worried. She says she'll come just as soon as she can, but she has to get some personal affairs in order first."

Aunt Ruth lived in Montana, in a place where the earth was so wide and the sky so big it seemed ready to swallow you up. It had been even longer since we'd visited Montana than our last visit to Whistling Ridge. I could remember Aunt Ruth only vaguely, like a smudged watercolor painting. She lived on a farm with somebody we called Uncle Andrew, though I'd never been sure if they were married or not, and they didn't have any kids. My memories of him were even dimmer—blond hair and cowboy boots and a big, booming laugh.

"What exactly does that mean?" Daddy asked. Mama shrugged.

Aunt Agatha stood and hugged Mama. Not a few-seconds hug, but a hug that lasted as long as an indrawn breath, like Mama was Aunt Agatha's oxygen. "I'm glad my secret is out, Marianne," she said. "Worried, too. But mostly relieved."

Mama looked Aunt Agatha in the eye. Even with Aunt Agatha looking so much older now, you could see the resemblance between them: Aunt Agatha's eyes were darker, and the lines in her face were sharper, but they both had the same silver-white hair, the same golden-brown skin.

Right now, holding on to each other in this simple kitchen in Whistling Ridge, both of them glowed, brighter than Mama ever had on her own.

"Ruth will come," Mama said. "Daniel and I are stuck here until we can afford to get the transmission fixed. We can stay longer than that if we need to. I promise, you won't have to do this thing alone."

"Thank you," said Aunt Agatha. And somehow, even though she didn't look any younger than she had two minutes ago, looking at her now, you didn't notice the wrinkles and the paper skin quite so much as before.

That night, Mama spent the dusk hour in Aunt Agatha's backyard, catching fireflies to fill the jars they'd prepped. It was the kind of thing nobody else could help with, because only fallen stars could whisper the wish-magic back into the fireflies. Aunt Agatha offered to help, too, but Mama took one look at her tired-old-lady face and declined.

"Oh well," said Aunt Agatha grumpily, "you always had more of a knack for it than I did, anyway. I've gotten out of practice, all these years living in one place. I'm better with my plants."

Still, she went outside with Mama all the same. And when the two of them thought nobody else was looking, I saw them lace their fingers together and lay their free hands on the ground, just like Mama had done near Silverwood Lake. Both star sisters glowed brighter and brighter, until they practically lit up the whole backyard.

But the gleaming veins of golden light that spread outward from their fingers looked all wrong, flickering in and out of being like a lightbulb does when it's getting ready to die, like all of Mama's and Aunt Agatha's light still couldn't fight the darkness that was humming below Whistling Ridge.

Mama had told me before that star-magic worked because everything in the world—trees, dirt, people, even water—had been created from elements born in the hearts of stars, billions and billions of years ago. When things started to go wrong, fallen stars like Mama and her sisters could whisper light into the broken places, helping to infuse a little bit of stardust back into the world.

The world needs light, Ivy, Mama had said once, *and we stars have light to give.*

But I'd never seen Mama's magic-tending look like this—like all the stardust she poured into the earth was not enough. Like the brokenness was too enormous to be healed.

Finally, the backyard went abruptly dark, the glow from Mama and Aunt Agatha extinguished like somebody had thrown water over them.

When they came back in a little later, Aunt Agatha walked as though every step hurt her, and Mama's hands trembled on the firefly jars.

It had been years since my mama had worked together with either of her sisters. How could the darkness in Whistling Ridge swallow the light of *two* fallen stars?

11.

When I woke up at Aunt Agatha's on Saturday—the morning after my doctor's appointment, the morning after Elena and I had found the apples filled with smoke—I felt like under-steeped tea, weak and watery, like the reminders of my fever had traced themselves through my skin.

"How long are we going to stay?" Elena asked at breakfast. She, Sophie, Mama, and I were the only ones at the table; Daddy had gone off to call his editor and pitch a bunch of articles, and Aunt Agatha was out on the front porch, tending her flowers.

Mama shrugged. "As long as it takes to get the money to repair Martha, and for Ivy to get all the way better. And we can't leave until Ruth and I can help Aggie figure out what's draining the magic from the town. Ruth texted me this morning—she's got her plane tickets and will arrive next Friday." Mama looked tired. "I hope that will be soon enough."

And maybe, I thought, my fingertips tingling on my cereal spoon, *we'll stay even longer.* The memory of those nine wishes rising into the air of the Silverwood campground was so vivid I could almost reach out and touch the fireflies. The certainty I'd felt when we'd crossed the Whistling Ridge town line Thursday, that this was the place I was meant to be, was even stronger this morning.

Even after only two days in Whistling Ridge, it already felt like home—there was a real bedroom with a door that could close, even if I did share it with Elena and Sophie. There was Coffee the cat and his elusive ("difficult to find") sister. There were the trees that ringed Aunt Agatha's property; I could already imagine what they would look like in the autumn, when the leaves would flame scarlet and gold. If only we could stay here, I might even get the chance to see a whole year of seasons.

Maybe all the disasters that had come from my wish would be worth it in the end, if it resulted in finding my forever home.

"Did you know," said Sophie, who had a milk mustache that made her look even younger than usual, "that almost every element on earth was made out of the fusion reactions that power stars? We're all made of stardust, and so are the ground and the trees and the animals and all that."

"Really?" Mama asked, even though she'd told me nearly the same thing before. Mama always treated the things we said like they were worth listening to.

Sophie launched into a long-winded explanation filled with technical terms I couldn't begin to understand, so I excused myself and took my writing notebook out to where Aunt Agatha was trimming dead blooms off a vine wrapped around the porch railing.

The notebook felt warm in my hands. Even without opening it, I could see the words on my list like they were burned in front of my eyes. Wish number three was *a garden*, just like the lush profusion of plants that spilled from Aunt Agatha's porch and filled her backyard. Aunt Agatha's whole property seemed almost to *breathe*, it was so filled with living things. You couldn't possibly have plants like that when you lived on the road. The best we'd ever done was a group of potted succulents that Mama kept on the dinette table for a few months, until even *they* had started having trouble with the constantly changing climate and Mama had given them away to somebody we'd met in Colorado.

I hugged the notebook to me. I'd been trying all morning to think of something to write; the whole atmosphere of Whistling Ridge seemed so *perfect* for writing, but no idea I thought of felt good enough.

"Sisters got to be too much?" Aunt Agatha asked sympathetically as I sat down on the porch swing and let it rock me back and forth.

I sighed. "Yep."

"As one oldest sister to another, I well know the feeling," said Aunt Agatha with a conspiratorial smile.

"What's that flower, Aunt Agatha? It's pretty." The living blossoms on the plant she was working on were full and lavender-colored, long, pointed petals stacked on top of one another until the effect was almost like a leafy vine covered in purple pom-poms, except much more elegant.

"It's a clematis," she said, gently guiding one of the vines that had drooped away toward the ground back to the pillar. "This variety is called 'Lovelace.' Lots of people in town have a Lovelace clematis somewhere. It's named after a very famous nineteenth-century mathematician, the Countess of Lovelace. But in Whistling Ridge, we grow them to remember a different woman—Lydia Lovelace, the town legend."

I stopped rocking on the swing and leaned forward.

"Really? Who was she?"

"Lydia Lovelace was one of the first settlers in Whistling Ridge. Nobody knows where she came from before she lived here. She had no family—she was an orphan—but she owned a little cottage on the south side of town where she grew the most beautiful garden anyone had ever seen. She was very beautiful herself, too, if you believe the stories—but not beautiful enough."

"What do you mean?"

"Lydia fell in love with a young man—the son of the town's first mayor. The story is that they were close friends, but for Lydia, the friendship became something more than that."

"And not for him?"

Aunt Agatha shook her head. "No. He loved a cousin who lived up North."

"His *cousin*?"

Aunt Agatha laughed. "Back in those days, people married their cousins rather a lot, though it does seem strange to us. Anyway, the story is that one night, Lydia confessed her feelings to the mayor's son, and kissed him under the starlight in her beautiful garden. But he didn't return her feelings, and married his cousin instead."

I stared at her. "What happened to Lydia?"

"She died. Of a broken heart, they say, though

admittedly that sounds a little suspect to a modern listener. Whatever happened, though, she just lost the will to live. She was buried in her own garden, and red roses grow over her grave still."

"Wow," I said, sighing again—a nice kind of sigh this time, the delicious kind of sadness that comes from tragically romantic things. "Kind of like Romeo and Juliet. But real. And in Whistling Ridge."

Aunt Agatha nodded. "She's a bit like the town's heart. People in Whistling Ridge love her, love how faithful she was to the mayor's son even when he'd broken her heart; that's why the Lovelace clematis is so popular. There are songs about her, books, there's even a Lovelace Festival the week before Halloween. . . ."

"That's it!" I said, surging to my feet. "Aunt Agatha, *that's it exactly!* I'll write something about Lydia Lovelace!"

Aunt Agatha smiled. "That sounds like an excellent idea, Ivy. And I expect you might even be able to convince your mother to consider it a local history study unit," she added with a wink. "You might ask at the library; the librarian, Christie Mendoza, has papers that belonged to Lydia, and she could show you around the cottage."

"Thank you, Aunt Agatha," I said, already scribbling

a list of ideas in my writing notebook. "It's perfect!"

And maybe my story would do more than just be a local history unit. Mama and Daddy were always telling us girls about the importance of history, and stories, and remembering our roots. Maybe writing something about Lydia would show them how deep and how romantic the roots of Whistling Ridge were.

More importantly, maybe writing this story would show them *me*—the Ivy they always seemed to be too busy to see. Maybe they'd finally see the way I *needed* a forever home, needed it just as much as the Lovelace clematis on Aunt Agatha's porch needed to drink sunlight. Maybe my story would show them how Whistling Ridge had already worked its way into the deepest parts of my heart, even after only two days.

I leaned back in the porch swing with the notebook held to my chest, my whole body filled with a bubbly, fizzy kind of excitement. This project was the key, the start of a new life for the Blooms.

The moment where my name, *Ivy Mae Bloom*, became a promise, not a threat.

12.

"I got a call saying your prescriptions are in at the pharmacy downtown," Mama said later that morning. "Aggie said there's a park in walking distance. Ivy, would you please take your sisters there while I'm gone so Daddy can get some work done? I know it's Saturday, but he'll need to put in extra time if we're going to save up enough to repair Martha. Aggie's house is too small for everyone to be cooped up together."

I groaned, not looking up from the notebook I was scribbling in—ideas for my Lydia Lovelace story. I even had the perfect first line, one that reminded me of all the old ballads Elena loved to sing:

Deep under the soil where the Whistling Ridge apple

trees sink their roots, the town holds the memory of a great heartbreak.

"Do I have to?" I said. "I still feel crummy."

"The fresh air will be good for you," Mama said bracingly. "And I looked the park up on Google. It's closer than that orchard walk you took yesterday. You can take your notebook along with you and work on your story while your sisters play. I won't even make you take along the math work you *ought* to have finished yesterday. This is nonnegotiable, Ivy. You should be grateful that your daddy and I aren't giving you some sort of worse consequence for stealing all those wishes. Pneumonia seems like a pretty significant punishment. Still, it may be awhile before we trust you with quite so much freedom again."

"Can I stay here with Daddy?" said Elena, and I knew she was thinking of a park filled with strangers, the kind of friendly Southerners who'd ask her name and want her to tell them all sorts of things about herself. Even when she was Sophie's age, Elena hadn't much liked public places with lots of people.

"Not this time," said Mama, and I could tell her patience was wearing thin. "You're all going. Take books to read, take games, I don't honestly care *what* you do there as long as you *aren't* doing it in Aunt Agatha's house. I'll pick you all up on my way back from the pharmacy. Understood?"

Elena nodded, face pale.

Sophie stayed silent, but I hadn't missed the quick, nervous look she'd given me when Mama said we all had to go together. *Good*, I thought viciously, glad Sophie knew I hadn't forgiven her yet. It would take longer than four days to get over the simmering anger I felt when I remembered how she'd told Mama and Daddy about the wishes I'd stolen.

I thought of the night we'd left Silverwood, the way Mama had told Daddy it seemed like too much of a coincidence for my wish *not* to have caused all the calamities that had happened since. If Mama was going to blame me for my pneumonia and Martha's transmission and whatever it was that was funneling the magic from Whistling Ridge faster than Aunt Agatha could heal it, I could certainly blame Soph for turning me in.

The wren was back on the camper top when we got outside. It cheeped as we walked by.

"I think I saw that there yesterday," said Sophie.

"I did, too," I said, temporarily forgetting to be grumpy with her as I craned my neck to look at the bird. "It was stuck under one of the solar panels, and me and

Elena helped it get free."

"I wonder why it came back," Elena murmured. "It seemed so upset yesterday."

"Curiouser and curiouser," said Sophie, sounding just like Alice in Wonderland as she squinted at the bird.

Mama had been right when she said the park was close by. Aunt Agatha's house was hardly out of sight when the park came into view—a nice old park with towering trees and a big lawn and a wooden play structure built to look like a castle. On the far side, where a wide paved trail wound past a soccer field with a game in progress and then disappeared into the forest, I could see the glimmer of sunlight on water.

"Ooh," said Sophie. "Cool castle."

"You don't have some opinion about how it should be built better?" I asked, unable to resist the barb.

Sophie raised her chin, like a queen who was too good to rise to anger. "Architecture isn't my area, Ivy."

"You should go play over there." The idea of being stuck at the park all morning with Sophie hovering at my elbow was scarier than the smoke-apples.

Sophie shrank back a little and clutched her thick textbook. "I just want to read."

Happy cries from Sophie-size kids playing on the playground echoed over to us, mingling with cheers and whistles from the soccer field. "Come on, it will be fun."

Sophie eyed the other kids for a minute before finally sighing and shoving the textbook into my arms. "Fine. But only because I want to see what the castle is like up high."

"Try not to be too weird!" I called after her.

Even with the heavy astrophysics book in my arms, I felt my shoulders relax as soon as Sophie crossed onto the bark-chipped earth of the playground. There was something about the park that breathed stillness and peace—even in this week full of disasters.

"Why didn't she want to go play?" I asked Elena.

"It's not easy for everyone to make friends like you do," Elena said. I thought of Ada and the RV Girl bracelet I'd tossed into the lake at Silverwood. Friends were easier to make than to keep. "Sometimes kids are mean to her. Haven't you noticed?"

I thought back to other parks, other states, other sunny days, and honestly couldn't remember. "She always seems like she's in control of everything." *Annoyingly so.*

"Not always," Elena said.

"Well, I'm going to sit in the shade and work on my story."

Elena followed me to an enormous oak tree that sat

not too far from the playground. It had branches as thick around as my waist that spun out from the trunk, so that one tree seemed almost like a small forest all by itself, filled with magic and mystery. It was exactly the kind of tree under which stories *ought* to be born. I could feel it, how my Lydia Lovelace story would come to life in this place, the magic of this moment seeping into the pages.

I settled onto the grass underneath the tree, letting my spine sink against the trunk. If I stayed very still, it was almost as though I could feel the tree breathe.

Elena sat next to me, her knees drawn up to her chest and her arms wrapped around them. Sometimes, when we were in a public place like this, Elena seemed to turtle in on herself, going into observation mode: always watching, but never comfortable being watched herself. I reached out and squeezed her hand, *one-two-three*— our sister code for *I love you*. I'd started doing it when Elena was younger than Sophie was now, when she had a tendency to cry anytime we were around big groups of people. Three squeezes were a way to reassure Elena *I'm here. We're together. Everything's okay.*

After everything Aunt Agatha had told us in her kitchen the day before, I wasn't 100 percent sure that everything *was* okay. But still, I could feel a little of the tension draining out of Elena's fingers as she squeezed back.

* * *

We'd been at the park maybe ten minutes, and I'd gotten so deep into my scribblings that I was hardly aware anymore of the sounds of the soccer field or the whisper of the wind through the leaves above me, when something sailed out of the tree and clonked on my head so hard I saw stars.

"Ouch!" I shouted, dropping my notebook and pen so I could rub the sore spot on my head. A *shoe* landed on the grass next to me—a scraggly-looking running shoe, gray with white stripes, its laces untied and flapping to the sides.

"Sorry! Oh my gosh, sorry, sorry, sorry!" hollered a voice from the tree above me.

The branches rustled.

I looked up to see a stocky boy about my age with skin and hair so pale it glowed in the sunshine. One of his feet had on a sneaker that matched the one on the ground next to me, but the other only had a sock. He was climbing monkey-like down through the branches, his arms and legs seeming to know just where to go, like he'd climbed up and down this tree a zillion times before.

In hardly any time, he had made it all the way to the lowest branch. He grabbed onto it and dangled for a minute, long legs hanging, before dropping to the ground.

"I'm so sorry," he said, panting. The boy spoke so fast it could've been a competitive sport, his speed totally at odds with the gentle drawl that wove its way through his words. "I was trying to figure out the likelihood of getting the Whistling Ridge parks department to let me build a tree house in this tree—it's the best, isn't it? It's the biggest oak in the whole town. It's why they named this Oaktree Park—and I wasn't paying any attention and then my shoelace got loose and boom, I took one more step and the shoe was gone before I even knew what had happened. Does that ever happen to you when you're concentrating on something, you just kind of forget to pay attention to anything else? It happens to me all the time. Drives my moms crazy. Anyway, I'm really sorry. I didn't even realize y'all were down there. Um, would you mind passing me my shoe?"

I handed the shoe over but couldn't find anything to say in reply, like the blond boy had sucked up all the words from everyone in the park with one very long paragraph. I thought of the wish list in my notebook. *A tree house* had been on there.

"What's your name?" the boy asked, not seeming to notice or care that I hadn't responded. Beside me I could feel Elena radiating unease. The boy stuck his hand out like he was going to shake mine, but then snatched it back at the last minute and wiped it on his shirt. "Oh, sorry, I'm covered in tree sap. I'm Simon Welcher. My Mom and my Mama have an apple orchard up the hill. There's some kind of apple disease all over town right now where all our apples have this weird smoky rot inside, so that sucks, but normally it's totally awesome. Are you new in town?"

"Ivy Bloom," I said, feeling a little shy myself in Simon's onslaught of chatter, reaching out to shake his no-longer-sappy hand. "We're visiting my aunt Agatha."

"Oh!" Simon's face lit up. "I know her. She lives right near our property. HEY, RAVI!" he shouted without warning. I jumped a little. "This girl Ivy's visiting Miss Agatha! Come meet her!"

The tree branches above me rustled ominously again, and—unbelievably—a second set of sneakers came into view, this one attached to a dark-haired boy with bronze skin and a large notepad clutched in one of his hands.

"Catch," the second boy called, and dropped the pad into Simon's waiting hands. A zippered pencil pouch came flying after it a minute later. Before long he, too, was on the ground, brushing oak leaves from his striped T-shirt.

"Hi," I said, a little guarded. Did *everyone* in Whistling Ridge make a habit of hiding up trees? How many more boys might be obscured in the branches, waiting to drop out at any moment?

Elena was doing her best to fade into the tree bark next to me. If our whole family had been different types of stars, Sophie would've been a hypergiant—a huge, unstable star that's full of energy and might explode at any minute. Elena, though, would've been a white dwarf, a super-faint star that doesn't have as much fuel and is okay to just hang out, letting the bigger stars steal the spotlight.

"I'm Ravi Sidana," the second boy said. Up close, I could see that he had brown eyes ringed with long, dark eyelashes, the kind that were really *not* fair on a boy.

He smiled at me, a smile like sunshine and birdsong.

I smiled back.

"Ravi's a really great artist," Simon rattled on, holding up the notepad—a sketchbook, I could see now. "He draws all the time, and his drawings and paintings are so good."

"Sorry if we scared you," Ravi cut in. His voice was quieter than Simon's, almost musical, and he had the same kind of nowhere-everywhere accent as my sisters and I. "When Simon said he wanted to climb the big oak, I decided to go, too. It was a pretty good vantage point for sketching. The whole town looks different up there."

"I didn't even realize you two were down here until just before I dropped my shoe!" Simon said. "Is this your sister? What's her name?"

Elena curled further into herself. I reached out and took her hand, squeezing one-two-three. "This is Elena. And my other little sister, Sophie, is playing at the park. She's eight."

"Cool! I have a sister who's eight, too! She's playing soccer right now. That's why we're both here, me and Ravi. His little brother and my little sister are on the same soccer team. Neither of us play, though. When fall soccer starts up, all the Whistling Ridge kids who don't play end up spending half our Saturday mornings here. It can be boring, but it can be fun, too. We're like the town misfits."

"Misfits?" I asked.

"You know. The ones who aren't coordinated, or who don't like to get sweaty, or whatever. The sports atheists."

"You don't . . . believe in sports?" I asked, confusedly trying to remember the definition for *atheist* in my pocket dictionary.

"Something like that. There's me and Ravi, and then there's Charlie"—he waved at a teenage girl with dark brown skin and corkscrew curls who sat reading a thick book on a bench nearby—"and Joel and Leah"—this time he gestured to a pale, freckled boy who looked between Sophie's and Elena's ages, and a red-haired girl about the same age, playing at the playground.

"We always seem to end up here on Saturday mornings," Simon concluded. "Since nearly everyone has a sibling who plays soccer."

"Except Charlie," Ravi said. "She just likes to read in the park. Says it's nicer than reading at home or the library."

"It's very nice to meet you both," I said.

"Please don't tell me you're going to join the soccer team," said Simon. "That would be really embarrassing."

I laughed. "I've never been on a soccer team."

"Really?"

"My family lives on the road. It's hard to join a team when you don't stay in one place longer than a few weeks."

"You'll fit right in, then," Ravi said with a smile. He had the kind of voice that sounded quiet and serious even when he was grinning. If the way Simon spoke was like a runaway kite on a windy day, Ravi was the string keeping it safely anchored. Ravi nodded at the notebook I was still clutching to my chest. "Do you draw, too?"

"No," I said, my breath half-held. Part of never having a forever home was never knowing how new people were going to react when I gave them little pieces of me. "I write. Stories, sometimes poems and things."

"Cool," said Ravi, and the way he said it made it clear he really *did* think it was cool.

I felt a warm little glow ignite somewhere in my chest. It reminded me of watching the fireflies spiral away when I'd released them by Silverwood Lake.

Over by the road, I heard the echo of a car door slam, and a minute later Mama's silvery hair came into view.

"Ivy! Elena! Sophie!" she called, waving at us. She held a white paper bag, which I guessed had my medicines. "Time to go!"

I was used to people doing a double take when they saw Mama, but Simon and Ravi didn't bat an eyelid. Then again, they'd probably seen stranger things than that, sharing a town with Aunt Agatha. Simon had mentioned an apple disease that sounded an awful lot like the swirling smoke Elena and I had found.

I shivered a little.

Mama came forward and put a hand on my shoulder. "I'm glad to see you girls making friends. Who are these young men, Ivy?"

Simon stood up so tall his chest puffed out a little. "Simon Welcher, ma'am."

"And I'm Ravi Sidana," Ravi added.

"You must be related to the pharmacist," Mama said, holding up the bag. "I just met your daddy."

"Yes, ma'am," Ravi said.

"You should come back next Saturday, Ivy," Simon said. "We're here every Saturday morning."

Mama's hand was warm where it rested on my shirt-sleeve. "I'm sure Ivy would love that, if she's feeling well enough. She's been sick lately."

"Not *sick* sick," I added hastily. The way Mama had said it made it sound like I'd had something *terrible*, for goodness' sake. "I'm fine."

"Well, hopefully we'll see you then!" said Simon.

Beside him, Ravi gave a tiny nod, his deep brown eyes bright. The way Ravi met my gaze—serious but happy, too—made me feel as though my insides were made of stardust.

After Mama had hugged the anxiety out of Elena and rounded up Sophie from the park and loaded us all into Aunt Agatha's car, I lay against the passenger-seat window, the chill of the glass nice on my cheek. The twenty minutes I'd spent at the park felt like they'd siphoned away an entire day's worth of energy—but beneath the tiredness, and the little squeeze in my lungs that whispered to find my inhaler, there was a fizzing, bubbling kind of happiness.

In my whole life, I didn't think I'd ever felt so very close to having a forever home of my own.

13.

Mama made me take a nap after lunch, like I was younger than Sophie.

"You're still recovering," she said with one hand on her hip, the most quintessential ("a perfect or typical example") *mom* gesture in the world. "I can see it in your eyes, Ivy. You're not feeling yourself. Your body needs rest."

"Fine," I said, half because I really was annoyed at being babied, half because it hurt my pride to admit she was right. Lying down in the guest bed was a relief. For the first time all day I could take a deep breath— and not just because the pneumonia had triggered my asthma, but because it felt like I'd had to hold all my cells together all day, keeping myself upright and moving through force of will more than force of muscle.

When I woke up, it was late afternoon. The sunlight that streamed through Aunt Agatha's white lace curtains was golden, so rich that I could have taken a spoon and sipped it from the air around me.

Daddy was at the kitchen table, his face pulled into tight, resolute lines as he hammered away at his keyboard, like he could drown out the house's noise if he concentrated hard enough. The others were in the family room, Sophie needling at Elena to get her ukulele out and sing something, Elena blushing and casting furtive glances toward Aunt Agatha. Aunt Agatha was sitting in her favorite armchair by the fireplace, a new crochet project—this one green—in her lap.

"I don't bite, child," Aunt Agatha said.

Elena blushed harder. If she had trouble just talking to people who weren't me, Sophie, Mama, and Daddy, I couldn't even *imagine* her sharing her music with anybody else. Elena's music was like her heart, the way my writing notebook was mine.

"Your mama said you like old ballads?" Aunt Agatha went on. "There's some nice mountain songs to learn around here, if you get talking to the old folks in the town."

"Are there ballads about Lydia Lovelace?" I asked,

thinking of the story that was beginning to take shape in my notebook.

Aunt Agatha nodded. "At least one, very famous around here."

"Would you . . . sing it to us?" Elena asked, her voice so timid it was almost a whisper.

Aunt Agatha scowled. "I don't think you want me singing anything. It's not a talent I was blessed with."

"Please?" I asked.

Aunt Agatha's expression softened. She let the yarn and crochet hook drop to her lap. "Oh, all right. I can't remember all of it, though. I'll have to look up the rest of the lyrics and give them to you later. I know I'm missing verses in the middle there. The part I know goes like so:

"'Twas years ago in a valley green
That I gave my heart to him
In love and faith we pledged ourselves
Till the light we shared grew dim.

Let roses grow where they lay me down,
Let starlight kiss me, too;
Let all the world feel my broken heart—
How it everlong beat true."

The tune was sweet and lilting, even in Aunt Agatha's admittedly scratchy voice.

"Could you write that down for me?" Elena asked. Aunt Agatha nodded and got up to find a piece of paper. Trust music to bring out every little bit of Elena's courage. Pride swelled inside me like warm air into a hot-air balloon, making me feel happy and light.

Staying here would be so good for all of us. Maybe even Elena would be able to find a place to bloom, here with gruff Aunt Agatha and her cats and her apples.

"Ivy," Mama said when Aunt Agatha had finished transcribing the verses she remembered and handing it to Elena, who held it like it was made of silver. "Aggie and I need to go out for a while. We're going to examine the town and see if we can find the place the magic's leaking from. Hopefully the two of us together will be able to accomplish more than Aggie alone could. Your daddy needs to *work*—preferably in peace and quiet— and it's too hot for him to hole up in Martha. Why don't the three of you go for a walk?"

"Elena needs her knife back from that orchard," said Sophie immediately. "Leaving it there could be considered littering, and I don't know what the laws in North Carolina are, but in a lot of states—"

"Yes, thank you, Soph," said Mama. "Go retrieve

Elena's knife. That sounds perfect. Ready, Aggie?"

Aunt Agatha tucked her yarn and crochet hook into the basket at the foot of her chair and followed Mama out through the front door.

"You don't have to come, if you're not feeling well enough," Sophie said, squinting at me like she could gauge my temperature if she just wrinkled her eyes hard enough.

"I'm fine." I slipped my flip-flops on. "Besides, I'm supposed to exercise, remember? Let's go."

The three of us tumbled out onto the front porch; Aunt Agatha's car was just pulling out of the driveway, the crunch of gravel under tires loud in the quiet afternoon air.

"Do you remember which way we went yesterday?" I asked Elena. She nodded. Directions, details, and things like that were *not* my strong suit. Daddy always told me it was a good thing I'd been born into the era of personal GPSes, because otherwise I'd have been doomed to a long, lost life.

Sophie, unsurprisingly, chattered the whole time we walked. "Did you know that at least half the stars in the sky come in multiples?"

I rolled my eyes, but Elena smiled. "No."

Somehow, she always had patience for Sophie, which

made me feel even more surly and disagreeable. In two years, when Elena was as old as I was now, would she feel the same irritation prickling under her skin all the time? Lately, when I snapped at Sophie or said something cranky to my parents, Mama would look at me with sympathetic eyes and make a comment about how *adolescence is always a difficult time.*

But sometimes I wondered: Was Mama right, or was I just naturally beastly?

"There's binary stars," Sophie said, "where two stars are in the same gravitational orbit. But there are also star systems that have three or four stars in a group. All rotating together, held in place by the same gravity."

"Like star sisters," Elena said.

"Like Mama and Aunt Agatha and Aunt Ruth," I added.

"It's not very scientific, but yeah," said Sophie. "Most scientists say shooting stars are meteoroids, not stars." She shrugged. "Even scientists don't understand everything."

I looked around at the apple trees rising up all around us, thinking of the apple Elena and I had cut into, the gray smoke that had curled out of it.

What would a scientist make of *that*?

Sophie was opening her mouth to launch into

something else about stars, or maybe about the fact that I kept having to stop every few feet to cough; it felt like the whole of the gray-green French Broad River that wound its way past the outskirts of Whistling Ridge had settled into my lungs sometime during my nap. So before she could, I opened *my* mouth instead.

"I've decided I'm going to make it so we stay in Whistling Ridge forever," I said, hugging my writing notebook to my chest—full, now, with ideas for my Lydia Lovelace story, and even a few more lines after that perfect beginning.

Deep under the soil where the Whistling Ridge apple trees sink their roots, the town holds the memory of a great heartbreak.

A long time ago, a woman named Lydia came to Whistling Ridge. She was beautiful, with pale alabaster skin and eyes the color of chocolate. Everyone in town loved Lydia Lovelace, but Lydia only loved one man: the mayor's son.

I hadn't known the name of the mayor's son, so I'd stopped there. But the story was sizzling under my skin, which was how I always felt when I found a project that was absolutely, completely *right*.

I wouldn't tell my sisters about it, not yet. Not with the way Sophie had told Mama and Daddy about the wishes the literal second she could. And I didn't want to hear them tell me that one story wasn't enough to make Mama and Daddy change our whole way of life, when one story was the only weapon I had. But I wanted them to know that I had a plan.

"No more Martha," I went on. "No more road. We could be neighbors with Aunt Agatha. I bet they have science fairs and stuff here, Sophie. And Elena, you could take music lessons. You'd learn so much more from a real live teacher than you can from YouTube."

Mentioning the science fairs felt like a big concession on my part. I didn't have to *like* Sophie, but if I wanted my plan to stay in Whistling Ridge to work, I needed her at least a little on my side.

Elena shook her head back and forth, a small, fast movement, like the little wren on top of the camper. "We couldn't, Ivy. Mama's work is too important."

I flapped a hand dismissively, like Elena's words were a cloud of midges I could wave away. I had avoided thinking too hard about Mama's magic-tending; it was the one gaping hole in my dream, the one thing I didn't have an easy answer for. "She'd figure it out. Maybe we could keep Martha and Mama could check all the magic once a year or something. And just think how nice it would be to stay in one place. We could have *friends*."

I thought of the boys at the park yesterday, Simon and Ravi. What would it be like to spend my Saturday mornings with people my own age, people I wasn't related to? People who couldn't just ghost me, like Ada had done, because our only relationship was over email?

"I don't know," Elena said. "Don't you miss Martha? Don't you miss it just being us?"

"Not even a little bit." How could Elena, who I loved as much as my heart could love a person, be so wrong about this?

"I don't want to stay," Sophie said. "It's nice here, but I don't want to stay. Besides, usually science fairs don't allow kids younger than the fifth grade, and they're only open to public schoolers. So they probably wouldn't take me, anyway."

"You'd figure out a way," I said, letting the acid creep back into my voice. Every time Sophie spoke this week, it was like I could feel again the rush behind my belly button as I released the fireflies by the lakeside—and hear Mama's and Daddy's disapproving voices when I got back to the campsite. "Everyone *loves* you so much. Perfect, genius Sophie."

Sophie shrank back, like I'd scratched her.

"Ivy," said Elena tentatively, "maybe—"

"Look!" Sophie interrupted, pointing at the ground. "It's your knife!"

Elena's knife lay nestled at the base of the apple tree whose fruit we'd cut into. The knife blade was still extended. She bent to pick it up, wiping the blade off on the grass before closing it and putting it into her pocket.

She wiped extra hard, I noticed, even though I couldn't see any dirt or wetness on the stainless steel. Like by wiping and wiping, she could rub away the memory of that smoke-filled apple.

I looked up at the tree. I hadn't noticed it when we were here yesterday, but now that I looked closer, I could tell that even the bark didn't look quite right. It was graying—not a silver-gray, like some trees get in patches as they age, but a dull, sick-looking gray, like the color of the tree was draining right out.

Like a tiny hole in a basin, the magic has been seeping out of this town for years, Aunt Agatha had said.

"Poor tree," said Sophie. "It looks sicker than you, Ivy."

I growled in frustration.

"I just meant it looks bad, not that *you* look bad."

I rolled my eyes. "Whatever. But you're right. It doesn't look good at all."

All three of us fell silent for a moment, our eyes on the tree, the same question on all of our hearts.

What could be doing this to the tree? To Aunt Agatha? Maybe to the whole town?

But right after that came another question, one I was pretty sure my sisters didn't share.

Did I *want* the magic fixed, if it meant we'd leave Whistling Ridge?

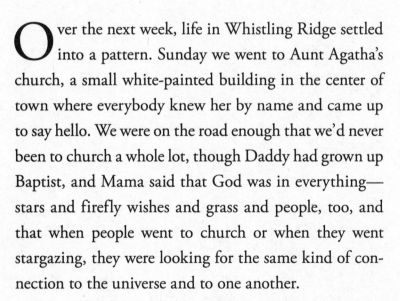

14.

Over the next week, life in Whistling Ridge settled into a pattern. Sunday we went to Aunt Agatha's church, a small white-painted building in the center of town where everybody knew her by name and came up to say hello. We were on the road enough that we'd never been to church a whole lot, though Daddy had grown up Baptist, and Mama said that God was in everything—stars and firefly wishes and grass and people, too, and that when people went to church or when they went stargazing, they were looking for the same kind of connection to the universe and to one another.

So it somehow didn't surprise me, knowing Aunt Agatha sat there in her pew every Sunday, letting her heart fill up with that connection.

For the next few days, my sisters and I found places inside the house or out in the orchards to do schoolwork ("because even half a dozen disasters aren't enough reason to stop learning," Mama said severely when I'd grumbled about it). Homeschooling is different than most people think. Usually, people figure it means we spend the whole day sitting at the table while Mama gives us assignments and grades things and writes on a whiteboard, like a regular teacher, but it's not like that at all. Mama supervises us and tells us what to do, and sometimes she'll walk us through lessons or check our work afterward, but most things we can do on our own. It's the best part of homeschooling, if you ask me—the chance to choose what you want to do and where and when.

While we settled into a rhythm with school, Daddy worked on a piece about Whistling Ridge's apple farms, and Mama and Aunt Agatha either had their heads together working on the mystery of Whistling Ridge's magic, or else were out in the evenings collecting fireflies for Mama to sell to the slow but steady stream of wish-seekers knocking on Aunt Agatha's door.

Even that was a trouble, though. Wednesday evening, Mama had come in from the forest behind Aunt Agatha's house with her face screwed up in frustration and only half the jars in her arms filled with wishes.

"There have been fewer every day we've been here," she'd complained to Daddy.

"The change of seasons, maybe?" Daddy suggested.

Mama shook her head. "They should continue another few weeks, weather-wise. It's not that. It felt . . . harder, last night, harvesting wishes. Like there was less to pull from."

"No magic, no wishes," said Aunt Agatha, guilt and worry written all over her lined face.

Friday afternoon, after Mama had looked hard at my eyes and then told me I still looked pale and washed-out and made me take a nap like a preschooler *for the third time that week*, Aunt Ruth arrived.

She pulled up in a black sedan driven by a college-age white dude with a scruffy blond beard and a lip piercing who wore a shirt that said *Asheville Is Uber Cool*. He gave one of those little chin-up nods as she got out of the car, and didn't even get out to help her take her luggage from the trunk. The second she'd stepped away, he backed out of Aunt Agatha's gravel driveway so fast the wheels screeched.

"Quite a gentleman," Mama muttered under her breath, striding forward to help Aunt Ruth with her bags. There were more of them than I'd have expected—three big suitcases and a duffel bag.

"Is she moving in for good?" Sophie whispered, and I didn't shush her because I'd been wondering the same thing.

It had been a few years since I'd seen Aunt Agatha. She'd never been as much a part of my growing up as my Bloom grandparents, who lived in Alabama and whom we visited every year or two for Christmas or summer break. But Aunt Agatha was still more familiar to me than Aunt Ruth. Maybe because Mama had spent years living in Whistling Ridge alongside her sisters, or maybe because the sagebrush in Montana made Daddy sneeze, we hadn't made it out to Aunt Ruth's place nearly as often as we'd visited Whistling Ridge.

Now, as she walked with Mama toward Aunt Agatha's porch, she seemed like the most familiar stranger I'd ever seen. She had the same golden-brown skin and silvery hair as Mama and Aunt Agatha, the same ice-blue eyes like the winter sky, the same willowy sway to her walk. But there was something different about Aunt Ruth; something breakable, like she didn't fill quite as much air as Mama and Aunt Agatha. Like a stout breeze could pick her up and carry her away like dandelion fluff. Aunt Ruth was older than Mama—the second star sister in their trio, the second star that fell to earth in Whistling

Ridge all those years ago—but even though her face had more lines on it, she seemed younger, smaller, less substantial.

Above her head, the little brown wren twittered frantically, flying from the RV top to a tree to Aunt Agatha's roof and back again, over and over. I couldn't tell if it was excited by the activity out in the yard, or if Aunt Ruth's arrival had disturbed it. Even more, I couldn't figure out why it was still *here*: every day, all week long, we'd seen it. It mostly hung out on Martha's roof, and Sophie swore she'd seen it embarking ("beginning a course of action") on the beginnings of nest building behind one of the solar panels.

I hope not, Daddy had said, looking out Aunt Agatha's window with a frown. *I can't imagine it would be safe once we get Martha back on the road.*

Aunt Ruth only glanced at the bird once, a distracted look on her face, before stepping up onto the porch and pulling Mama and Aunt Agatha both into a hug. When all three of them were together, their hair and skin glowed brighter than I'd ever seen it, like the three of them were filled with a secret electricity that pulsed from sister to sister to sister.

"Ruth," Aunt Agatha said. "I'm so glad you made it. Was the flight okay?"

"Mmm," said Aunt Ruth, which wasn't really a yes or a no.

"Come in and get settled," said Aunt Agatha, her arm still around Aunt Ruth's shoulder. "We're a full house by this point, so I put you on an air mattress in the sewing room. I hope that's all right; it was the only place left that would fit a bed."

"Of course," said Aunt Ruth, her voice as soft and light as the wren's chatter. Like her words, too, might just blow away with a big enough gust of wind.

Mama followed them into the house, leaving me and Elena and Sophie on the porch alone.

"Did she seem a little strange to you?" I asked in a low voice.

Elena shrugged. "There isn't anything wrong with being shy," she said, and I didn't think I was imagining the defensiveness shading her tone.

"She was exhibiting signs of a heightened pulse rate," said Sophie.

I sighed. "Is it too much to ask that you maybe sometimes could talk like a normal human girl?"

"I thought it was very interesting," said Elena, rubbing Sophie's back.

Sophie looked hurt. "I always try to answer questions as specifically as possible. It's a trait that's extremely important in a scientist."

"I'm just saying, something seemed a little strange," I said.

"Everything here seems strange," Elena said, as the three of us stared at the front door where Mama and her sisters had disappeared a few minutes ago.

A few hours later, after Mama and Aunt Agatha had cooked an entire kitchen's worth of food for a welcome feast, Mama poked her head into the living room, where Elena was finishing up today's chapter of *Little Women* and Sophie and I were listening—me while doodling in my writing notebook, Sophie while sorting flash cards with astrophysics vocabulary words.

"Girls, time for you to earn your keep," Mama said. "Elena, could you come squeeze some lemons for lemonade? Sophie, you get to set the table tonight. Ivy, I want you to go find your father and Ruth and tell them it's time for dinner. Daddy's working—he might be in the RV—and Ruth's napping in the sewing room."

Elena put down the book, tucking a bookmark into it—a slip of card stock with a doodle of Martha driving down a curving road. Sophie had drawn it a couple of weeks ago while we were traveling from Nebraska to Kansas. She may have been a genius, but Sophie still drew like an eight-year-old, all blocky shapes and crayon that couldn't quite stay inside the lines.

I knocked on the sewing room door twice. Finally, I heard Aunt Ruth's whispery bird voice telling me to come in. I pushed open the door hesitantly; even though we'd been here for a week, I'd only glimpsed Aunt Agatha's sewing room as I passed it in the hallway, never gone inside. There were tall shelves filled with fabric and yarn arranged by color, and a funny-looking brown table with spindly legs and three different levels where the sewing machine sat. Draped over it was a half-pieced quilt, a little like the one on the living room wall—this one all in shades of blue and silver, like sunlight on water.

Aunt Ruth sat on the edge of the double-high air mattress. In the light from the big window, the skin under her eyes glinted a little. Like it was wet. Like she'd been crying, and her tears hadn't quite dried yet. On the mattress next to her curled another cat—this one pale, almost white. Coffee's shy sister, Cream, I guessed, who apparently lived in the sewing room.

Aunt Ruth gave a wan smile, and I tried not to stare.

"Hello, Ivy," she said. "It feels so long since I've seen you! You've become quite a young woman."

"Mama says it's time for dinner," I said, not knowing how to respond to the *young woman* bit. Grown-ups were always going on about how quickly children changed, when as far as I was concerned, growing up was the slowest process known to mankind.

Aunt Ruth nodded. "Of course. I should've been in there helping. Oh, jet lag." She sighed, but stood and followed me into the kitchen.

The whole time we ate dinner, I could tell that Sophie and I were both watching Aunt Ruth extra close. Our eyes kept meeting; it had been weeks since I'd felt like Sophie and I were on the same side.

"One thing is for sure," she whispered to me later, after we'd gone to bed. "She may not look old, like Aunt Agatha, and maybe the magic in Montana is just fine, but something is *definitely* going on with Aunt Ruth. Did you see how she looked like she was always just a breath away from crying?"

"Yeah," I whispered back, staring into the darkness of Aunt Agatha's second guest room, wondering what could possibly be wrong with the middle star sister.

15.

Saturday morning, when I asked if I could go back to Oaktree Park, Daddy said yes immediately. Mama and her sisters had been gone before I'd even woken up; Daddy said they were planning to drive the borders of Whistling Ridge, to see if they could find any weak spots in the town's magic and try to get a feel for whether or not the magic loss had gone beyond the town line. The whole house smelled like the herbs they'd burned this morning, looking for any clues the smoke could give. I wondered if Aunt Agatha and Aunt Ruth had star-metal divining plates, like Mama's.

"Take your sisters, too, please." Daddy's face was painted with stress. "I'm trying to budget out how many articles I need to do to pay for the transmission so we can get on the road again before you're sixty. It's not going well."

"Please can I stay?" Elena asked, biting her lip, and I could see the shadow of the week before on her face, the way she'd shrunk into herself when Simon and Ravi had fallen from the tree above us. Sometimes I wished I could hug the anxiety right out of Elena, so the world no longer seemed quite so terrifying. Sometimes, her fear was so palpable ("so intense as to seem almost tangible") that I ached with it. If Sophie annoyed me just as much as Amy March in *Little Women*, Elena was like Beth, her quiet nervousness hiding the great big soul inside her.

I'd asked Mama once a few years ago, after Elena had gotten so anxious at one of the campgrounds we'd stayed at that she couldn't stop shaking and crying, why we couldn't use one of the fireflies to wish a little courage for her. Mama had looked at me, her ice-on-water eyes big and serious, and told me never to try that. *Elena is perfect the way she is, Ivy*, she'd said. *I'd no sooner wish away her anxiety than I'd wish away your asthma. Trying to use a wish to change something that's* part *of somebody is dangerous—you never know what may happen.*

These days I'd pretty much had my fill of wishing, anyway.

Daddy sighed and rubbed his face with one hand.

"Sure, honey. I just won't be much company until I've finished these spreadsheets."

"That's okay," Elena said, her shoulders sagging with relief. "I don't need company."

"I'll go!" Sophie said brightly, her shoes already halfway on.

"Do I *have* to take her?" I asked Daddy.

"Yes," said Daddy. "You do."

"She'll just be in the way," I said under my breath, even though I knew it wasn't strictly fair. "She just wants to go because I'm going, and she's a little copycat who always has to stay in the spotlight."

Daddy looked at me with a pained expression. "Maybe she *does* just want to go because you're going, Ivy. She loves you. She wants to be like you. You're her big sister, and she looks up to you. Aunt Jenny was the same with me when I was your age. I bet if she'd been a little girl and not a fallen star, Mama would've been the same with *her* sisters."

"Yeah, right," I said. "That's why Sophie spends all her time making my life miserable and trying to prove she's smarter than all of us."

"If you want to go to the park today, Sophie goes with you. That's final. I need her out from underfoot today. I have a feeling that as soon as your mama gets back, she'll be flooded with customers."

Saturdays were always busy days for wishes—somehow, when people weren't spending most of their time and energy focusing on their jobs, or making dinner, or getting homework done, the wishes that they spent most of their time ignoring spooled through their hearts, like the weekend was a megaphone to their deepest desires. Already, through the last few days, people in Whistling Ridge had begun to stream up to Aunt Agatha's house, asking in low voices to speak to Miss Aggie's sister, please. I was starting to understand why neither Aunt Agatha nor Aunt Ruth dealt in wishes. Wish-bartering and staying put in the same place didn't seem to go together very well.

Mama had spent two hours at twilight the night before catching fireflies to get ready for today, Aunt Agatha and Aunt Ruth keeping her company. (*It's been so long since I caught wishes, I don't think I could even remember how to do it*, Aunt Ruth had said with a laugh. *Now, if you have a sick cow that needs diagnosing, I'd be a lot more help!*) The three of them had wandered through Aunt Agatha's yard and then traipsed into the woods and orchards beyond it, watching for the pinprick glow that gave the lightning bugs away.

When they found one, they'd all stayed very still until it blinked again, then Mama had reached out with wind-swift hands and caught it between her cupped palms. Before she put it into a glass jar covered with cheesecloth for safekeeping, she'd whisper something to the little bug in her hands, and the firefly would glow ten times as bright as normal as its magic woke up. Mama had complained that the fireflies were still fewer than they should be, but she'd managed to fill a few glowing jars last night anyway.

Before we left, I cornered Sophie in our bedroom. "It's just you and me, no Elena. So . . . try to act as much like a normal kid as possible, okay? Don't embarrass me."

Sophie nodded solemnly, her baby-blue eyes big. "I promise I will try to keep my observations to myself and endeavor to simulate the behavior of an average third grader."

It was all I could do not to chuck my writing notebook right at her head, Lydia Lovelace story and all. "Arrrgh! You are *completely* impossible."

The first person Sophie and I saw when we stepped into the park was Charlie, the teenage girl from last week. She was lying on her back on the same park bench as before, reading a nice thick book with a dark-skinned girl in a power pose on the cover. She sat up as soon as she saw us, one finger stuck into the book to mark her place.

"Hey," she said tentatively. She had a gently roll-ing mountain accent, like soft pillows and warm days. "Simon said your name is Ivy? You're the ones visiting Miss Agatha, up on the hill, right?"

I nodded.

Charlie hesitated, squeezing her book hard. "Some-body told me that your mama—well, that she can—"

I have a feeling that as soon as your mama gets back, she'll be flooded with customers, Daddy had said.

"You mean about the wishes," I said, when Charlie didn't seem able to finish her sentence.

Charlie nodded. "It's true?"

"Yep." I thought of those nine fireflies in the darkness by Silverwood Lake.

Charlie cleared her throat. "Do you think maybe I could, like, talk to her?"

"Of course," I said, because Mama was good at talk-ing, and she always had time for people who needed it. But I had a feeling that talking wasn't all Charlie wanted. I wondered what kind of question hovered inside her that a wish would feel like the only right answer.

When I took my next breath, it rattled a little, even though the steroid the doctor had prescribed me the week before had made me feel lots better. That rattle felt like a warning, a reminder.

Wishes can be unpredictable.

"Mama is really good at listening," I said carefully. "And yes, she barters wishes. Just . . . they don't always work out quite the way you expect them to, that's all."

Then again, my wish had brought us to Whistling Ridge, hadn't it?

"Okay," said Charlie softly. "Thanks, Ivy. I'll keep thinking about it."

She lay back down on the bench and lifted her book again—but it seemed like an awful long time before she turned another page.

I'd had hardly a minute to shake off the muddle of my conversation with Charlie before Simon Welcher hurtled from one of the wooden castle turrets, waving and calling out. "Ivy Bloom! You came back!"

"Don't let him scare you off," Ravi called from where he sat under the big climbing oak, his sketchbook on his lap. "I promise we're not all like that."

But I liked Simon's exuberance.

"Thank goodness you're here," Simon said as he drew closer. His white-blond hair was plastered to his forehead with sweat. "My little sister's soccer game just got out and she's had me up there playing pirates. I'm ready for a drink of cold water and some shade, stat."

Simon waved in the direction of Ravi and the oak tree. "You should bring your notebook and write in the shade."

"Go play, Sophie," I said, with a significant look toward the play structure. Sophie opened her mouth like she was going to protest, but I raised my eyebrows and she shut it fast and ran off to the playground.

Ravi had a look of intense concentration on his face as he pulled his pencil along the page of his sketchbook. Under the pencil tip I could already see a picture emerging: Charlie lying on the park bench, her book held above her, her corkscrew curls falling off the side, a pensive, thoughtful look on her face.

"Wow," I said without meaning to. "You're really, really good."

Ravi blushed, his face turning pink, but he smiled, too. "Thanks. I've liked drawing as long as I could remember. My mom always says I got it from her dad, my Nanaji. He taught art history at Columbia after they moved to New York from India when my mom was a baby. He's retired now, but always sends me gift cards for art supplies."

Simon plopped down beside him and fished for a bottle of water that had been stowed by the tree trunk. "So—what are you working on, Ivy?"

Now it was my turn to flush; more than anything, I

wanted to make Simon and Ravi smile, wanted them to think that I *was* awesome, wanted them to be as enthusiastic about my ideas as I was. That was the hard thing about moving around so much: every time I met someone new, I felt the dizzying swoop of uncertainty all over again, the anxiety of wanting somebody to like you and not knowing if they would.

When I first met Ada, I'd shown her my writing notebook and let her read the things in it. She'd thought they were so cool, and even after we'd left her town, she always asked me to email her stuff I was writing when I'd finished it. I'd spend hours typing up the poems and stories from my writing notebook and sending them to her to read.

But over the last year, that had stopped. Even back when she was still answering my regular emails, Ada started ignoring the ones with stories or poems. When I asked her why, she said she just didn't have time to read anymore, but I couldn't shake the suspicion that behind those words she really meant *this is boring*.

Now, Simon and Ravi were both looking at me expectantly.

Would their enthusiasm end the same way Ada's had?

I took a deep breath. "I'm writing about Lydia Lovelace," I said in a rush. "My aunt told me about her, and it's such a romantic story. I thought it would be neat to write a story about her. A story especially for Whistling Ridge."

Simon was so excited sparks were practically coming off his skin. "That sounds amazing! You should ask at the library! Miss Christie, the librarian, she knows all about the town history. She could probably take you to Lydia's cottage, too. It's still there, though technically no one is supposed to go there until the city council gets it restored, because there was a fire there a while ago, when we were little kids, and it's not safe to go inside and stuff. But I bet Miss Christie would take you and at least let you look around, if it was for research."

"That's what my aunt said, too."

"And you know about the Lovelace Festival, right?" Ravi asked. "It happens every October. Any kid who wants can submit some kind of art about Lydia for a display. They set the projects up in city hall, so anyone can look at them. The city council picks the best project and the creator gets an apple pie."

"Ravi always enters," Simon said. "His paintings are amazing. He's won two years in a row."

"Hey," said Ravi, "what if we did a project together and entered it?"

I ignored the little twinge of worry I felt when Ravi mentioned October. Aunt Agatha had said the festival was just before Halloween, which was still a month and a half away. We'd already been in Whistling Ridge for more than a week, since the beginning of September.

I couldn't remember the last time we'd stayed in one place for two whole months. Would we really still be around to enter a project in the Lovelace Festival?

Still, I couldn't help the way my chest was filling up with glowing embers as Simon spoke.

"We could do, like, a multimedia thing," he said. "You could write a story, and I could build a little model of Lydia's cottage. My uncle is a cabinetmaker. He has a shop downtown and he helps me build whatever I want."

"I could paint some backdrops," Ravi interjected. "Nanaji—my grandpa—just sent me new paints for my birthday. Thirty-six colors of acrylics."

"Yeah!" said Simon. "Then, I don't know, we could print your story off and stick it inside the cottage or something. We could decorate the walls with Lovelace clematis. . . ."

"And roses," said Ravi. "Lydia was famous for her roses, right?"

I felt like somebody had just poured a pitcher of joy over me and now it was settling, liquid and bright, into all my hollow places. I could see, suddenly, what it might be like to stay in Whistling Ridge. I'd come to the park every Saturday, get Ravi to teach me painting, listen to Simon talk like he was being timed. I could turn thirteen and have a real birthday party, with balloons and cake and friends. I could go to sleep in a bed with sheets that didn't have to be custom-ordered from an RV supply company. I could talk to my friends whenever I wanted, without worrying about going years without seeing them face-to-face.

The wishes on my list could all come true.

I could have a forever home.

And maybe Simon and Ravi would help that happen. Maybe working on this project together, the three of us, would make all the difference.

Mama always said that blessings come in threes. Maybe me, Simon, and Ravi could bring a little of that rule-of-three magic to convince my parents how much I needed to stay.

I thought about the nine golden wishes spiraling into the sky near the lake in Silverwood, Oklahoma. And even though I still felt the ping of guilt thinking about Martha's broken transmission, and even though every time I took a deep breath the rumble of sickness lurked in my lungs, and even though I carried a little purse of worry for Aunt Agatha's wrinkled face and Aunt Ruth's wet eyes—

I still couldn't help but hope that those nine wishes were spreading their magic over me and Mama and Daddy and my sisters, doing their very best to turn Whistling Ridge into our forever home.

That wish-glow lasted right up until Sophie ran up and tumbled to the ground next to me, her arms cocooned around her head. She looked like she was folding herself together to protect from falling debris.

"Soph?" I said, forgetting for a minute to be mad at her. "Are you hurt? What happened?"

"I'm not hurt," Sophie said distinctly from inside the cover of her arms. "But can we go home now, please?"

I pried Sophie's arms away from her face. Her light skin was flushed red, and there were tear tracks on her face.

"Stop being dramatic," I said. "We just got here. What on earth happened?"

Sophie darted a glance at the playground. A little girl, as pale and blond as Simon, stood at the edge of the bark-chipped play space, looking grumpy.

"Uh-oh," said Simon, following Sophie's gaze. "That's Hannah, my sister. She has a habit of talking before she thinks. Sorry."

"No idea where she gets that from," Ravi deadpanned.

"Did she say something, Sophie?" I asked.

Sophie nodded. "She said I was weird," she mumbled so quietly I could hardly hear her. "I was just explaining that the way stars appear to twinkle is an illusion, caused by earth's atmospheric turbulence, since the stars are so far away that their light becomes disturbed as it passes through the atmosphere. She didn't even let me finish. She just stuck out her tongue at me and said I was weird."

It was strange: Sophie was the one person on earth who annoyed me more than I could stand, and most of the time, I would have happily strangled her with my own bare hands, especially after she'd tattled to Mama and Daddy the night I stole the wishes. But right now, even so, I felt a fiery protectiveness, a burning willingness to smite anybody who crossed Sophie.

"What a brat," I said, not caring that the girl was Simon's sister. "It wasn't true what she said."

Even if it *was* kind of true—even if Sophie *was* weird, and even if I'd told her the same thing a million times—she was *my* weird sister.

"I tried not to say anything too outrageous, but . . . I couldn't help it. She was *wrong*," Sophie said in a strangled whisper, her eyes leaking tears again. "See, Ivy? This is why I don't want to stay. This is why it's better to be in Martha."

I leaned over and squeezed her shoulder. "You're not outrageous," I said, even though I was the one who'd told her to be less outrageous in the first place. "You shouldn't have to hide who you are. People who love you—we'll like you for it. Whether we're on the road or not."

And I was almost surprised to realize that right in that moment, sitting underneath the biggest oak tree in all of Whistling Ridge, the little ball of protective fire inside my chest did feel an awful lot like love.

16.

Monday morning, Elena and Sophie and I were sitting on Aunt Agatha's porch when Aunt Agatha's chrysanthemums bloomed.

Sophie and Elena were in the porch swing, rocking gently back and forth. Elena was writing an essay about why students should be allowed to use calculators in school more, humming the Lydia Lovelace ballad Aunt Agatha had taught her under her breath as she wrote. Papers that Daddy had printed off for her on Aunt Agatha's printer were scattered across her lap and the swing bench beside her, holding all the facts and arguments she'd found online to support her argument—one I definitely agreed with, since math was *not* my strength. (We both hoped that if Elena's essay was good enough,

Mama might be convinced to let *us* use calculators.)
Sophie was playing a brain teaser on the tablet, her little
face screwed up in concentration.

I was lying on my stomach on the porch, *supposed* to
be doing a geometry worksheet, but I'd gotten distracted
by the border plants growing in the little garden that ran
on either side of the porch steps. I thought of the list in
my notebook. *A garden.* I wished I could be rooted as
deeply as the plants in Aunt Agatha's borders, tethered
to the soil the way they were. Moving around so much
felt like a gardener coming and ripping a plant up by its
roots—every time I had the chance to settle in for a few
weeks, start to make connections and feel comfortable, I
got pulled up and had to start all over again.

Lots of the plants in the garden were herbs. I'd seen
Aunt Agatha run out and pinch some bright green
umbrella-shaped basil off its stalk when she'd been making pesto the night before. *There's nothing like fresh herbs
to make a regular meal taste special,* she'd said, blend-
ing the basil up with almonds and oil and fresh-grated
Parmesan cheese. She was right, too. When she'd put
spoonfuls of glistening green pasta on our plates, it had
tasted like heaven.

Planted in between and around the herbs, Aunt
Agatha's front garden was full of flowers: black-eyed

Susans, their centers shining and dark; little purple asters; old-fashioned dahlias staked up with tomato cages.

And chrysanthemums, which until today had been tightly closed up into buds, just the smallest hints of yellow and orange and red at their tips.

It's strange, Aunt Agatha had said, frowning at the chrysanthemums while she'd picked the basil. *The mums have usually bloomed by now.*

In the week and a half since we'd arrived in Whistling Ridge, summer had begun to whisper out as the calendar inched toward mid-September. The hot mugginess had gone, leaving behind clear blue skies and warm afternoons that smelled like cinnamon and gave way to cooler nights. There was a little breeze teasing its way through the garden now, as I lay on the porch with my chin in my hands. It had been overcast all day, but as I watched, the cotton-candy cumulus clouds scudded away and the sun, bright and yellow-white, shone right onto Aunt Agatha's little white house.

(*Scudding* was one of the words from the list in the back of my notebook. I'd learned it in the spring, when we'd stopped in Virginia to watch a sailing competition, and it was a lot more fun than saying "blown by the wind.")

Just as the sunlight hit them, the chrysanthemums bloomed.

They unfurled slowly, their petals relaxing and opening, revealing—

Before I knew what I was doing, I'd screamed and surged backward, knocking my head hard enough against the bottom of the porch swing that Elena dropped all her papers.

"What's the matter?" Sophie said, blue eyes wide.

I stood up and stepped back to the edge of the porch, my own eyes fixed on the chrysanthemums.

"Go get Mama and the aunts," I said, my voice sounding like it came from somebody else's throat. "Quick!"

Inside the chrysanthemums, there was none of the color that the buds had hinted at; the half-dozen regular petals that ringed the centers had fallen off as soon as they'd opened. Instead of flowers, the mums were blackened skeletons—dried-out, wrinkled things the color of soot and ash.

From the center of each chrysanthemum, glimmering black beetles crawled, their claws clicking like teeth.

That night, when I was supposed to be in bed, I overheard the star sisters talking when I got up to get a drink from the bathroom.

"I don't know what's wrong," Mama said.

"Why isn't anything slowing it down?" Aunt Ruth asked, the memory of tears in her words.

"It's getting faster," Aunt Agatha said. If I closed my eyes, I couldn't picture my own aunt's face at all; her voice was trembly and old-sounding. That night at dinner, I'd seen her squeeze her hands together under the table, trying to stop the shaking that had started up soon after we'd arrived. "I can feel it now, tugging at me all the time. Like the tide."

"Feel what?" Aunt Ruth asked.

"The void," said Aunt Agatha, so quietly I had to strain to hear.

All weekend, Mama and her sisters had been huddled together at Aunt Agatha's kitchen table with the silver instruments Mama always used to find problems with the world's magic: the star-metal divining plate, the pendulum that looked like a shooting star, the bowl that held water to reflect starlight at night. They'd taken long walks through the town, plucking at the roots of Whistling Ridge's magic and trying to see where things had gone awry. But none of their divining or tending or muttering together had helped them find the source of the magic draining from the town.

And no matter how much light and stardust they

poured into the earth, it was never enough.

I'd never seen Mama look so worried: usually it was easy, or at least *looked* easy, for her to tend to the world's magic, feeding extra in where there were bare spots and calming it when there were places with too much. It was no harder for her than it was to remind the fireflies of their origins among the stars—easier, maybe, than it was to send the wishes away with people who brought her their worries and their fears clutched in tight fingers.

It had never been hard like this before, not for as long as I could remember.

What did Aunt Agatha mean by *the void*?

"It's taking everything we give and swallowing it up," Mama was saying now. "Like . . . like darkness. Like night."

"What could do that?" Aunt Ruth asked.

"I don't know," Aunt Agatha said.

"What . . . what if we can't stop it fast enough, Agatha?" Mama asked.

"Then the town will unravel," she said, and then was quiet so long I thought she'd finished talking. I was tiptoeing back to my bed when I heard her speak again.

"And I'll unravel with it."

17.

The steroid the doctor had given me made it hard to sleep. More and more, I'd lie in my bed for hours after Mama sent me there, itchy with wakefulness, my eyes gritty, my arms and legs tense—until finally, at eleven or twelve or whenever I stopped staring at the illuminated face of the alarm clock, I'd fall restlessly into sleep until the sun streamed in through the window the next morning.

Tonight, the insomnia was worse than ever, my stubborn awakeness full of memories of what Mama and the aunts had been saying.

Getting faster.

Like the tide.

Unravel.

Darkness.

And Aunt Agatha, voice reedy and thin, saying, *The void.*

What had she meant? In more than twelve years of living, I'd never heard Mama talk that way, or mention any kind of void at all, except for the way she sometimes called people who lived in regular houses and never moved to a new town *devoid of imagination.*

If Mama and her sisters fixed Whistling Ridge's magic too quickly, I'd have no chance to convince my parents that we needed to stay for good.

But if they didn't fix it, did that mean Aunt Agatha might . . . die?

Surely that wasn't possible. I'd never heard of a star-woman just *dying* before, only returning to the sky when their human work was done.

I rolled over in Aunt Agatha's guest bed. Nowhere felt comfortable; every spot seemed harder and lumpier than the last. In the darkness, I could see the gauzy white curtain on the guest bedroom window breathing slightly, teased back and forth by the tiniest hint of a breeze that slipped in through the cracked-open window.

And suddenly, in that way that bad ideas have of seeming extremely sensible when it's hours after you were supposed to be asleep, I knew I couldn't stay in bed anymore.

I'd never snuck out before—well, except for the time

in Silverwood when I stole the wishes. But sneaking out of a real house, with wooden siding and a front door with a dead bolt and a cement foundation, felt different.

But it was surprisingly easy, sliding the bedroom window open more—it creaked, but Elena and Sophie both slept like the dead—and taking the screen out and putting it on the bedroom floor and then climbing right out of the window. I had to let myself drop a few feet, but the grass underneath was soft on my skin, and my feet only stung a little.

I was in Aunt Agatha's backyard, a little square of grass with raised garden beds along the back fence and a little rose-covered arch over the gate that led into the woods.

Aunt Ruth sat on the tree swing, gliding slowly back and forth, glowing silver in the moonlight. The shy white cat, Cream, was curled on the grass at her feet.

"Ivy."

I stood, frozen, underneath the window, feeling a little like I'd been caught stealing the wishes all over again.

Aunt Ruth shrugged. "Don't worry. I won't tell." The swing ropes made a little *snick, snick* sound as they rubbed against the leaves of the maple tree.

I stepped forward into the yard, enough so my voice

hopefully couldn't be heard too easily inside the house. "I couldn't sleep."

"Me neither," Aunt Ruth said. She slid off the swing and lay down on the grass, her white hair fanning out around her like a comet's tail. The darkness made her golden-brown skin pale, like stars look before the sun has fully set. She patted the ground beside her. "Come lie down with me, honey. The sky is beautiful tonight."

I padded forward, the grass springy and ticklish under my bare feet. She was right. Once I'd lain down next to her, the stars overhead were so vivid and bright it felt as though we were swimming through the cosmos, the black velvet of the night reaching down to wrap us in its arms. I almost felt dizzy with it, all that sparkling beauty.

I wondered, sometimes, if Mama and her sisters ever missed being stars.

As if she'd read my mind, Aunt Ruth sighed. "It's hard sometimes, Ivy, being human."

I thought about the way my stomach twinged when I saw Aunt Agatha wrinkly and shaking. The simmering anger Sophie always seemed to be able to call up in me. The way I still felt a wash of shame and grief when I thought of Ada ghosting me.

"Yeah," I said. "It is."

Aunt Ruth laid a shining golden hand on her chest. "These hearts—they're so easy to wound."

She said it like she knew what it was to hurt deep inside. The way I'd felt all summer when I'd emailed Ada over and over and heard nothing in return. What was Aunt Ruth's secret sorrow? Did it have something to do with Uncle Andrew? I hadn't seen her make a phone call since she'd arrived, or video chat, the way we'd all video chatted Daddy when he'd flown to Alabama for a week to help Aunt Jenny build a new shed.

Neither of us talked much after that. We just lay there for a long time, surrounded by the diamond glitter of the sky, until my eyes got heavy and time started to slip in strange ways, and then I was dreaming about sailing through the stars in a boat made of silver and gold.

When I woke up, I was in my bed at Aunt Agatha's again. Aunt Ruth was nowhere to be seen.

18.

Mama kept me so busy with schoolwork for the next two days that I hardly had time to work on my Lydia story, though I thought about it constantly. I'd never seen any pictures of her, but I could imagine her so clearly: dark velvety eyes, a smile that was sweet and funny all at the same time. I hadn't wanted to bother Mama or the aunts about taking me to the library—especially when Daddy kept taking the only functioning vehicle for drives along the Blue Ridge Parkway for research—and so for now, I'd contented myself with imagining Lydia however I wanted to. She'd live in a cottage covered in Lovelace clematis, just like Simon had suggested. And her garden would be the envy of the town, filled with roses more colorful than any that had ever been seen before.

I did my best not to think of the conversation I'd eavesdropped on Monday night—*darkness, swallowing, void*. The whole memory of that night was wrapped up with the feeling of lying on the cool grass with Aunt Ruth and seeing the stars wheeling overhead; it all was dreamlike, surreal, so that I almost wondered whether any of it had actually happened.

I wandered into the kitchen Wednesday afternoon for a snack and found Mama and the aunts sitting around the table, looking over a map of Whistling Ridge and the towns beyond it.

"It's spreading along the ley lines," Mama said, pointing at the map. "It's got to be. See how Silverwood and Whistling Ridge connect, here?"

"And before you got here, I had to travel to St. Louis, here, to deal with some flooding," Aunt Agatha said. "But if it's already spreading past Whistling Ridge . . ."

Aunt Agatha didn't say anything more, but the stricken looks on all their faces said plenty. I thought of what Mama had said back in Silverwood when I'd asked what would've happened to the city's magic if we hadn't come along.

More people would've gotten hurt.

The shrill clanging of the old-fashioned phone on

Aunt Agatha's kitchen wall was a jolt of electricity in the tense quiet of the house. Aunt Ruth, who was closest, picked it up. "Hello? Oh, no, this is her sister, Ruth." A pause, and then, "Oh? Yes, she's here. One moment."

But instead of handing the phone to Aunt Agatha, Aunt Ruth turned to me. "It's for you, Ivy."

"For *me*?"

Aunt Ruth actually *winked* as she passed me the phone receiver. "It's a boy."

Sweat prickled on my palms as I set down my water glass and took the handset from her. I'd barely gotten a hello out when Simon's voice crashed into my ears, a little tinny over the phone, but as fast and as cheerful as ever.

"Hi, Ivy! I hope it's okay that I called. Miss Agatha's number is in the phone book, and anyway, my moms know her really well, so I figured it must be okay. I was calling to see if you maybe wanted to go to the library this afternoon. Ravi too. We got out of school at three and we had hardly any homework today, so it's perfect. Remember how I said Miss Christie knows everything about the town's history? I could introduce you. Well, plus I have three books that are overdue and my Mama said I'd better turn them in or my parents will take the money out of my allowance. But I thought if you came with us, you could learn about Lydia, too. I bet Miss Christie has all kinds of papers stashed away somewhere—"

"Hang on," I interrupted. I wasn't sure that Simon ever would've stopped otherwise. I covered the phone speaker with my hand and looked at Mama. "Could I maybe go to the library with some friends? To do research for a project?"

"Who?" Aunt Agatha asked.

"Some people I met at the park. Simon Welcher and Ravi Sidana."

Aunt Agatha smiled. "They're such nice boys."

I looked at Mama. "So—could I go?"

Mama's eyes were flicking between me and the map on the table, and I could tell she was only half paying attention, her mind still fixed on the problem of Whistling Ridge's magic. *The void*, whatever that was. For a minute, I was halfway grateful for the mysterious force sucking away at Whistling Ridge; at least it kept Mama's thoughts focused on something *other* than the nine wishes I'd stolen in Silverwood.

"Are you done with school?" Mama asked.

"Completely done."

Finally, she nodded.

"That's fine," she said distractedly, "but please be

back by dinner. What are your sisters doing?"

I shrugged. "I think Sophie is making Elena help her with an experiment." As if to confirm, the sound of a small explosion came from the backyard. Mama winced.

I put the phone back to my ear. "Yes. I can come."

19.

Simon's Mama, a plump, shortish woman with the same white-blond hair and friendly smile as Simon, who told me to call her Miss Brenda, picked me up in a silver minivan. Simon and Ravi were already buckled into the middle of the van, so I got the front seat. It took us only a few minutes to get to Whistling Ridge's Main Street. The street looked like it could have been listed in a dictionary next to terms like *charming, classic,* or *small-town*; all the buildings were brick, with colorful awnings advertising stores like *Blue Rose Café* and *Ye Olde Sweete Shoppe*. The narrow road had a long median filled with flowers, and half the shops had American flags hung from them, the stars and stripes almost glowing in the September sunshine.

When we got to the library, Miss Brenda didn't come in.

"I've got some errands to run," she said, sticking her head out of the rolled-down driver's-seat window. "I'll be back in an hour or two, all right?"

"Yep," Simon said, already halfway inside. The library was a funny-looking brick building, tall and skinny, with a bright red door and *Whistling Ridge Community Library* painted on the windows.

I hung back a little as Ravi followed Simon through the door. For a family who liked to read as much as mine did, for a girl who loved words as much as me, I hadn't spent a whole lot of time in libraries. When you don't have a permanent address, nobody will give you a library card—and there wouldn't be much point in one, even if they would. Sometimes when we were in a town long enough to find the library, Daddy would go there to do some research, or Mama would drag us girls through to find a book to read to back up something we were learning in school. But since we could never check them out, the best we could do was skim.

My writing notebook dug into the skin of my arms where I held it. I thought of the wish list inside, and how when I'd begun my current notebook, I'd written *A library card* right underneath *A pet*.

Stepping into the Whistling Ridge library felt almost dangerous—like if I got too close to that dusty book smell and saw the way the librarian smiled, it would make leaving Whistling Ridge even harder.

If my Lydia Lovelace story couldn't convince Mama and Daddy of how much I *needed* to stay.

Simon popped his head back out the door. "Ivy! Come *on!*"

I took a deep breath and went inside.

It was dim after the sunny brightness of Main Street. Ravi and Simon were heading toward the big front desk inside the door; I trailed behind them, waiting for the librarian to turn and pay attention to us. She had light brown skin and shiny, straight black hair that had been pulled into an extremely symmetrical bun on top of her head.

Simon cleared his throat. "Miss Christie? Could you help us with something?"

The librarian looked up from sorting through books in the return basket. I guessed I didn't have to worry so much about her smiling warmly; Miss Christie looked as ferocious as her hair was neat, like it was her personal responsibility to guard the books in her collection and she was willing to give her life—or our lives—to do it.

"If you want tutoring, you'll have to inquire at school,

Mr. Welcher. The library doesn't provide that service."
Miss Christie raised her eyebrows at Simon.

"Not tutoring," Simon said, waving a wild hand in my direction. "It's actually not me who needs help. This is Ivy Bloom. Her family is visiting, staying with—"

"You're Agatha's niece, aren't you?"

I nodded.

"Hmm," said Miss Christie, her lips pressed together in a way that could've been either good or bad.

I cleared my throat, summoning up every bit of bravery within me. "I'm looking for information about Lydia Lovelace," I said, my words tripping over themselves on their rush to get out. "Simon thought you'd have some stuff about her. I'm writing a story about her for the Lovelace Festival showcase thing this fall. But I only just learned about Lydia, and I don't know all that much, and—"

Miss Christie was looking at me with a little frown between her eyebrows. I could tell she was sizing me up. My heart fluttered when she opened her mouth again; all of a sudden I couldn't quite breathe, like all the oxygen had been pulled out of my lungs when I'd come through the library door. Maybe I was wrong in thinking that my story could convince Mama and Daddy to stay in Whistling Ridge. Maybe it was all just wishful thinking.

Then again, with all the things I'd seen in my life, I couldn't really discount *any* kind of wishing. Those nine fireflies had gotten me here, hadn't they?

"That sounds like a very good idea," said Miss Christie, the wrinkle on her forehead relaxing a little. I could have sworn her brown eyes were *twinkling*. "Children your age should be more interested in a place's history and less interested in what's on television."

"Well, my family doesn't have a television, anyway," I said, talking almost as fast as Simon out of pure relief. "We live in an old Winnebago named Martha and only stay put for a few weeks at a time, so there's not really room, plus Mama says that too much TV prevents you from being truly engaged in the world around you, and—"

"Come with me," Miss Christie said, stepping out from behind the desk and waving Simon and Ravi and me to follow her. Her black high heels were as shiny as her hair. Over her shoulder, she called, "My name is Christie Mendoza. You may call me Miss Christie. I happen to agree with your mother, by the way. It's good for children to look out from behind their screens every now and then."

Ravi rolled his eyes at me behind Miss Christie's back.

"Parents *love* Miss Christie," he whispered, his voice

barely a breath in the library's quiet.

A giggle bubbled up, warm and full in my throat; I swallowed hard to keep it from getting out, but couldn't stop myself from grinning back at Ravi anyway.

We followed Miss Christie into an elevator and up to the third floor of the brick building. "The archival room," she said as the elevator rose slowly, creaking and shaking the whole way. Simon's white skin looked a little green, and I couldn't blame him; the elevator had to be at least fifty years old, probably more. Miss Christie kept talking. "The general public isn't allowed up here but may come by special permission, if accompanied by a librarian."

"Thank you," I said. The elevator dinged and opened onto a small room filled with bookshelves and filing cabinets.

Miss Christie went straight to one of the farthest cabinets and rattled a drawer open, thumbing through the files quickly until she found what she was looking for.

"She does *not* waste time," I whispered to Simon and Ravi. Ravi shook his head, his eyebrows up, while Simon mimed Miss Christie's brisk shoulders-back-head-straight way of walking. I bit back another giggle before Miss Christie turned around, a manila folder in her hand.

She set the folder down on a table. "I am going to ask you not to touch any of the contents of this file," she said, giving us each a severe look until we nodded like a row of bobbleheads. "They are extremely old and quite delicate. However, if you'd like to read any of the things in here, Ivy, I'd be happy to help you photocopy them to take home."

"What . . . are they?" I asked, feeling almost like I needed to whisper.

Miss Christie opened the folder. "These are Lydia Lovelace's personal papers." She pulled out a yellowing sheet that had been folded and creased so often it was nearly falling apart in the middle. It was typed—typewriter typing, not computer printing—but some sections were in looping, perfect cursive that looked almost too beautiful to be real.

"The deed of sale for Lydia's cottage," Miss Christie said, pointing a finger at a line on the top of the paper, where *Lydia Lovelace* had been written in that picturesque scrawl. "In 1888, when Lydia moved here, there were only a handful of houses in all of Whistling Ridge. Most of the town didn't even exist back then."

I stared at the document. The archival room was quiet; the whole library felt hushed, as though it were awed in the presence of this tiny slice of history.

"It's like art," said Ravi, almost reverently.

Miss Christie nodded, smiling a little. Her smile softened up the rest of her face so much I almost couldn't remember why I'd thought she looked so fearsome at first.

Next, she pulled out something written on cream-colored stationery. The cursive on this wasn't quite as perfect as the one on the deed; here, you could tell that the writer was a real human person, who sometimes crossed things out or got ink splotches in the margins.

"A letter," Miss Christie said. She checked a little list printed on the side of the folder. "Sender unknown. It's dated sometime after the deed of sale, though—1893. Unfortunately, it was water damaged at some point and the writing is completely unreadable."

"How old was Lydia when she came to Whistling Ridge?" I asked. Had she pulled up in a carriage? Or ridden up on a horse? Or just gotten here on her own two feet? Had there been trains through the mountains back then, or roads?

"I'm not really sure. We only have one incomplete diary from Lydia, and the handwriting has deteriorated enough that the dates aren't very legible. Her great love story is assumed to have happened in the late 1880s or early 1890s, so presumably she was an adult by then.

There isn't a lot of recorded history from that period in Whistling Ridge."

The last thing in Miss Christie's folder was a leather-bound book, which she opened carefully. Some of the pages had fallen out of their binding and been set back in place; others were crinkled with water damage, or their ink was faded and gray.

"Lydia's diary," said Miss Christie. "It's been ages since I've opened it. You can see here, at the end, there are pages missing—it ends right after her heart is broken. I've never been certain whether the pages fell out because they were old, or whether Lydia ripped them out herself."

"Can I . . . can I read it?" I asked, my toes trembling in my flip-flops. The book seemed almost to *breathe*; how many secrets, how much life, did it hold inside?

Miss Christie pursed her lips. "I can't let you take it home, of course; it's much too old. But as I said, I can photocopy it for you." She thumbed through the book, gentle as a mother bird. "It's not terribly long. Let me get the rest of these things put away and I'll bring it back downstairs to the copier."

I couldn't stop my hands from twitching, my feet shifting side to side, as we took the elevator back down and then watched Miss Christie copy the pages of the diary. When she handed me a stack of papers, still warm from the copier and smelling of ink and heat, I held them so tightly to my chest that they might have become part of my own skin.

"I hope it helps with your project," Miss Christie said. She didn't seem quite so fierce now that she'd shown us her special upstairs room and taken ten whole minutes to copy page after delicate page from Lydia's journal. Maybe she was more of a kindred spirit than she'd seemed at first glance. "I'll keep an eye out for your display this autumn at the festival."

"Thanks," I said, cheeks flushing. It was strange, hearing people talk about my story. It had been so long since I'd told anybody but Mama and Daddy and my sisters about my writing. And Ada, of course, but being pen pals with Ada was starting to feel like something that had happened a million lifetimes ago.

"Miss Christie?" Simon had been quiet so long he almost seemed like a different person; I didn't even know he *could* stop talking. "I was thinking, I know you're one of the people in charge of making sure nobody visits Lydia's cottage while it's unsafe, but I thought maybe since Ivy is writing a story, it would help her to see where Lydia lived, and maybe you could show us—I mean her—around sometime, and Ravi and I are going to make Ivy's story into a multimedia project, too, so if you had any pictures of it, especially old ones, that might—"

Seeing Miss Christie's perfectly curved eyebrows raised nearly into her hairline, Simon stopped abruptly and took a breath.

"He was quiet so long I was starting to think he was sick or something," Ravi whispered so low that only I could hear it, and I had to cough to hide my giggle.

"You're right that the city council, for whom I am a consultant on matters of town history, has forbidden access to Lydia's cottage until repairs can be made," Miss Christie said sternly. "The fire damage is fairly extensive. It is *highly* unsafe, and they particularly wanted to keep curious children who might endanger themselves or others away from the premises."

She paused, letting the silence draw out until it was thin and glossy, like the sides of a soap bubble ready to pop any second. Simon looked queasy. I thought of the fire in Silverwood, the way that factory had been blackened and charred, and goose bumps rose on my arms.

"*But*," Miss Christie continued once we'd all gotten sufficiently close to what Sophie would call a *significant cardiovascular event*, "I'm willing to make an exception in this case, given the nature of your interest, Miss Bloom. The library closes early on Thursday afternoon;

if the three of you can meet me here tomorrow around four, I will show you the cottage. But *only*," she added with a meaningful look toward both Simon and Ravi, "if each of you promises to be extremely circumspect and to stay out of the cottage itself."

We nodded.

"Good. Now go," said Miss Christie, straightening back into her buttoned-up librarian persona like she was buckling herself into a suit. "I have books to catalog."

20.

Lydia's looping, old-fashioned script was tricky to read. Mama had made sure I knew how to write in cursive by the time I started middle school, but Lydia's writing wasn't anything like the cursive I knew; it was fancier, with capital *A*s that looked almost like little stars, and capital *H*s that were so strange I only puzzled out what they were because she kept writing about somebody whose name ended with *e-n-r-y* and I figured it was a lot more likely to be *Henry* than *Mlenry*.

The ink she was writing with blotted or smeared sometimes, and here and there she had crossed out words and scribbled corrections in letters so small, they could've been written by mice. And as if all that weren't bad enough, between the fact that it was more than a hundred years old *and* the fact that it had been photocopied, parts of it were so faded I couldn't make them out at all. I couldn't even be sure of the dates—most of them looked like they could be 1888, but then halfway through there was a jump into what looked like 1891 but *might* have been 1897.

No wonder Miss Christie had said nobody was sure when Lydia's love story had taken place.

"What are you scowling at, Ivy?" Daddy asked Wednesday evening. We'd just finished dinner, and the star sisters had driven off in Aunt Agatha's car to try once more to slow the magic draining inexorably ("in a way that is impossible to stop or prevent") out of Whistling Ridge. They planned to visit a bunch of places that were important to the town—the city government buildings, the home of the first settler in Whistling Ridge, the apple tree that was rumored to be the first planted—and see whether pouring stardust into one of *those* places made any more of a difference than the other things they'd tried.

It was Elena's turn to do the after-dinner dishes, so I sat at the table with Daddy—him typing away at his article, me grimacing at the pages from Lydia's diary.

I pointed. "Lydia Lovelace's diary. The librarian copied it for me earlier. I'm doing research for the story I'm writing. Me and Ravi and Simon want to make it into a multimedia display for the Lovelace Festival. But it's *really* hard to make sense of any of it."

Daddy peered over at the paper on top of my stack—the first page from Lydia's diary. He whistled.

"You aren't kidding, Ivy Mae. That's quite the chicken scratch." He squinted. "It looks like she's saying something about, um, the apple harvest . . . and somebody named Henry? And maybe . . . good grief. I have no idea."

I sighed. "Yeah, me neither. I think I'll give up for tonight. I'll try again tomorrow, when my brain is fresh."

At least I'd learned one thing, though: the mayor's son was named Henry. I pulled my notebook out and opened it to where I'd started my Lydia story.

Deep under the soil where the Whistling Ridge apple trees sink their roots, the town holds the memory of a great heartbreak. A long time ago, a woman named Lydia came to Whistling Ridge. She was beautiful, with pale alabaster skin and eyes the color of chocolate. Everyone in town loved Lydia Lovelace, but Lydia only loved one man: the mayor's son. Henry was handsome and smart and rich, and the first time Lydia saw him, it was love at first sight.

But she didn't know that underneath his beauty, inside all his jokes and flattery, lurked a cruel heart that would break her own.

A thrill of excitement zinged through my fingers as I put the pen down. It had been a long time since I'd started a project that felt this promising. There was something about Lydia's story that crept right into my bones and settled there, like a memory from another lifetime, like a thing that had always been a part of me even if I hadn't known it before.

Somehow or other, this story was going to change my life.

21.

The sky was hazy the next day, the blue painted over with milky yellow clouds, the kind that made you think of storms and sorrow. Mama and the aunts were grim at the breakfast table. Coffee prowled back and forth through the kitchen and out again, like he'd been infected by the restless mood in the house.

"There were hardly any fireflies out last night," Mama said as we ate.

Aunt Agatha's head dropped into her hands. "It's my fault. I should have called you both sooner. If I hadn't been so arrogant—if I hadn't been so sure I could fix it on my own . . ."

"Stop that," Aunt Ruth said, her voice sounding stronger than it had since she'd arrived. "It's not your fault, Aggie. None of us have encountered anything like this before. You couldn't be blamed for assuming you'd eventually get the better of it."

The words they'd spoken a few nights ago hung in the silence:

Getting faster.

Like the tide.

Swallowing it up.

"I think we all need a morning off," Mama announced. "Whistling Ridge has held out against this mysterious threat this long—it won't implode in the next two hours."

"Let's walk to the creek," Aunt Ruth said. "I haven't been there for ages. Is it still the same?"

"It's still wet, if that's what you mean," said Aunt Agatha drily.

"There's a creek?" I asked, the memory of Silverwood Lake and those nine fireflies rising up all around me.

"Just a small one," said Aunt Agatha. "Your mama is right. It'll be good for all of us to clear our heads a little."

"Elena, get sunscreen," Mama called as she stood and started clearing dishes from the table. Mama was always worried about us having enough sunscreen, since we'd all inherited Daddy's easy-burning skin and not Mama's magical complexion that never changed in the sunlight.

Elena had eaten quickly and then disappeared back into our bedroom. She had been figuring out how to play chords for the Lydia Lovelace ballad Aunt Agatha had taught her, so she could accompany herself on her ukulele as she sang. Now, I could hear her quiet voice singing, "*'Twas years ago in a valley green,*" while she plucked at the strings. She and Aunt Agatha had looked up the words to the rest of the ballad while I'd been gone at the library yesterday—something about Lydia feeling hollowed out by her heartbreak.

"Ivy, would you fill the cats' bowls before we leave?" Aunt Agatha asked. "The cat food is in that cabinet down there."

I rooted through the cabinet Aunt Agatha had pointed to until I found the bag of cat food and carefully poured it into the dishes that sat in a corner of the kitchen. As soon as the pellets hit the metal of the bowl, Coffee shot back in, too excited even to pretend he didn't care. After a moment, even bashful Cream crept from the hall into the kitchen, slinking along the walls like we might not notice her if she was careful enough.

I wondered what it would be like to live the way Aunt Agatha did, with four solid walls around me and a pair of cats who came running every time I fed them.

When Coffee brushed past me on the way to his dish, the soft silk of his fur felt like belonging.

* * *

The creek *was* small, and shallow enough that we could splash all the way across it without getting wet past our shins. The sight and sound of the water as it burbled over the rocks felt the way chocolate tastes as it slowly melts over your tongue—sweet and rich, the kind of thing that made you want to sigh in contentment and never leave. I couldn't believe we'd been in Whistling Ridge for two weeks and nobody had mentioned that Aunt Agatha lived fifteen minutes from a literal paradise.

As soon as we got there, Sophie ripped off her shoes and socks and waded into the creek. Elena hung back while Mama and Aunt Ruth sat on rocks by the water. Aunt Agatha, though, came to where I stood at the edge of the creek, letting the little current froth over my toes.

Aunt Agatha sighed. "Even the creek is fading."

"What do you mean?" I squinted at the creek. It looked fine to me.

"The water used to go all the way up to that bank there." Aunt Agatha pointed to a dark, vanishing tide mark on the opposite bank . "It used to be deep enough to swim in. Just ask your mama."

"What happened to it?"

Aunt Agatha reached down and picked up a smooth stone from the bank. She rubbed wide circles over it with her thumb; I could see dirt from her garden lodged under her fingernails. Her hands still trembled, just a little bit, all the time.

"Whatever's stealing the magic from Whistling Ridge," Aunt Agatha finally said, releasing the stone and letting it skip over the water, "is taking the life from the town, a little bit at a time. The creek drying up. The apples filled with smoke. The chrysanthemums you saw in my garden the other day. See how even the sky is losing its blueness?"

"But you're going to be able to stop it, right? You and Mama and Aunt Ruth?"

"I hope so, Ivy."

The words were as hard and heavy as the rock Aunt Agatha had let fly a moment ago. I didn't know how to respond, didn't even know how to sort out the tangled-up desires flaring inside me. Fixing the magic meant leaving Whistling Ridge, which meant giving up the chance to create a forever home here, in this mountain town that already felt like part of my own skin.

But *not* fixing the magic might mean the end of Whistling Ridge *and* Aunt Agatha, who didn't seem quite so much a stranger as she had two weeks before.

Aunt Agatha cleared her throat and gave a wry smile. "The honest answer is, none of us really know what *will* happen, because nothing like this has ever happened before. Magic-tending has always been second nature for me and your mama and Ruth. It's what our kind do, the way Elena sings or Sophie memorizes facts. Magic is usually like the weather—it fluctuates, it has good times and bad times, but it always returns to a baseline eventually."

"But not this time?"

"Not this time," Aunt Agatha confirmed. "Now, how far *you* can skip a stone?"

We took turns slinging rocks across the water and counting the skips; my best was three, but Aunt Agatha won with a whopping six. And even knowing that the creek was drying up, even knowing that the fine lines around Aunt Agatha's eyes and mouth and her feathery hair were not good signs—even then, I couldn't help but feel a swell of happiness, there with my sisters and aunts and mama by the glittering water.

22.

Daddy had agreed to give me a ride to the library that afternoon so I could meet up with Simon and Ravi and Miss Christie. He'd been hesitant, at first, to send me off with a librarian he'd never met—*I believe in letting children have their freedom, Ivy Mae, but even I have limits*—but Aunt Agatha had assured him that Miss Christie had lived in Whistling Ridge nearly as long as she herself had, and that the librarian was one of the most trustworthy souls she'd ever met. Privately, I thought that nobody would dare cross Miss Christie; I wasn't convinced that she wasn't capable of *actually* breathing fire.

A warbling chirp greeted us as we made our way past Martha and toward Aunt Agatha's car. I looked up in surprise; I'd almost forgotten about the little wren Elena and I had saved. It was still up there, hopping back and forth on Martha's roof. It didn't seem nearly so distressed as it had before—more curious, like it wanted to be our friend.

Daddy followed my gaze. "Well, I'll be," he muttered, the twang in his voice deepening with his surprise. "Hang on just a sec, Ivy Mae."

He doubled back around the Winnebago and climbed halfway up the access ladder until his head popped up over the camper's roof. The wren stilled, wary now. I heard Daddy blow out his breath hard, and then he jumped down to Aunt Agatha's gravel driveway and raked a hand across his stubbly chin.

"Sophie was right," he said, half to me, half to himself. "That dadgum bird went and built itself a nest behind one of the panels up there. I dunno what we're going to do when it's time to ship out—or heck, when it's time to get Martha towed to the mechanic's. . . ."

The wren was back to its cheerful chirping, peering over at us from the RV top like we might be some previously undiscovered species of rare, enormous bird. Daddy sighed. "I guess we'll figure it out when the time comes."

Still, he kept glancing in the rearview mirror at Martha until we'd turned out of Aunt Agatha's long driveway and onto the main highway that led through Whistling

Ridge. Right at the end of the driveway, I turned to look, too. Even from here, I could see the glint of light on the bird's wings as it busied itself with nest tidying.

I'd stolen nine wishes, contracted pneumonia, accidentally broken Martha's transmission, and maybe even sped up whatever was happening in Whistling Ridge just to build myself a home away from the RV.

Why was this little bird so eager to do the opposite?

Ravi was waiting alone at the library, sitting on a bench outside the door with a book in his lap, when Daddy pulled up alongside the curb.

"Make sure you're back home in two hours," Daddy said as I got out.

It wasn't until I'd closed the door and he'd driven away that I realized he'd said *back home*, not *back to Aunt Agatha's*. A little glow of something that felt suspiciously like hope hovered inside me, threading its way through my spine, tingling at my fingertips.

"No Simon?" I said, sitting down on the bench beside Ravi. He tucked a bookmark into his book—a colorful hardcover with two kids riding bikes on the front.

"He came down with strep last night. He can't talk at all. It's killing him."

I smiled in spite of myself. Strep was awful anyway,

but for somebody who talked as much as Simon, it had to be *torture*.

"His parents wouldn't let him come. He was pretty mad." Ravi pulled a smartphone with a shiny camera lens from his pocket. "I had to promise to take lots of pictures."

"What're you reading?"

He held it up so I could see the title: *The Parker Inheritance*. "It's a mystery. Buried treasure and everything. It's really cool so far."

"Do you read a lot?"

"My mom's a poet. Like, she's had poems in magazines and stuff before. Our house is full of books. It's actually my first memory, her reading to me."

"I thought your parents owned the pharmacy."

"Yeah. They do. My dad worked at a chain drugstore for a long time down in Durham, and my mom worked at a law firm, but my parents always loved the mountains and had this dream of opening a pharmacy up here. Plus, I was born, and my brother, Nikhil, a few years later, and my mom wanted more time with us. So we moved here and they used their savings to buy Main Street Drugs.

"Now my mom helps my dad while Nik and I are in school, and then she comes home when we do and somebody else works in the pharmacy. She says being a lawyer was her job, and being a mom is her calling, but poetry is her passion. She loves to sit and talk about things like *how traditional Indian poetry influences the culture of Bollywood films* when we're all around the dinner table. I got an A in English last year because I could explain all these different poetic forms, thanks to Mom."

"That's cool," I said, a little green shoot of envy twining its way through my heart at the idea of something that tied a whole family to one place, like Ravi's pharmacy.

At that moment, Miss Christie came through the library door with a key ring in her hand, locking the door behind her as brusquely and efficiently as she did everything else. "Miss Bloom, Mr. Sidana. I'm parked over here."

We followed her to a cherry-red car that looked a whole lot like a convertible with the top up. I eyed Miss Christie appraisingly. It wasn't exactly what I would've expected.

Miss Christie drove in silence—down Main Street and then farther, until the brown-brick buildings of the Whistling Ridge town center had all fallen away and the forest rose up around us instead. The houses here looked especially old—falling-down and mostly abandoned, not cute renovated twentieth-century cottages like Aunt Agatha's.

After a few minutes we pulled onto a dirt track hemmed in by kudzu-covered trees. The lane was already becoming overgrown, vines and grassy weeds crunching under the tires of Miss Christie's car as we made our slow way down it. I shivered. The overcast sun seemed even darker out here, like it couldn't quite shine its way into the loneliness of the abandoned property.

"It's been awhile since anyone was out here," Miss Christie said. "It's gotten more ramshackle than I remembered."

She pulled the car to a stop by a tumbledown cottage. It should have been charming—all peeling white paint and a cute front porch and Lovelace clematises massed on trellises that climbed the sides. In the weedy garden, rosebushes grew taller than Miss Christie, their blooms wild and bright.

It *should* have been charming. But instead, I shivered again. There was something about Lydia's cottage, something I couldn't quite put my finger on. Like it was crouched in wait, ready to swallow anything that came too close—me, Ravi, Miss Christie, the town, the sunlight, the stars.

"The homestead used to be open to the public," Miss

Christie said, picking her way through the overgrown rosebushes. "Years ago there was an electrical storm, and lightning struck the cottage. The fire department managed to save the exterior, but there's a lot of structural damage. The city council has planned to restore it ever since, but there are always more pressing budgetary priorities."

Her mouth thinned, and I hid a smile, remembering her tirade in the library about young people and history. Creepy vibes or not, I could see how the Lovelace homestead would be exactly Miss Christie's speed.

"I've never been out here," said Ravi, coming to stand so close to me that I could feel the heat from his arm, like it was creating an electrical charge in the space between it and my own. He talked more without Simon here, I was noticing. Like Simon spilled enough words for two people, and when he was around, Ravi retreated into the background.

"It's been closed my whole life," he went on. He pulled his phone from his pocket and started taking pictures: the clematis run wild, the tangled rosebushes, the brooding shape of the cottage itself.

I folded my arms over my chest like armor. The homestead felt *hungry*. Had it always been this way, or did it have something to do with the lightning-struck fire so long ago? I could almost see it—crackling white fingers reaching from heaven, orange flames roaring up in response, smoke pouring into the night sky. My lungs tightened at the image, reminding me how it had felt to lie in my RV bed, swimming in and out of consciousness, hardly able to breathe.

I put a hand on the reassuring bulge of my inhaler in my pocket and took a deep breath.

"Well," said Miss Christie impatiently, "are you going to look around? Gain inspiration for your literary aspirations?"

I nodded, even though most of me was screaming *not on your life*.

I followed Ravi toward the front of the house. Up closer, I could see the way the porch sagged in toward the ground; through a scratched and dirty window, I caught a glimpse of what looked like blackened boards hanging down from the ceiling where it had caved in.

"It's *so* much cooler than I imagined," Ravi said, taking close-up pictures that showed the texture of the peeling paint, the way carpenter ants had chewed their way through whole sections of the porch steps, leaving piles of sawdust behind.

"It doesn't feel . . . weird?" I glanced at him out of the corner of my eye. He stood on tiptoe, his hands around his eyes to shield the light as he peered in through a front window.

"Weird how? I mean, it's kind of sad it's been completely ignored for so long, yeah. Think how cool it would be if they fixed it up and reopened it to the public!"

I squeezed my fingers around the edges of my writing notebook. I'd brought it along because I'd been sure the homestead would be inspiring, and I'd get so close to Lydia that her story would pour out of me right onto the page.

Instead, I felt paralyzed. It hurt, thinking of beautiful, loving Lydia connected somehow to this broken-down, burned-up place.

The way Ravi acted like he didn't notice the gloomy foreboding that hung over the whole property was strange. It reminded me of the way regular people went through their whole lives without ever seeing the magic that wove through the world around them. *Humans don't always know what they don't know*, Mama had said once when I'd asked her about it. Unease prickled at the skin of my arms.

"Come on, let's go around to the back," Ravi said.

I followed him around the side of the house into the backyard, which was even more of a mess than the front—the garden was so full of runaway flowers and shrubs and waist-high weeds that we could hardly squeeze ourselves in between it and the back of the house. Kudzu and English ivy wove their way over and through all the other plants and made their way up the siding of the cottage, green tendrils like slender creeping animals.

A door jutted from the back wall, hanging haphazardly off its hinges, like it might fall at any moment.

"Whoa, it's a mess in there," Ravi said, waving me over to look.

I peered inside. The room through the door might have been a kitchen once; along the opposite wall hulked an enormous old-fashioned woodstove. Everything else had fallen apart, literally. The plaster from the walls lay in clumps all across the floor, and the ceiling *was* caved in, light from the attic streaming down into the room.

Ravi glanced around to make sure that Miss Christie was still out front and then lifted a finger to his lips and stepped through the door. After a minute, he popped his head out and waved. "Come inside, it's so cool! Just for a second. We'll be out before Miss Christie knows we broke her rules, I promise."

Anxiety churning in my stomach, I followed him into the cottage. The wooden floor was still strong enough to hold us, though I could see a few places in the corners where mice had chewed depressions in the floorboards.

"The light in here is amazing," Ravi whispered, snapping a photo of the ruined ceiling. "I'm going to try to paint it. It's like those old paintings of saints, where they're glowing."

I walked gingerly around the kitchen as Ravi took pictures, running my fingers over the cold cast iron of the woodstove. Beside the stove was a wooden trunk, the kind with metal inlaid across the top. It had a lock, but the damp had rusted away at it so much that it didn't even protest when I opened the lid.

There wasn't much inside it except for a half-dozen spiders that crawled grumpily away from me—and, at the bottom of the trunk, a bundle of papers that looked *very* familiar.

The papers from the end of Lydia's journal.

I lifted them out of the trunk carefully, shaking them over the floor just to make sure there were no more spiders in residence. They were fragile, but not really in any worse shape than the rest of the journal had been when I'd seen it in the library the day before.

"We'd better get out of here," Ravi whispered. From outside, I could hear the crunch of Miss Christie's boots on dried leaves as she came around the back. Quickly, I slipped the journal pages into my writing notebook and then followed Ravi out the door, back into the wild of Lydia's garden.

23.

"Hmm. This garden is in a terrible state." Miss Christie clicked her tongue, looking around at the overgrown backyard. "It's disgraceful."

She nodded toward a nearby red rosebush, tangled over with vines. "That's Lydia's grave, though you can't see much of it right now."

"Wow!" Ravi held the phone up and snapped photo after photo, before picking his way carefully through the overgrowth and holding the thorny canes aside. Underneath them was a worn-out marker made of gray stone, so old that the carving was barely readable. "Come look at this, Ivy!"

I swallowed hard but followed him, ducking under a low-hanging climbing rose to kneel in the grass beside the headstone. I lifted a finger to trace the letters in

Lydia's name. I couldn't stop myself; even though it was creepy, it felt magnetic, like it was drawing my hand to it. The stone was cold, the kind of cold that slithered all the way through to my blood.

A verse of poetry was carved underneath *Lydia Lovelace*:

Let roses grow where they lay me down,
Let starlight kiss me, too;
Let all the world feel my broken heart—
How it everlong beat true.

"It's the ballad," I said. "The one that tells Lydia's story. Or part of it, anyway. My aunt's teaching it to my sister."

There weren't any dates—or if there were, the stone was so old they'd been rubbed away.

"What's that beside the stone?" Miss Christie asked, peering over our shoulders.

I turned to follow her gaze, and my heart paused. Beside Lydia's grave, still as a painting, there was a bird. A tiny wren, like the one that had made its home on top of Martha—except this one was dead, its wings splayed like a ballerina mid-leap. And not only dead: it was like death had drained the bird of color, plunging it into gray scale, so that it looked like something from a black-and-white photo. Not only *gray*, like a regular gray bird, but bleached, colorless, desaturated.

"Curious," murmured Miss Christie, frowning.

Ravi, of course, took a picture. "Poor bird. A fox or something must've gotten it. If we had a shovel, we could give it a burial." He paused for a moment, then stood and stepped over a patch of ivy that foamed almost like water, taking more photos of the back of the house. "This is going to make the most amazing project. I can't wait to get started."

I mumbled something that kind of sounded like agreement, immobilized on the ground before Lydia's grave. Before we'd come, I'd been itching to decode Lydia's diary and get my story written—I could *see* it, the way Ravi would paint a backdrop and Simon would build a little miniature cottage and we'd drape it with Lovelace clematis, just the way he'd promised. And everyone in town would get to see their work and read my words. And maybe, just maybe, Mama and Daddy would *finally* understand how much it would mean to me to make Whistling Ridge our forever home.

Now, though, my fingers were frozen where they curled around my writing notebook. The thought of getting my pen out and writing something down about Lydia felt wrong—*dangerous*, even, like an invitation to whatever horrible thing was lurking in Lydia's homestead to take up root elsewhere in the town, too.

Wait.

I turned and stared at the back of Lydia's cottage, feeling the way the brooding darkness of the place seemed to seep right into my skin.

Earlier, the homestead had felt *hungry*.

I thought of my eavesdropping the other night, the words Mama and Aunt Agatha had used:

Swallowing.

Unravel.

Void.

That feeling the star sisters had described sitting around Aunt Agatha's table—the feeling of whatever was sucking the magic right out of Whistling Ridge . . .

That feeling was concentrated here, in Lydia Lovelace's forgotten cottage.

What if Lydia Lovelace hadn't died of a broken heart all those years ago?

Whatever it was that was stealing the magic from the town, whatever was turning Aunt Agatha into an old woman right before our eyes—

What if *Lydia* had been its first victim?

24.

Ravi kept trying to draw me into conversation on the drive back to Aunt Agatha's, talking about how cool the homestead was, how he'd paint the kudzu, what the porch must've looked like before it caved inward. I gave one-word answers, hardly even hearing what he said.

"You okay, Ivy?" he asked, his eyebrows drawn together. Somehow, I didn't think I could stand an entire ride with Miss Christie's eagle eyes fixed on me, seeing everything; even now, I caught her glancing sharply at me in the rearview mirror more than once.

"Fine."

"Okay," said Ravi, but the wrinkle in his forehead didn't go away.

I couldn't stop seeing the ruin of Lydia's cottage. Couldn't stop feeling the way the place pulled at me, like a living thing. Like a dark, devouring beast. I clutched my writing notebook to my chest; I could almost *feel* the pages from Lydia's journal tucked inside it, whispering secrets. Secrets that maybe nobody else in Whistling Ridge had ever found. The real story of what had happened to Lydia. The key, maybe, to whatever horrible force had swallowed her and then destroyed her cottage . . . and now, was working its way to all of Whistling Ridge.

I should tell Mama and her sisters as soon as I got back. I knew that. This—the homestead—it *had* to hold the key to the mystery they'd been working on ever since we landed in Whistling Ridge with a broken transmission and a case of pneumonia.

I should tell them. But sitting in Miss Christie's cherry-red car, I couldn't figure out how I'd form the words. They were all already so stressed out. Daddy had been writing article after article to send to his editor; his pace would probably have to get even faster, now that Mama was having trouble catching many firefly wishes. And I thought of Mama and Aunt Agatha in the garden the week we'd arrived, pouring their magic into the earth only to have it burn out and leave them aged and shaking.

This morning at the creek, Aunt Agatha had said, *None of us has any idea where we should even start.*

Would telling them about Lydia's cottage give them a place to start—or just add to all the things they couldn't do anything about?

And deep inside the darkest, most selfish part of my heart, another honest question lurked:

Did I really want them to know, if telling them might mean we'd leave Whistling Ridge sooner?

Ravi leaned over and gave me a hug before I got out of the car at Aunt Agatha's house.

"You seem like you could use it," he said. He smelled like warm, musky clove, mixed with the sharp scent of paint. The whole thing made the back of my throat feel scratchy. We'd only been here for two weeks, but Simon and Ravi already felt like friends, like they were just as much a part of me as my family and the aunts and the way stargazing on a clear night made me feel.

We couldn't leave Whistling Ridge. Not yet.

I couldn't let these friendships with Simon and Ravi spark out, like the friendship I'd *thought* was so strong between me and Ada. The three of us were *meant* to be friends; I could feel it deep inside. *Blessings come in threes.*

"See you Saturday," I said as I slid out of the backseat.

"'Kay," said Ravi, and before I'd closed the door, he'd already slid the bookmark out of *The Parker Inheritance* and folded open the spine.

That evening, after we'd eaten dinner and Mama had gone to catch the few fireflies she could find while Daddy worked on his latest article, I snuck out to the backyard with the photocopied pages of Lydia's journal and my writing notebook. I'd tucked the pages I'd found in the cottage into a box under my bed. I should give them to Miss Christie, I knew; she'd want to put them back in the diary, or at least keep them safe in the archival room. But I couldn't bear to do it quite yet, before I'd had a chance to look at them myself.

I sank into the grass with the notebook opened in my lap and the photocopies spread before me. Maybe, if I could decipher what Lydia had written, I'd be able to make sense of the things I'd felt at her cottage.

Could it be, I wondered, that Lydia's heartbreak and death had pulled the town's magic down with it? Could it be that she was so bright, so wonderful, treated so badly, that when she died . . . something about Whistling Ridge died, too?

I chewed on my bottom lip. I didn't know if that made sense, exactly—not when it had been so long since Lydia had been here. Whistling Ridge had been fine for more than a hundred years since that moment. So why, just now, had it . . . stopped being fine?

Whatever it was, Lydia's diary might hold a clue. Maybe, in addition to helping me with my story, the diary could provide an answer to the question Mama and her sisters had been asking ever since we'd arrived:

What was draining the magic from Whistling Ridge?

It was like there were two Ivys inside me—the one who wanted the star sisters to succeed, wanted the lines to recede on Aunt Agatha's face and the creek to fill up and the apples to have flesh and seeds inside them. And then the other guiltier, sneakier Ivy, who couldn't stop thinking about how solving the mystery meant giving up my whole wish list and getting back on the road as soon as Martha's transmission got fixed.

And it wasn't like the town was on the brink of destruction. The sun still shone from behind the clouds, the birds still sang, all the ways Mama had taught me to look for magic in the world still existed. There was no lurking volcano belching smoke and ash, no fire raging out of control.

Surely holding on to this secret for just a *few* more days couldn't hurt.

For now, I'd try to figure out Lydia's diary without explaining anything to my mama. And maybe once I knew what secrets Lydia's life held—maybe once I knew whether they had anything at all to do with the magic of Whistling Ridge—*then* I'd tell.

Unfortunately, figuring out the diary was easier said than done. I squinted at the printouts, turned them from side to side, and still I couldn't make any sense of the chicken-scratch writing. I sighed and turned to my notebook instead. Maybe if I could finish the beginning of my story, it would energize my brain cells enough that they'd be ready to tangle again with the mystery of Lydia's penmanship. Trying to decipher it made that hot, itchy anger that always seemed a breath away these days rise to the surface, so that I had to take deep breaths to keep my fingers from crumpling up the pages with their incomprehensible words.

I put the journal away and opened to a clean spot in my notebook instead. The best thing about writing had always been the way it let me forget where I was, what I was doing, and what was bothering me in my life. As I wrote, Aunt Agatha's backyard got smudgier and smudgier around me, like an Impressionist watercolor that had gotten too much water mixed in with the paint, and it was almost like I could see Whistling Ridge the way it had been when Lydia was alive 130 years ago: dirt roads, wagons, a few small houses here and there.

I tried not to picture Lydia's own house, though, with

its lavender clematis and sherbet-colored roses and that deep, dark, sucking hunger.

I started by making a list of characters. Lydia, of course, who I pictured as having raven-dark hair. And Henry, who was sandy-haired and strong-jawed. Henry's fiancée, who I decided was named Antoinette, because it sounded extremely fancy, and who I pictured as blond and snooty. And Henry's parents, the mayor and his wife, who thought their son was too good for an orphan nobody like Lydia Lovelace.

That was enough to start. Anybody else could get added in later.

More of Aunt Agatha's backyard disappeared as I wrote, my thoughts coming too fast for my pen to keep up with, until I was so deep inside that old-fashioned version of Whistling Ridge that I wouldn't have been surprised if I'd looked up and seen a horse-drawn buggy riding down the orchard road. I was so preoccupied with my notebook that when Aunt Ruth tapped me on the shoulder, I jumped, my pen flying off into the grass beside me.

"Sorry," I said, grabbing the pen and blushing.

Aunt Ruth smiled—a watery smile that held the memory of the tears I'd caught her crying the night she'd arrived.

"Your mama got back and wasn't sure where you

were," she said. "I think she wants you to keep your sisters away if any wish-seekers come calling. Especially since she keeps running out of wishes and having to turn people away—one gentleman became very cranky this afternoon while you were out with your friends. Agatha had to threaten to set the cats on him before he finally stomped away in a huff."

I groaned before I could stop myself. Aunt Ruth's smile deepened into a real, genuine grin.

"Tending your sisters isn't your favorite thing, hmm?"

I shook my head.

"Well, maybe I won't tell her you're out here just yet." Aunt Ruth gave a conspiratorial wink. "I know what it's like to need to be alone sometimes."

"Is that why you moved out to Montana all by yourself?" I'd always been curious about that; the few times we'd visited her, it had seemed so lonely, so remote, so utterly far from Aunt Agatha's warm home in Whistling Ridge, where the star sisters had lived since their earliest human days.

"Yes, that was part of it."

"And the other part?"

Aunt Ruth laughed. "I see you haven't gotten any less curious as you've gotten older, Ivy Mae."

That was the kind of thing adults said about me a

lot, along with using words like incorrigible ("not able to be corrected, improved, or reformed") and irrepressible ("not able to be controlled or restrained"). They said the same things about Sophie, too, sometimes. Mama was always trying to convince me that Sophie and I didn't get along because we were so alike, but that idea made me itchy between my shoulder blades.

"The other part of it," Aunt Ruth went on, choosing her words as carefully as though she were picking her way around cut glass, "was that I fell in love. I visited Montana once when you were young, and I decided to stay, because I loved someone there."

"Uncle Andrew," I said.

Aunt Ruth nodded. "Yes. Part of what tied me to Montana was love."

Tied. Was. I thought of all those suitcases Aunt Ruth had brought when she'd come to Whistling Ridge, the ones that were piled up in Aunt Agatha's sewing room now, and the way she always seemed one wrong word away from tears. "Not anymore?"

The sad smile was back on Aunt Ruth's face. "I know I'm overly fond of my secrets, but I'm not ready to let this one go yet. I'll tell you the whole story someday, Ivy honey."

I nodded, chastened. Maybe Aunt Ruth, the second

star sister, really *was* like Elena—the quiet one, the shy one, the one who liked to keep her thoughts close to her chest. Of course, if that were true, it would make Mama like Sophie, which I wasn't sure I could *ever* imagine.

Maybe being a fallen star with magic running through your veins mellowed you out, even if you *were* the youngest of three sisters.

Aunt Ruth cleared her throat. "So, what are all these papers? Mind if I join you?"

When I nodded, she sat cross-legged on the grass beside me. I spread out the pages so she could see them. Maybe, if I didn't tell her my suspicions about Lydia being the first victim of the Whistling Ridge curse, Aunt Ruth could help me figure out what the journal entries said without understanding why they were important.

"You know about Lydia Lovelace, right?" I asked. Aunt Ruth nodded. "These are copies of her journal entries. Miss Christie at the library made them for me. I'm writing a story about Lydia for a display at the town festival next month. Well, it's more than a story—my friends and I are going to make it into a big project. They're building a diorama of Lydia Lovelace's cottage, and we'll print the story out and put it in there."

If we're still here next month.

"That sounds wonderful," Aunt Ruth said when I

didn't add anything else. "So what do they say?"

"That's the problem," I said. "I practically can't read the writing at all. So I'm mostly having to make things up, but it would be a lot better if I could use some real facts, too."

"Hmm," said Aunt Ruth, pursing her lips. "I worked as a medical aide for a year or two and got pretty good at figuring out doctor handwriting—this can't be too much harder, can it?"

"You mean you'll help me?"

"Sure. I mean, until my conscience overcomes me and I send you back to mind your sisters so your mama can barter her wishes in peace and privacy." But she winked at me, and I had a feeling that wouldn't be anytime soon.

"So, let's see," Aunt Ruth said, pulling the first page of Lydia's diary closer to her. "If we can figure out how she generally shapes her letters, we can probably stand a good chance of training ourselves to read the whole journal. See, here, how her *h* has that big swoop and then almost no hook. . . ."

And for almost the first time since Miss Christie had driven her car down the long drive to the Lovelace homestead that afternoon, a glimmer of excitement burned deep inside me.

25.

A unt Ruth never did make me go in and watch Elena and Sophie—she and I worked until dark on Lydia's papers. Guilt writhed in the space below my collarbone, but I told it to go away. Living all together in a couple hundred square feet, I hardly ever did anything without my sisters. Mama could fend them off by herself for one evening.

When we had finished translating the first few diary entries and made our way back inside Aunt Agatha's cottage, Elena and Sophie weren't even anywhere near Mama where she sat at the dining room table, trying to gently explain to a worried-faced wish-seeker why she didn't have any more wishes to barter today. The wish-seeker was a woman who looked about Mama's age; her eyes were puffy and red and her cheeks were shiny, like she'd been crying.

"I'm so sorry," Mama said in the kind of gentle voice she usually saved for animals or hurt children. "I truly wish I could help you."

The stranger didn't reply, just shook her head and looked anguished. As I passed down the hall toward my bedroom to put the photocopies away, I could hear the front door slam when she left.

My sisters were lying in wait for me in Aunt Agatha's guest room.

Elena had a pinched, anxious look on her face, and Sophie's jaw was set hard and tight, like she was ready to march into battle.

"Ivy," Sophie said as soon as I stepped across the threshold of the bedroom, "we need to talk."

It was such a funny, grown-up phrase coming from such a little girl, even one who made a habit of saying things that should've come from college professors, that I started laughing. Sophie's scowl deepened.

"We don't think you should write that story about Lydia." Elena's words tumbled over one another on their way out.

"It's creepy," Sophie added. "Too much dying."

I hugged my writing notebook and photocopied

papers closer to my chest. "What are you talking about? Has anybody ever said Romeo and Juliet were creepy?"

I tried hard not to think about the grayed-out bird, feathers splayed, next to Lydia's grave. Whatever had hurt Lydia, whatever had pulled the color from that bird, whatever it was that lurked in the clematis and kudzu at Lydia's homestead—it wasn't like writing about her would bring that stealing through our windows.

Right?

"Besides," I said when Sophie opened her mouth like she was going to say something else, "I got the idea from Aunt Agatha. And if I don't write it, how are we going to convince Mama and Daddy to stay in Whistling Ridge?"

"*That's* your big plan to keep us here?" asked Sophie.

I shrugged, not wanting to hear her say it was a stupid idea that would never work. I thought of the way it had felt to spend so many hours with Simon and Ravi since we'd come. The way the three of us together felt magical. I wasn't going to let Sophie tell me I had no chance to hold on to that magic.

"Well, we don't *want* to stay," Sophie said.

"Not forever," Elena said. "Not after Mama and the aunts fix Whistling Ridge."

"I miss Martha," said Sophie stubbornly. "I don't like it here. Kids are mean and everything looks the same all the time."

"Mama's work is important," Elena said. "You know that, Ivy."

I flopped onto my bed and turned away from my sisters. "What are you, those people who interrogate criminals? Go away. I need to finish drafting this scene."

"But—" Sophie started. I put my hands over my ears. Elena shushed her, but that didn't really reassure me; Elena might have been the shy one in the family, but being shy didn't mean she wasn't as stubborn as the little wren building its nest on top of the RV. When Elena wanted something, she did not give up.

Still, at least they were leaving me alone.

For now.

I finished my schoolwork as quickly as I could on Friday so I could spend the afternoon alternating between scribbling in my notebook and poring over Lydia's journal. Aunt Ruth was right—the more I looked at the scrawly script, the easier it became to understand. I could read whole passages now. Her diary entries weren't very regular; sometimes she'd go for weeks without writing, and then write every day for four or five days in a row. Mostly, Lydia wrote about regular kinds of things: how much flour she'd bought at the general store, what the new hat she'd ordered looked like. She kept records of her gardening, writing down soil amendments and fertilizing schedules and how certain plants did in certain areas. The way she wrote about her garden reminded me of the way Mama showed people our baby pictures—like a proud, clucking hen, standing guard over her nest.

I was a few pages into the diary before Lydia mentioned Henry. His full name was Henry Asbury, and just like Aunt Agatha had said, he was the son of Whistling Ridge's first mayor. He'd been gone when Lydia had first appeared in Whistling Ridge—just like Miss Christie had warned, the diary didn't give any clues as to *where* she had come from—but a few months after the journal started, Henry had come home after finishing law school up north. He'd bumped into Lydia, literally, one afternoon when she took her horse to the blacksmith after it had thrown a shoe.

Lydia wrote about him like he was the handsomest person on the whole planet (though I'd been wrong, and his hair was red, not sandy). It was clear from the minute he apologized for running into her that she was smitten ("deeply affected with or struck by strong feelings of attraction"). And at first, it seemed like he liked her the same way. Lydia talked about how he'd pick her up in his buggy and they'd go for drives in the countryside, or how they'd walk through the orchards and Henry would pull down the sweetest apples and give them to her.

They are like no apples I have tasted, Lydia wrote, *as though an apple had grown inside a beehive, its fruit sweet honey on the tongue.*

By the time dark had fallen that evening and Mama had shooed us girls off to bed, I had the whole first scene of my story done, with Henry bumping into Lydia on the street as she waited for the blacksmith. And I'd written about Henry's parents, the mayor and his wife, who hadn't been mentioned much in the diary yet but who I was sure were important in keeping Henry away from Lydia.

Mayor Asbury and his wife loved money and fancy things. They lived in a house on the highest hill in Whistling Ridge, where they could look down on the whole town. And nobody was as far beneath them as orphan Lydia Lovelace.

I turned off the lamp by my bedside with a smile: creepy gardens and meddling sisters notwithstanding, tomorrow I'd have a whole first scene to show Simon and Ravi. And we'd have our multimedia project done in time for the Lovelace Festival next month. And as long as I could convince Mama and Daddy to stay in Whistling Ridge until the end of October, they'd come and see the project and read my words, and they'd be so proud and thrilled and overwhelmed that they'd *know*, the way I knew, that I *needed* Whistling Ridge to be my forever home.

That night I dreamed about Lydia's cottage. The whole dream was as colorless as an old black-and-white silent film, filled with birds that swooped in distress and roses whose thorns shone as bright as swords—and a deep, dark, brooding hunger that oozed like mud from the walls of the little house and pooled beneath the marker on Lydia's grave.

But by the time I woke the next morning, all I could remember was the vague feeling of it, like spiders crawling down my spine.

26.

By the third Saturday in Whistling Ridge, my parents seemed to assume that Sophie and I would be going to Oaktree Park.

"You can come, too," I said to Elena. She was sitting cross-legged on her trundle bed, picking at her ukulele, working on her arrangement of the Lydia Lovelace ballad. The melody made me think of Whistling Ridge in September, all golden light and apple cider, happiness shot through with just a little bit of wistful melancholy. Elena's silver-sweet voice was perfect for the song, with its fierce, sad words. *Let roses grow where they lay me down . . .*

Elena stopped strumming and shook her head. "I'd rather stay."

"Maybe next week. I like your song. I can't wait to

hear it when it's all finished."

"Thanks," said Elena, her smile like the scent of autumn in the orchards, fresh and joyful.

I paused before leaving the bedroom. "Elena, do you think something happened to Uncle Andrew?"

Elena cocked her head to one side. "Who?"

"Uncle Andrew. You know, Aunt Ruth's . . . whatever."

Elena shook her head. "I don't remember Aunt Ruth's house at all."

If I'd been eight the last time we'd visited Montana, Elena would've been six. I guessed it wasn't a shock that she didn't remember any of it.

"I just kind of think something happened," I said. "Aunt Ruth seems so sad all the time. And she brought all those suitcases, like . . . she's planning to stay awhile."

"Do you think her heart is broken?" asked Elena. "Like Lydia's?"

I shrugged. "That's what I'm wondering."

Sophie and I made it to the park without fighting a single time, which might have been some kind of record. With every day we stayed in Whistling Ridge, I could feel the anger from the wishing night loosening a little, fading just the smallest bit from my skin.

Maybe as long as Sophie gave up on the idea that moving was better than staying, we would be okay.

When we got to Oaktree, Sophie hesitated. Without having to ask, I knew that she was keeping a wary eye out for Simon's sister, Hannah. *Kids here are mean*, she'd said yesterday. Were kids anywhere else better, though, when it came to people like Sophie? Nowhere I ever remembered visiting had people who were especially good at accepting when somebody was really, really different.

Last week, after Hannah had called her weird, Sophie had said, *This is why it's better to be in Martha*. Maybe it wasn't so much that she felt like people would be nicer elsewhere, I realized: maybe it was just that Sophie figured as long as we moved around often enough, she wouldn't have to ever stay to deal with how not-nice people could be.

But I wasn't so sure I agreed. I thought of the pain of my empty email in-box. If life on the road meant the best friend I'd ever had could disappear without a trace, it wasn't a life at all.

"I think Hannah's at her soccer game," I said carefully when I didn't see any signs of white-blond hair in the turrets of the wooden castle. The only kids I could see playing right now were Joel and Leah, the freckled boy and red-haired girl a little older than Sophie who Simon had said were fellow non-soccer players. "But Soph, even if she's not . . . you'll be okay. Just remember that you're who *you* want to be, and nobody else matters."

Maybe today could be the start of something new. A better, nicer Ivy, without that sense of simmering anger I'd carried with me all summer long. Maybe staying in Whistling Ridge could change me. This morning, with my writing notebook clutched to my chest and a whole scene done in my Lydia story, anything felt possible.

Sophie hugged me, light and quick, before she ran off to play.

Ravi waved at me from where he was sketching under the tree again. Simon wasn't with him, but the slightly ominous way the oak branches were rustling gave me a pretty good idea where he was. Charlie was on her usual bench—sitting up this time, her book closed in her lap. Like she'd been waiting for me.

When she saw she'd caught my eye, she patted the bench next to her. I sat.

"Look," she said, quietly enough that Simon and Ravi couldn't hear us. "I've been thinking all week about our conversation last Saturday. About your mom, and the wishes. The thing is . . ."

She trailed off, looking down at the ground, before swallowing hard. "My mom. She has cancer. It's the second time, and . . . things aren't looking super great. Prognosis-wise, I mean."

"I'm so sorry." I said it like a reflex, because that's

what you say when somebody's mom has cancer and things aren't looking super great. But I meant it, too.

"My parents, they haven't given me all the details, but I'm pretty sure the doctors have run out of things to try. And then y'all showed up two and half weeks ago, and I started hearing rumors about what your mom does. Do you think . . . do you think she could help me? Help my mom?"

I thought about what I'd said to Charlie the week before, what Mama and Daddy had drilled into me for as long as I could remember: *Wishes don't always work out quite the way you expect them to.* I didn't know nearly as much about wishes as Mama did, but I had a feeling that cancer might be one of those things a wish couldn't fix completely—like my asthma, or Elena's anxious days.

But maybe a wish could do *something*. Maybe it could bring hope. Maybe it could help Charlie and her parents on the long road ahead.

"I don't know if a wish could do exactly what you want it do," I said honestly. "But you should go see my mama anyway. She's having trouble harvesting enough wishes here lately, but . . . it's worth a try."

"Thanks, Ivy," said Charlie, reaching over and giving my hand a quick squeeze. "You're a pretty good listener, you know. For a kid."

I smiled halfway. "Thanks yourself."

As Charlie let go of my hand, it was almost like she looked a little different—a little lighter, a little brighter, like the air around her was glowing just the tiniest bit. Like, for maybe the first time in a long time, she had hope.

And even if Charlie's wish didn't fix her mama's cancer—even if her mama still got sicker, even if she someday died, even if nothing worked out the way Charlie and her parents wanted it to—maybe that hope would be enough.

I almost felt guilty, knowing that if I succeeded in getting my parents to settle down, Mama wouldn't be bringing that kind of hope to people all over the country anymore.

But the minute I turned from Charlie and saw Ravi sitting under the tree, my heart closed a hard fist around that guilt. There would always be magic in the world. There would always be sources that desperate people could turn to. Right now? It was *my* turn to hope.

"I brought you something," Ravi said as soon as I'd sat down beside him on the grass. Carefully, hesitantly, he flipped to a different page in his sketchbook and pulled out a sheet of thick watercolor paper.

"Oh. *Wow*," I said, taking the painting from him. It was Lydia's cottage. Ravi had captured it perfectly: the way the porch sagged, the dark rotting boards that showed through the places the whitewash was peeling away from the siding. It was good—*really* good. Simon hadn't been kidding when he'd called Ravi an artist.

"Me and Simon won't build it like it is now, obviously," Ravi said, taking the paper back. "I mean, all crumbling and old. I just did this for practice. I've got another one I'm working on that shows it how it probably looked when Lydia was alive."

Maybe that other one wouldn't make me feel like I'd walked into a spiderweb. I held my body very, very still, so I couldn't shiver even if I wanted to.

"You're really good," I said, because I couldn't say anything about the painting, about the way Lydia's house seemed to *watch* me from the page.

What had happened at Lydia's cottage? I felt like I'd wondered that same thing so many times in the last two days that it had worn grooves in my brain, like a trail that's been walked over and over again until it's just clear dust cutting through the trees. Whatever had happened, I *knew*—in the same way I knew that Whistling Ridge was meant to be my forever home—that it was something bad.

My stomach churned uncomfortably. I couldn't keep this from Mama and my aunts much longer. Aunt Agatha had looked as old as the hills this morning, her movements slow and her lined face drawn with pain.

I couldn't shake the feeling that my secret-keeping was making her worse, feeding the thing that was sucking the life from her with every day that passed.

"Look out below!" Simon bellowed from the branches above us, and a minute later he'd dropped to the grass beside us, brushing leaves from his shorts. "Hi, Ivy!"

"Hi," I said. "Is your throat all better?"

"Oh, yeah. My Mom took me to the doctor pretty quick, and the antibiotic cleared it right up. It was *horrible* not to be able to talk! Seriously, Ivy, the *worst*."

Simon clutched his chest dramatically. Ravi and I exchanged a laughing look.

"Hey," Simon said, "is that your writing notebook? Have you started on your Lydia story yet? Did Ravi show you his picture? It's so cool, right? Can we read your story so far? I mean, it's okay if you don't want to share it yet, but—"

"Here," I said before Simon could talk himself into an early grave. I shoved the notebook at him, trying to ignore the anxious little bird swooping in my stomach. I'd never actually shown my writing to many people other than my family. I chewed on my lip, thinking of Ada and the way she'd stopped reading all the stories and poems I'd spent so long typing up to send her.

Simon plopped down on the grass next to Ravi, and they opened the notebook together. It took a hundred years for them to read it. *Please don't hate it.* I sent a little prayer out into the universe. If Simon and Ravi didn't like my story—if they didn't want to go through with our multimedia project . . .

Once it got to the point where I was actually positive that I'd died and my ghost was still waiting to hear what they thought, Simon looked up and grinned. "Oh my gosh! It's so good! You need to write more, like, today, okay? I can't wait to read the whole thing!"

Ravi nodded beside him.

I blushed so hard I could feel the redness creeping up past my hairline. But even with the blushing and the funny feeling in my stomach, there was something else there, too: excitement, pride, even a little relief.

Somebody liked my story. My story.

All I had to do was make sure we stayed until the festival. It was exactly five weeks from today. Never had five weeks felt so short and so long, all at once.

I tried not to think of Elena and Sophie confronting me in our bedroom Thursday night, telling me they didn't *want* to stay. They were wrong. They had to be wrong.

Didn't everyone—Aunt Agatha, me, Lydia, even the little wren on the camper roof—didn't everyone want a forever home?

27.

All weekend I was as restless and unsettled as the gray sky outside. At night, I'd lie in bed for hours, torn between excitement over my Lydia story and the nameless, creeping dread I'd felt at the Lovelace Homestead. I dreamed about the cottage over and over again—the kudzu choking everything, the caved-in ceiling, the lines from the ballad etched on Lydia's grave. In my dreams I heard them sung in Elena's voice.

Aunt Agatha looked worse every day, like it was hard just to hold herself together. There were no more walks to the creek or stone skipping; she hardly even paid attention to Coffee, who paced restlessly through the house over and over, or Cream, who had come out of hiding to follow Aunt Agatha like an anxious shadow. Every day that passed, she seemed a little less substantial, sitting in her fireplace armchair crocheting or at the table with Mama and Aunt Ruth, going over and over things they might try to fix Whistling Ridge.

It was like Aunt Agatha was slipping into a world made of fog and smoke.

By Monday, I knew I couldn't keep the secret to myself any longer. I couldn't keep convincing myself that Aunt Agatha would be fine if the magic loss wasn't stopped; the evidence for the opposite was right in front of my eyes. Even all the wishes on my wish list were starting to seem less important than my real-life, flesh-and-blood aunt, who had fed me cider and talked to me like a grown-up and let us all into her life like we belonged there.

Sophie was already at the kitchen table, started on schoolwork, by the time I made it out of my room. Even though she was a super genius when it came to science, Mama still made her do lots of regular third-grade sorts of things: handwriting practice, easy essay writing, social studies. Sophie may have been able to tell you the exact history of the Hubble Telescope, but she still sometimes wrote her *Z*s backward and got her *I*s and *A*s out of order in words like *wait* and *faith*.

Mama sat across from her, nursing a cup of tea,

looking tired. She wasn't glowing as brightly as normal; her skin seemed dull and ashy, and her silver-white hair hung limp around her shoulders.

"Ivy," she said, mustering a small smile when I walked in. "Good morning, honey. You sleep okay?"

I shrugged. "Where are Aunt Agatha and Aunt Ruth?"

"Aggie's still sleeping. She's not been feeling herself the last few days. Ruth is reading."

"You aren't going out again this morning?" Magic-tending instruments were scattered all over the table between Mama and Sophie: the silver star pendulum, the star-metal scrying plate where she burned herbs, the maps she and the aunts had been studying.

"Not right now, at any rate." Mama sighed, big and gusty. "Everyone needs a day off once in a while. And really, we've run out of ideas. I have no clue what we'll try next."

I thought of the conversation I'd overheard days ago.

Unravel.

Darkness.

Getting faster.

"What are you looking for, exactly?" I asked carefully.

A wrinkle appeared in Mama's forehead. "You've seen me tend magic before. Usually, it's not hard for me— or Aggie or Ruth—to find the center of a problem. It will feel *wrong*, like if you've put one place setting upside down at the table. Like something doesn't fit."

"Like those 'one of these things is not like the others' puzzles?"

Mama laughed, her light brightening, just for a moment. "Yes, quite a lot like those puzzles. The most it's ever taken me before is three days, maybe four, to find. Usually even if something is all knotted up, I can identify it without much trouble, and fix it without help.

"But this—I've never seen anything like this. And no matter what we try, we can't seem to find any answers. Anyway—" Mama's shoulders straightened and her gaze sharpened. "I shouldn't be telling you any of this, Ivy Mae. You don't need to worry about it. It may be a riddle, but we'll get to the bottom of it."

"I think I found a clue," I said before I could talk myself out of it.

"What?" Mama asked, eyes wide, the mug of tea in front of her forgotten. "But—how could you—"

"Thursday, when Miss Christie took us to the Lovelace Homestead," I went on quickly. "I should have told you then, but . . . well . . ."

Mama's eyebrows climbed higher with every second I spent dithering ("being indecisive") over my response. From across the table, Sophie looked up from her work, fixing me with a considering sort of stare. I ignored her and plunged on.

"It felt wrong, Mama. Awful and creepy and wrong. I don't even know how to describe it. It felt so dark, and . . . hungry. And there was—there was this little bird, right by Lydia's grave. It was dead, but it wasn't just *dead*, it was like all the color had been drained out of it. Just like the smoke in the apples, or the beetles in the chrysanthemums. Just like the magic, draining out of Whistling Ridge."

"But—you're *sure* of this, Ivy? Could it have been something you imagined?"

"I don't know. Maybe I *am* imagining it. But Ravi and Miss Christie just thought the place was cool. Nobody else noticed a thing. You know, like how you always say people are too busy to notice the magic under their feet, and we can only do it because we know to look."

"Hmm," said Mama, her thoughts a million miles away. Maybe off in the Andromeda Galaxy, which I knew from Sophie was more than two and a half million light-years from earth.

I waited. For a *long* time.

Finally, Mama stood and went over to drop a quick kiss on Sophie's head. "Ivy, I don't know what it was you felt, or thought you felt. But it's certainly more of a lead than we've had all week. I'm going to go wake Agatha now. She knows your librarian, right? We'll get in touch and see if we can go see the cottage." She came and wrapped her arms around me in a quick hug, her glow brighter than it had been since I'd come into the kitchen. "Thank you, Ivy."

As I watched her float down the hallway toward Aunt Agatha's bedroom door, I wondered if I'd just given Mama the key to send us all away from Whistling Ridge.

Back to Martha.

Back to the road.

Back to life without a forever home.

Mama and the aunts left for the cottage right away. I could hardly pay attention to my schoolwork all morning. I carried my language arts workbook from the kitchen table to the living room sofa to the front porch swing to the backyard, trying to find a place where my thoughts didn't feel so jumbled-up and useless, but no matter where I sat down, it took only a minute before I couldn't focus on the book at all. My brain felt stuffed full with words and worries.

I was in my bedroom, the language arts book spread out on the bed before me with the outline I was supposed to be filling out still completely blank, when the front door flew open and then closed, a minute later, with a slam.

The first thing I heard was a dry, rattling cough. Then Aunt Ruth's voice. "Get her some warm tea, Marianne. Aggie, are you certain you don't want to go to a doctor?"

"What's the use?" Aunt Agatha asked, only her words were underlaid by an exhausted tightness.

I sat, immobile as a Whistling Ridge apple tree, afraid even to breathe too deeply, while I listened to the star sisters.

What had happened at the Lovelace Homestead?

"You should go to bed, Aggie, if you won't go to the doctor," Mama said. I could hear her in the kitchen: the water running to fill the teakettle, the cabinet doors opening and closing as Mama retrieved the tea bags. "Elena, will you grab me that mug? Thanks, honey."

"All right," said Aunt Agatha, sounding exasperated. "But I'll be *fine*, Marianne. Stop flapping around like that. I'm not one of your children."

A minute later, I heard Aunt Agatha's footsteps down the hallway. She stopped for a minute to lean against my doorframe; was I imagining the way that her chest heaved with every breath, or the gray tinge to her golden skin? I could feel myself staring but didn't know how to stop.

"Thank you, Ivy, for telling your mother about Lydia's cottage," Aunt Agatha said. "It is the first time in many months that I've felt we're close to any kind of a breakthrough. You're right that something is very wrong in that place."

Her words were completely at odds with the way she looked. How could a *breakthrough* have left her looking older and sicker than ever?

"Aunt Agatha?" I whispered. "Are you . . . okay?"

Aunt Agatha smiled, a sad little grimace. "I just need a little extra rest, that's all. See you soon, Ivy."

After I heard her bedroom door open and shut, I closed my schoolbook and wandered past Elena and Sophie, who were at the kitchen table peering through a microscope at something they'd found in Aunt Agatha's backyard, and into the living room. Mama and Aunt Ruth stood with their shoulders together, looking out the window. The world outside was gray and washed-out-looking, almost like a sepia photograph. It hadn't been truly sunny in days—just this skim-milk sky and a gray-white light, like a flashlight beginning to run out of batteries.

I'd been so preoccupied with trying and failing to concentrate on my schoolwork that I hadn't even noticed that the apple trees in the orchard next door looked *strange* today. Their leaves seemed darker than normal, as though the little veins through which the leaves drank had turned black.

Maybe they had.

"What happened at Lydia's cottage?" I asked. My voice sounded funny and squeezed in my own ears. "What happened to Aunt Agatha?"

Mama turned and gave me a tired smile. "Nothing you need to worry about, Ivy honey. Ruth and Aggie and I will sort it out. You and your sisters just focus on school."

The prickling, simmering anger that never seemed far away these days was back. How could Mama just assume I'd be okay with that kind of dismissal? How could she not realize that I *needed* to know what was wrong with Aunt Agatha, with Whistling Ridge, with the places and people that had become part of my heart even after only a few weeks? Sometimes it felt like Mama treated me and my sisters exactly the same—like she didn't realize that I was almost thirteen. Not a baby anymore.

"But why is Aunt Agatha sick?" I pressed.

"We don't know," said Aunt Ruth. "We'd only been at the Lovelace Homestead for a few minutes when Aggie started feeling poorly."

"Ruth and I are going to go back another day, to see if

we can untangle what's wrong there," Mama said. "But for now, Aunt Agatha needs rest. And you need to finish your work for the day, Ivy Mae. We may be up to our ears in calamities, but school still takes precedence. Your sisters are nearly done already."

"Okay," I said, but couldn't keep the resentment out of my voice.

But as I turned to go back to my bedroom, I glanced one more time at Mama. It was like her thoughts were written across her face, an invisible script that showed up in the pinched look around her cheekbones and the dark circles under her eyes. Worry for Whistling Ridge. Worry over whatever had happened at the Lovelace Homestead. Worry, probably, for the whole world.

Because if all the magic drained from Whistling Ridge, what would become of everything else?

28.

Mama and Aunt Ruth went back to Lydia's cottage the next day, armed with the silver pendulum and a pitcher of starlight-infused water that shimmered like the star-sisters' hair. *Two of us won't be as good as three,* Mama had said grimly to Daddy, *but Ruth and I will see how much light we can pour into that dark place on our own.*

Aunt Agatha stayed behind. None of the star sisters said so, but I could see in the way Mama and Aunt Ruth looked at her when they thought she wouldn't notice: they worried that another excursion to the Lovelace Homestead would be even worse for Aunt Agatha than the first. I could understand the worry. Aunt Agatha still didn't seem herself; she'd gotten out of bed at her normal time Tuesday morning, and seemed cheerful enough, but she moved slowly, like her joints ached, and she still had that rattling cough.

In the skim-milk light filtering through the window, even her skin looked wrong. It wasn't glowing, or even its normal bronzy gold. It was dull, almost gray, and chalky, like the color was being sucked out of Aunt Agatha as surely as the magic was being sucked from Whistling Ridge.

Watching her shuffle around the kitchen getting breakfast Tuesday morning, I couldn't get the image of the little gray bird beside Lydia's grave out of my mind.

Had beautiful Lydia lost all her color, too, before she'd died?

I shivered hard. I couldn't say for sure whether it was the nip in the September air, or the thought of Aunt Agatha fading, pulled into whatever "void" was stealing the life from her town.

The phone rang while Mama and Aunt Ruth were gone. I sat with Sophie at the kitchen table, helping her with her spelling words, since Mama wasn't there to do it. Sophie jumped up as soon as the phone rang, beating me to it. "It's for you," she said, handing me the receiver. I was more than happy to be done helping her with spelling words, which had to be the absolute *worst thing* Mama had ever asked me to do. The only thing worse than having to help take care of younger sisters is having to help teach younger sisters who are positive they're a hundred times as smart as you are.

"Hello?" I asked, putting the old-fashioned phone to my ear.

"Hi! Ivy? It's Ravi," said the voice on the other end.

"Oh," I said, a sneaky little happiness blooming in my chest and chasing away the spelling-word-induced grump that had haunted me all morning. "Hi."

"Simon's here, too," said Ravi, and I heard a faint "hello" that was unmistakably Simon. "We're on the bus. Today's a half day at school, and I'm going to Simon's for a while. Want to come over? He lives pretty close to your aunt's house, and Miss Brenda said she could pick you up if you wanted to come. Or you can walk through the orchard and we'll meet you halfway."

I looked at the kitchen table. Sophie was putting away the spelling book, but a bunch of other stuff was scattered across it—my geometry worksheets, the computer I was supposed to use for a biology lesson before Mama got home, a bunch of colored pencils Elena had gotten out to sketch the RV wren. Each of us sisters had a big plastic tote with a handle where Mama put all our school assignments, so we could easily carry them around if we were doing school outside the RV. Right now, it looked like all our totes had been sucked up in a tornado that had deposited the contents right here in Aunt Agatha's kitchen.

I put my hand over the phone mouthpiece and called to Daddy in the next room. "Daddy, Ravi called and said it's a half day and he's going over to Simon's house for a while and they want to know if I could go, too. It's really close, and Aunt Agatha knows Simon's parents really well. You met Miss Brenda when she came to get me to go to the library last week, remember?"

"How much work do you have left?" Daddy asked.

"A lot," I said honestly, looking back at the table. "But the public school has a half day, so shouldn't we get one, too?"

Daddy stood and came into the kitchen doorway, rumpling his hair absentmindedly. "I guess I don't see why not," he said finally, "as long as you're back by this afternoon."

Even though the sky outside was still gray and the light still looked all wrong, I felt like I was bathed in sunshine.

"I can go," I said, lifting the phone back to my ear. "Tell me where to meet you?"

* * *

I followed Ravi's directions through the orchard, trying my best not to think of the swirling smoke inside each apple that hung overhead, until I found where he and Simon waited.

"See?" Simon said, bouncing a little on his heels as he led us farther away from Aunt Agatha's. "You can already see my house through the trees over there. It's not far. It's so cool that you can come! When I was growing up, I always used to wish that Miss Agatha had a kid so we could meet up in the orchard here. I used to pretend like I was a spy, or a pirate, and hide out in the orchard. Last year I tried making a tree house in that tree over there, but my mom found out and wasn't very happy with me because I hadn't asked permission and the tree house would've interfered with the apple harvest. That's why I decided to try to build one in Oaktree Park instead."

"Did you get permission?" I asked.

Simon's shoulders slumped. "Nope. The city denied a permit because it's on public property and the tree is so old and famous."

"Sorry."

"It's okay. My uncle said maybe we can build some other kind of hideout next summer. Or a workshop! That would be cool. Maybe my moms would let me have some tools of my own for Christmas. And Ravi could paint there, and you could come and write."

"An artist's retreat," Ravi said with a smile. "That would be cooler than a tree house."

Next summer seemed a million years away. I'd never stayed in one place long enough to see all four seasons come and go; I couldn't even imagine it.

"I've always wanted a tree house," I said. I'd left my writing notebook at home, but even without it I could see the imprint of my list of wishes, burned against my eyelids. I'd written *a tree house* on it back in the spring, when we'd driven by one that was so beautiful it practically *breathed* magic, like it had been built for elves or fairies and not human children. What would it be like, I'd wondered as we passed it, to have a space that was all my own—not Mama's or Daddy's, not for any adults, but just for me and whoever I wanted to invite?

Simon patted my shoulder as we climbed up the steps to his back door. "Stay in Whistling Ridge, and I'll make sure we get the coolest artist's retreat ever."

Simon's house smelled like sugar and cinnamon as we walked in. Hannah was at the kitchen table, her face smeared with frosting from the cupcake she was eating. A woman with short gray hair stood at the counter, frosting the last few cinnamon-scented cupcakes from a big batch.

"This is my Mom," Simon said. "She used to be a chef in a restaurant before I came along."

Simon's mom pretended to swat at him with the spatula as he stole three cupcakes and passed one each to me and Ravi, but she laughed, too. Her laugh was the kind that felt like it could fill the whole world with cheer. "Nice to meet you, Ivy," she said, putting the spatula down and sticking a hand out to me. "I've heard so much about you already. You can call me Miss Harriet."

"Thanks for the cupcake," I said. It was a perfect blend of flavors—the cinnamon cutting through the sugar and creating something deep and rich and warm. The frosting swirled on top was silky, melting in my mouth in a burst of vanilla and spice.

"It keeps me out of trouble," Miss Harriet said with a wink. "Usually by this time of year, I'd be up to my ears in apples and spending the whole day baking apple cakes and canning applesauce to sell at the farmers' market, but this year our whole crop has been fighting a disease and we're just hoping we can manage to find enough whole apples to fill our existing contracts."

The smile slipped off her face as she talked about the apples, leaving Miss Harriet looking as tired and frustrated as my mama and her sisters. A minute later she shook her head, like she was forcing the worries away, and smiled again.

"Anyway, it's real nice to meet you," she said again.

"Come on," Simon said, licking the last of the frosting off his fingers and tossing the cupcake wrapper into the trash. "Let's go upstairs."

Ravi and I finished off our cupcakes in a few delicious bites, and then followed Simon up to his room. It was smaller than the guest room I'd been sleeping in at Aunt Agatha's, but it was all *his*, which made it seem like the biggest bedroom I'd ever seen. The walls were painted blue-gray, and there was a bay window with cheerful yellow curtains and a cushioned window seat.

"It's so nice," I said, the words almost a sigh. I'd never been in a friend's room before. Most of the friends I'd made in the past were fellow traveling families, and with the ones who weren't—like Ada—we didn't usually stick around long enough to get invited over.

Simon shrugged. "It's pretty normal. It's been my room since I was a baby."

I ran my fingers over a group of framed pictures on his wall. One was toddler Simon with his moms; he definitely took after Miss Brenda. Another was of him and Hannah dressed up for Halloween, only a year or two ago.

What would it be like to have slept in the same room for more than a decade? To have a house steeped in memories like this one?

"You okay, Ivy?" Ravi asked.

"Yeah," I said. I didn't know how to explain the jumble of emotions all knotted up inside me: envy for the life Simon had, worry for Aunt Agatha, worry that if Mama and Aunt Ruth fixed the magic at Lydia's homestead, we'd leave Whistling Ridge before the Lovelace Festival even had time.

But more than anything I felt grateful—grateful for the way that Simon had almost fallen out of a tree on my head at the beginning of September, and everything that had come after.

"Yeah," I said again. "I'm . . . good."

In stories, the number three is important.

Standing there in Simon's room, surrounded by the walls he'd grown up in, with the three of us held together by friendship like the points in a constellation . . . I was starting to understand why that was.

29.

Mama and Aunt Ruth got back from Lydia's cottage right as I made it home from Simon's house. The wheels of Aunt Agatha's car crunched on the gravel driveway as they pulled up; from the top of the RV, the wren burst into angry chattering and fluttered back and forth, like it was scolding Mama for the noise she'd made driving in.

Mama didn't even ask where I'd been, just gave a tired smile as the three of us climbed the porch steps and went inside.

"Any luck?" Daddy asked from the couch as we closed the front door. I stilled as Mama shed her jacket and kicked off her boots.

"No," Mama sighed. "None. That place is definitely

the source of the problem, but every bit of magic we feed into it just disappears. Both of us together, every drop of distilled starlight we've collected here—it's like the land just swallows it up and is still hungry for more. We'll go back again tomorrow and try again."

"But we're not taking Agatha back there," said Aunt Ruth, her whispery voice edged with steel. She glanced over at Aunt Agatha, who sat in the armchair by the fire. Green yarn was spread over her lap, another shawl like mine beginning to take shape. Her crochet hook was in her hand, but she worked more slowly than I'd ever seen her, each stitch its own act of strength.

I floated over to Aunt Agatha's chair, like somebody in a dream, and sat down on the floor beside it. Even now, Aunt Agatha smelled like starshine and apples; when I leaned against her legs, I could feel the soft brush of yarn against my cheek.

If I closed my eyes, I could almost forget the gray tinge to her skin, the way her hands shook as she held the crochet hook.

It had taken less than three weeks for Aunt Agatha to feel like an indelible ("impossible to be forgotten or removed") part of us. If I'd told Mama about Lydia's cottage sooner—if I hadn't been so stubborn—would Aunt Agatha already have recovered?

"I'm fine," Aunt Agatha said, the crabbiness in her

voice at odds with the way she brushed a gentle hand over my hair, just for a moment. "You're all old fusspots."

Aunt Ruth sank onto the couch beside Daddy. "Stop it, Aggie. You know none of this is right."

"What will you do?" Daddy asked.

"Keep trying," Aunt Ruth said. "We'll keep trying until we fix Whistling Ridge, or . . ."

She didn't have to finish the sentence for all of us to know exactly what she meant.

That evening after dinner, Elena and Sophie went for a walk in the orchard.

"Want to come with us?" Elena asked. "Maybe you could bring your notebook."

"I'm too tired," I lied. Really, I was feeling good— better than I had since the pneumonia had first started by Silverwood Lake. What I really wanted was some time to myself, time to be alone and hear my own thoughts and maybe look at Lydia's diary. Quiet is a strange and wonderful thing when you're used to spending all your time in a two-room RV with four other people.

"Okay," Elena said, but before they left she reached for my hand and squeezed three times. *I love you.* There was so much in that quick gesture; even if Elena was quiet with her words, she had a way of making herself understood anyway. Those squeezes, I knew, meant *it's not your fault*. They meant *it's going to be okay*.

They meant *sisters, no matter what*.

I was sitting cross-legged on my bed, deep into the middle of the diary entries, when Aunt Ruth knocked at my open door. "Mind if I come in?"

When I nodded, she came and sat on the bed next to me. Cream trailed after her and curled up between us, her bulk warm and soft against my legs. Was it a good sign that the cats weren't following Aunt Agatha as much? Or was I just reading things into the situation because I was so desperate for Aunt Agatha to get better—and for her sickness not to be my fault?

"I hoped you'd be working on this," Aunt Ruth said. "May I help? It's nice, having a challenge to think about, instead of . . ."

She stopped and laughed self-consciously. "Well. Anyway. It's nice."

What was she trying not to think about? Whatever had happened with Uncle Andrew in Montana that had sent her fleeing to North Carolina with all her belongings? Aunt Agatha, lying in the other room looking like an eighty-year-old, her light almost gone out? The way none of the star sisters had been able to stop the magic draining away from the town? The looming horror at Lydia's cottage?

"Sure." I scooted over so she could see the papers better. "So, I just got to the part where Lydia finds out about Henry and his cousin. She's been in Whistling Ridge for awhile now—a few years maybe, though the dates are a hard to be sure of—and she's *completely* in love with Henry. Like, she's already planning where they'll live, that kind of thing. She keeps writing about this 'golden-eyed girl' who visits her in dreams—I'm pretty sure Lydia thought the girl was her daughter. You know. With Henry.

"She's just waiting for him to actually propose, because she figures they're already practically engaged. From what I can tell, everybody else in town thinks the same thing."

"But not Henry's parents."

"Yeah. And, it turns out, not Henry, either. Because in this entry"—I shuffle the papers to find the one I mean—"Henry leaves to go back up north for a while, and when he comes home . . . Lydia starts hearing rumors that he got engaged. To somebody else. His cousin in Massachusetts."

"Ouch," Aunt Ruth said.

I nodded. "So in this entry, Lydia writes that she confronted Henry about the engagement. She tried to make it sound funny, like a joke, because she was sure it was just gossip. But . . . it wasn't."

"Poor Lydia," Aunt Ruth murmured, with a look on her face that made me think she wasn't thinking *only* of Lydia.

"That entry is even harder to read than the others. Her handwriting is all over the place. I think she was *really* upset."

"They do say she died of a broken heart," said Aunt Ruth with a sad little half smile.

I looked down, thinking of the little bird by the grave, of Aunt Agatha's graying skin. Death by broken heart had sounded kind of romantic when Aunt Agatha had first told me Lydia's story, but whatever it was that was lurking in the vines and rotting boards of Lydia's homestead was way worse than heartbreak. It actually *hurt*, a sharp pain behind my belly button, to think of Lydia meeting some terrible, magical fate, when all she had ever done was put love and light into the world.

Aunt Ruth and I alternated reading out loud to each other for a few minutes, pausing every now and then to figure out a tricky passage. As the page went on, Lydia got more and more desperate. *I must get him back*, she'd written a few days after Henry told her about his engagement. *I cannot live, cannot keep drawing breath, without him at my side.*

Aunt Ruth winced reading that. "A tad bit melodramatic, though I daresay that's often how it feels."

I thought of how I'd felt back in Silverwood, when I'd checked my email over and over, desperate for anything at all from Ada to show that we were still friends, that she still cared about me even if we never saw each other face-to-face. I'd been so upset that I'd been willing to steal nine wishes and break all of Mama's rules to get my way.

How much worse must Lydia have felt after she gave so much to Henry and he pushed her away?

I wake each morning drowning in sorrow, Lydia went on. *It feels as though my heart is tearing down the middle, and I would do anything to stop it. I must go to Henry one more time, with the weight of my full hope behind me. Perhaps that will be enough.*

"How could he be that horrible?" I asked, angry on Lydia's behalf.

Aunt Ruth shrugged. "There are always two sides to every story, and we don't know his."

"I don't need to know his to know he hurt her really, really bad."

"Let's keep reading."

Lydia was happier in the next entry, writing about how she'd gone to Henry one more time and *poured her heart out*, and something again about the weight of her hope being behind her. She'd told him how much she'd come to love him—she'd even told him about the golden-eyed girl in her dreams.

And Henry had actually listened.

His whole demeanor was changed, Lydia wrote. *And by the time I'd finished speaking, the hope I carried had grown strong enough to shelter us both, and we embraced, and I felt so full of joy I couldn't remember my pain.*

"Aunt Agatha didn't mention this part," I said, chewing on my lip. "I didn't know they got back together after he broke her heart."

"Real-life stories are always more complicated than we think they are," said Aunt Ruth, and I wasn't sure anymore if she was talking about Lydia or herself.

"Yeah?" I asked, hoping she'd say more.

Aunt Ruth gave me a sharp look, like she knew *exactly* what I meant. "I'm not ready to tell that story yet, Ivy. But soon, I think. I'll tell you soon."

She stood, nudging Cream off the bed. "I'm going to go check on Aggie. Thanks for letting me help, Ivy. Let's do more tomorrow?"

"I'd like that," I said.

30.

By Wednesday, the leaves had darkened even more. Iron-colored clouds swirled across the invisible sun; the air in Whistling Ridge felt thick, heavy, but it didn't rain.

Mama and Aunt Ruth looked like they hadn't slept in years. Aunt Agatha, when she pulled herself out of bed to sit on the porch swing for a while, looked like a ghost.

"That's pretty," I said, sitting down on the swing beside her and brushing a finger across the sage-colored yarn in her lap. The green shawl was growing slowly larger, like she was determined to keep at it no matter how quickly she was fading.

Aunt Agatha coughed—a deep, wet-sounding cough that somehow made the weight that sat on my chest feel even larger.

"It's for Elena," she said when she'd finished coughing. "It only seemed fair for each of you to have one. I was thinking yellow for Sophie, or maybe pink."

"Not pink," I said, wrinkling my nose. "Sophie says scientists can't wear pink."

"She's certainly mistaken about that," said Aunt Agatha, with a trace of her old wry smile. "But I'll go with yellow."

"That will be nice. Cheerful." *Something Whistling Ridge sorely needs,* I thought, looking up at the blackening leaves, the sullen sky. "Aunt Agatha, how are more people not noticing all these changes?"

"You might be amazed at the things people choose not to notice, Ivy. Though I think people *have* noticed—but what would *you* do, if you saw the sky darken and the leaves turn black and the apples fill with smoke, and you knew there wasn't anything you could do about it?"

I shrugged. "I guess just keep doing normal stuff?"

"Exactly. It's not like people stop needing groceries just because the world might be hurtling toward its end. People have an incredible ability to come up with explanations for inexplicable things." Even though she had to be feeling awful, there was still dry amusement in Aunt Agatha's scratchy voice.

I looked straight ahead, into the garden and the

driveway and the black-leaved apple orchard beyond. Beneath me the swing swayed gently, the long chains creaking with every pass forward and back, forward and back, as Aunt Agatha rocked it.

"What's going to happen if you can't fix it?" I whispered.

Creak. Creak.

"That's the question all of us are asking, Ivy Mae. That's the question all of us are asking."

At lunch that day, Mama made an announcement.

We were all squeezed in around the kitchen table, even Aunt Agatha. I was trying to ignore Sophie going on and on about something star-related, while discreetly pulling the tomato out of my sandwich and leaving it on my plate. Mama and Daddy had a rule that we had to try any food we didn't like at least twenty times, which felt *extremely* unreasonable to me.

"I know the last three weeks have been difficult for you girls," Mama said, interrupting Sophie mid-ramble. "I know that Daddy and I, and Aunt Agatha and Aunt Ruth, have been busy and preoccupied. The three of you have done a really good job of getting your schoolwork done—and staying out of trouble," she added with a significant look in my direction.

"But there's at least one spot of good news," Mama went on. "Daddy finished the articles he's been working on, and the payment for them should be deposited in our account by the weekend. If I can sell just a few more wishes by next Monday, we should have enough to have Martha towed to Al the mechanic, and have the RV fixed by the end of next week. Wishes have been hard to come by lately, with the way the magic's behaving, but I've got a small supply left. We're pretty sure we'll have enough."

"*What?*" I dropped my tomato-free sandwich onto the table.

"Does that mean we'll be leaving?" Elena asked.

"Not right away, no," said Mama. "We've got to stay until Whistling Ridge is fixed, or . . ." She trailed off, glancing furtively at Aunt Agatha. "But as soon as we've figured out how to mend things here, yes, we'll be able to get back on the road."

The lettuce and turkey and mayonnaise in my stomach churned. We'd been here three weeks, and Mama was already talking about leaving?

"The Lovelace Festival is still a whole month away," I said. "What about my project with Simon and Ravi?"

Mama sighed. "I don't know, Ivy. We're still thinking about it. If we can repair things in Whistling Ridge,

there will be other places that need attention, other rip-
ples we'll need to tend to. You *know* this stay was never
going to be forever."

"I'm full." I pushed my chair back and stood up.

"Ivy! You've hardly eaten anything."

"Upset stomach. I'm going to go work on my story," I
said, stalking off before anyone could call after me.

I ducked into the bedroom I shared with Elena and
Sophie to grab my notebook and Lydia's diary pages
from under the bed, but instead of curling up on the bed
like Aunt Ruth and I had done yesterday, I popped the
screen out of the window again and climbed out into the
backyard. I knew it was silly and would probably irri-
tate Mama and maybe Aunt Agatha, but I couldn't face
any of them again after the way Mama had cheerfully
announced that we would be able to leave Whistling
Ridge as soon as possible.

Like that was a *good* thing.

I didn't know how I was going to convince Mama and
Daddy to stay long enough for us to go to the festival.
Everything seemed to hinge on the chance to display
my project—showing my parents what was in my heart,
how badly I needed a forever home, of course. But also
making something real and tangible out of the tentative

connection I was building with Simon and Ravi. If we finished this together, made something solid that you could see and touch and read . . . maybe it wouldn't be as easy for them to cut me out of their lives as Ada had.

I lay back on the grass and looked at the darkened leaves of the maple tree above me. Even poisoned by the whatever-it-was that was afflicting Whistling Ridge, the maple tree was beautiful, wrapping its wide arms around Aunt Agatha's backyard. I bet in a few more weeks the leaves would be spectacular, flaming crimson and orange. The thought was a little lance of pain. Right there on the wish list in the notebook I held was wish number six: *the chance to see a whole year of seasons in one place.*

How could Mama and Daddy not realize how important those wishes were to me?

I didn't know what else to do except write, so I wrote. My pen flew over the notebook pages so quickly my hand cramped and my handwriting was almost impossible to read, but I didn't stop. I wrote about Lydia bumping into Henry Asbury on the street of Whistling Ridge. I wrote about their friendship, how it turned into love.

The more Lydia and Henry came to know each other, the more she knew they were meant to be together forever. Lydia could feel it in her bones, as certain as she knew that her roses needed love to grow.

But the day that Lydia learned about Henry's other
love, it felt like thorns had pierced her heart.
Lydia knew she had one last chance, one last hope,
to make Henry see that they belonged together
the way she knew they did.

When Henry had left her, Lydia had found a way to
fix it. She'd gone to him and made him see how important he was to her, and it had worked. I'd tried so hard to
make Mama and Daddy see my heart, see how important it was to stay in Whistling Ridge, and they *still*
planned to hit the road at the soonest possible moment.

What on earth could I do about it?

I'd just begun writing about their joyful
reconciliation—Henry's heart softening under the
weight of Lydia's pure love—when Cream the cat
meowed and brushed up against me where I was sprawled
on the ground. Her sudden presence startled me enough
that I dropped the pen into the grass and had to fish it
out again.

"Working on your project?" Aunt Ruth followed
Cream into the backyard. "I figured you might be out
here when you weren't in your room."

I nodded. "I'm almost caught up with the journal. I
just wrote the part where they get back together."

"Ah," said Aunt Ruth. "I've been thinking about that.

Such an interesting point in the story, knowing they must ultimately have parted ways again."

"Yeah. It's weird. Why would they, if Lydia wrote they were so happy?"

"Maybe the journal holds a clue," said Aunt Ruth. "Would you like to read some more together?"

I closed my writing notebook, the pen safely in the spiral binding, and nodded. Aunt Ruth sat cross-legged on the grass beside me.

We were almost to the end of the photocopied pages I'd gotten from Miss Christie at the library. We made quick work of them; the last entries on them were short, mostly just statements of what Lydia and Henry had done together. Things like *went for a picnic on the hill, the weather was fine.* It was almost like with Henry back, Lydia had less to say.

There was just one part at the end of the photocopies that was strange. *I can't seem to fix the roses,* Lydia had written. *They're dying, and nothing I do helps. It's as though my hands have lost the skill, grown clumsy and fumbling.* The next morning, Lydia said, *I woke this morning to find my vision hazy and strange. Perhaps I ought to consult a doctor.*

The photocopied pages ended right after that.

"Is that all?" Aunt Ruth asked.

I shook my head and pulled out the loose pages I'd found at the Lovelace Homestead.

"Where'd you get those?"

"I found them in Lydia's cottage," I said, hoping that honesty wasn't going to end up getting me grounded. "I'm going to give them to the librarian, I promise. But I wanted to read them first."

Aunt Ruth winked. "I won't tell if you don't. But why weren't these with the others?"

"When Miss Christie showed us the diary in the library, there were pages missing from the end. Like they'd fallen out, or been torn out. I found these in an old steamer trunk in Lydia's kitchen."

"I don't like the fact that you went into that tumble-down ruin, Ivy, because I suspect you had at least a fifty percent chance of it caving in on your head. But I admit I'm dying to see how Lydia's journal ends, so I won't tell your mama."

Before we could get started, though, Sophie hurtled through the back door. "Ivy! Mama says she's ready to look at your math problems with you. You're supposed to come *now*."

The sleeping dragon of my anger reared up inside me. Why did Mama have to make *Sophie* be the one to come get me? Her bossy little voice made trying to tear myself away from learning about Lydia twice as hard.

"Fine," I snapped. "Go away. I'll be there soon."

"Let's finish this tomorrow," said Aunt Ruth calmly, helping me discreetly tuck the pages back into my notebook so Sophie didn't see them. A sense of warmth spread through my chest, like hot chocolate on a cold winter's day. How had I gone my whole life without this kind of relationship with my aunts—the kind where we sat for hours working on a project together; the kind where we had secrets all our own?

Even with everything that was happening—even with Aunt Agatha's sickness, and the ominous look of the leaves above us, and the dark circles under Mama's eyes, and the sneaking worry that if I'd only told about the cottage sooner, it all could've been avoided—I couldn't bear the thought of our time in Whistling Ridge coming to an end.

I had to figure out a way to keep us around, at least until the festival.

31.

I could hardly pay attention as Mama talked me through my geometry lesson, my mind was so busy thinking up ways to delay us leaving Whistling Ridge. When she folded up the math book and said I'd done a good job with the lesson (even without a calculator, which she wouldn't let us use despite Elena's argumentative essay), I made a beeline for our bedroom, where I could hear Elena plucking at her ukulele.

She was singing a verse of the Lydia song when I got there—

"And with him gone, I hollowed was,
A shell of who I'd been . . ."

It was almost eerie, how much it echoed the diary entries Aunt Ruth and I had read earlier that afternoon.

I waited for Elena to be done with the whole ballad before putting a finger to my lips and sitting down on the trundle bed beside her.

"What's going on?" she asked in a low voice, setting the ukulele down.

"You have to help me," I said. "You *know* I have to stay in Whistling Ridge until the festival, Elena. Help me do something to make sure we can."

"Like what?"

"I have lots of ideas." I ticked them off on my fingers as I went. "When Martha and the magic are fixed, I could run away for a while. I bet Simon and his moms would be okay if I came and stayed with them for a couple of days, right? If Mama and Daddy don't know where I am, they can't leave, right?"

Elena's eyes bugged out. "You aren't serious, are you?"

"Or I could slash Martha's tires when they get her back from the mechanic," I rushed on, pretending like I didn't see the growing dismay on Elena's face. "How long do you think it takes to get old Winnebago tires ordered and changed? Or maybe I could release the wishes Mama has stored up, so she can't barter them this weekend. They said they *almost* had enough money, not that they *had* enough money, right? And Mama's had such a hard time finding wishes lately—maybe if I let the wishes go, it would take them a few more weeks to get the money to fix Martha."

"Ivy! Stealing wishes is what started all of this in the first place! Haven't you already gotten in enough trouble over that?"

"But what if I don't actually *steal* them, really? I wouldn't use them, I promise. I'd just . . . open the window and let them go, so Mama couldn't barter them. Nobody would get hurt, and it would probably take them at least a week or two to afford the mechanic. Maybe it would buy me enough time to finish my project and enter it in the festival. Then Mama and Daddy would *see* what Whistling Ridge means to me."

"Ivy," Elena broke in. "Are you listening to yourself? You sound . . . you don't sound like yourself. I *know* you want to stay—I understand, really—but these are all really, really bad ideas. You'd get in so much trouble! And what if something really went wrong, and you got hurt, or the RV did, or a wish-seeker in town?"

I could feel my jaw sliding into what Mama called my *stubborn face*. "Don't you want to stay?"

Elena shook her head. "Not really. You know that. I like traveling. And it's nice, when it's just you and me and Sophie and Mama and Daddy. I like the aunts, but . . . I miss it being us."

"Well, *I* want to stay. I've never wanted anything so much in my life. I did the most awful thing I've ever done in my whole life when I stole those wishes in Silverwood, and I would do it all over again if I had to. I'm not giving up my forever home without a fight."

"Please at least wait a few days before you do anything," Elena said. "Please? Just think about it. Maybe you'll feel differently by the weekend."

"I won't."

"If you feel the same, do it this weekend. But give it a few days to think about it first."

I sighed. "Okay. Fine. I'll wait a few days."

"Thanks." Elena leaned forward and gave me a hug. "I'm sorry about the festival."

"I'm not. I'm going to make it there, one way or another."

Just as Elena picked up her ukulele and went back to strumming, I heard the faintest creak outside, saw the subtlest wiggle in the cracked-open bedroom door. Like a breath of air had disturbed it on its hinges.

Like somebody had been standing there, and then had left.

"Did you hear that?" I asked Elena, but she was already absorbed in her composing again and shook her head.

Maybe I'd imagined it.

32.

Reading the new section of the diary with Aunt Ruth the next afternoon was a little easier than the photocopies, because the ink was darker and the words more distinct, though we had to be careful as we turned the brittle pages. We read them in Aunt Agatha's sewing room—Aunt Ruth sitting on a twirly office chair, me curled up beside her on her air mattress.

The old paper was so dry that sometimes corners would flake off as we touched them. By now, I'd read so much of the diary that Lydia's handwriting felt like an old dress that's gotten just a tiny bit too small—not exactly comfortable, but familiar.

But the new entries were weird. They picked up where the pages still in the journal had left off, only besides complaining about her roses and her vision, Lydia started complaining about Henry, too. *He stays with me, but I wonder why,* she wrote. *Sometimes I ask him something and he seems to forget to answer, like he doesn't hear me at all. Is it my voice that's disappearing, or his ability to hear it?*

The crumbling pages gave me goose bumps. The further we read, the stranger they got. *I tore out my favorite rosebush today,* one of them said. *Nothing I tried could save it, as though something were eating it from the inside out. Some days, I feel that way myself. Even with Henry by my side, happiness feels like more and more of a distant memory. I begin to forget why I gave so much for this love in the first place.*

"What's she talking about?" I asked, putting the pages down. "She got what she wanted, right?"

Aunt Ruth's forehead was wrinkled, and it took her a minute to answer, like her thoughts had her a million miles away. "I don't know," she admitted finally. "I honestly can't make heads or tails of it. You're right, Ivy. It doesn't make sense. It doesn't sound anything like the story I've always heard."

We read a few more pages, but the feeling of strangeness didn't go away. The more we read, the more Lydia seemed not only unhappy, but—*angry*. Her entries got more and more suspicious, like she was convinced Henry was hiding things from her. *He says he loves me,* she wrote, *but I have little reason to believe that's truly what is in his heart. Is this whole thing a shell of something real? I cannot shake the feeling that, deep inside, he's still thinking of leaving me and going back to that Yankee girl. His words of reassurance feel as hollow and colorless as the roses I pulled out and burned last week.*

Finally, when we were only a few pages from the end of the papers I'd found in the cottage, Lydia's paranoia came to a head. *I cannot keep up this pretense any longer,* she said. *I told Henry to go away today when he came calling. I let go of every hope I've clung to these past weeks and when I did, it was like a light came back into his eyes, and I knew he was remembering his love for that woman whose name I will not write here. Like everything I'd given up for him was meaningless, and even the memories of what we shared had gone lifeless. It was like I twisted a knife into my own heart, except that I couldn't have, because H carved my heart out and ground it under his boot the very first time he told me he loved another.*

My hands shook as I listened to Aunt Ruth read. There was something *dark* about the entry, something mean, like her bitterness about Henry was a living thing that was slowly swallowing her in its jaws.

"Let's stop," I said finally. I snatched the papers from Aunt Ruth in the middle of a sentence and stacked them all together, holding them in tight fingers, like they might fold themselves wings and fly away to accomplish some dark deed if I let them.

"All right," said Aunt Ruth, eyebrows floating up.

"I just—isn't it a little disturbing to you?"

"Disturbing?"

I chewed on my lip. "Like, how Lydia gets all mean and angry, even when things seem to be going fine. It's weird. It's not . . . not what I expected." Not like the Romeo and Juliet story I'd thought I'd find, where Lydia suffered gracefully through the pain of her heartbreak until her body couldn't live with it anymore, and then died peacefully in her rose garden. That's how I'd pictured it for my story.

"I don't know," said Aunt Ruth. "I suppose it's a little disturbing, yes, but I also think it's very *real*. Relationships are complicated, and sometimes the thing we think we want is the thing that's really the worst for us." She hesitated. "You know, when I—when I left Montana, I was incredibly angry."

"You were?"

"I was so angry that when your mama first called and asked me to come, I said no."

"You *did*?" Mama definitely hadn't mentioned that.

Aunt Ruth nodded. "I told her it was a bad time and that I was certain she and Agatha could figure things out without me there. I was so angry my voice shook."

"Angry at Mama?"

"Angry at everyone. Angry at Andrew. We'd had so many good years, and then at the end, things just . . . fell apart. I suppose I should've seen it coming for a while, but I didn't. But he came to me three months ago and told me he wanted to separate, and I was . . . shattered. And furious."

"Just like Lydia."

"Yes. And I was angry at Agatha and Marianne, too, for not recognizing that I needed space to deal with my feelings. And angry at the whole world, really, for existing, for being full of sunrises and flowers and cows munching on sweet grass, when I felt like I couldn't go on living because it all hurt so badly. That's why I finally decided to come here—to get away from Montana, from all the reminders of what I'd lost. We don't know what happened with Lydia and Henry. Maybe they were happy for a while, and then they drifted away. Maybe when she convinced him to come back to her, he never really felt it in his heart, and she could tell."

I thought of all the suitcases piled in Aunt Agatha's

sewing room. "So . . . what changed? For you?"

Aunt Ruth shrugged. "Nothing. I'm still angry, Ivy. Every morning I wake up with my jaw tight, my muscles clenched. But what I'm starting to realize is—" She paused, closed her eyes for a minute, took a deep breath. "What I'm realizing is that underneath the anger, there's just sadness. A lot of sadness. And it's terrifying, because—well, anger is something I can *work* with. When you're angry, you can do things, channel that anger, make the world change around you. Or at least it feels like I can. But sadness . . ."

"Is different?" I prompted, when she stayed silent.

"Yes. Sadness is different. Sadness feels startlingly like powerlessness. Like if you let it in too deep, it will *become* you, leave nothing left of the 'you' you used to be. With anger, you can feel powerful, you can feel *right*. Sadness, though . . . sadness is something that just has to be survived."

It made me think of the chapter we'd read in *Little Women* the day after I'd stolen the wishes, where Marmee tells Jo *I am angry every day of my life*. Was everyone, deep down, wrestling with their own fount of anger, the way I always seemed to be?

"So, you think Lydia became angry because it was easier than being sad?" I asked.

"Something like that, yes."

I looked down at the papers clutched in my hands. "I guess I can see that." Still, I couldn't shake the way those last entries had made me feel—like I'd been wallowing around in Lydia's darkness, like she'd reached out from the past and pulled me under the wave of her own rage.

"Want to push through to the end?" Aunt Ruth asked, eyeing the pages I held.

"Okay." I spread them out between us again, almost afraid to finish.

The final entries were filled with the same anger and frustration that Lydia had poured into the earlier ones. She wrote about Henry's fiancée moving to Whistling Ridge—she never called her by name, so I was sticking to Antoinette—and wrote all kinds of hateful things about her. *Harpy, minx, witch.* I didn't know for certain what all her insults meant, but the nastiness practically oozed through the page.

If only I could take all the pain I've felt and pour it into the two of them, Lydia wrote, *let it spread through their treacherous hearts like sap through a tree.*

I shivered. When we'd first started reading the journal, Lydia had seemed like I'd imagined her: funny, poetic, loving. But now . . . she was different, and I didn't know what had made her that way. In one of my favorite books, *The Black Cauldron,* one character dreams about another having a "black beast" sitting on his shoulders and goading him into being an awful person. That was how the end of Lydia's diary sounded—like she had a black beast of her own, digging its claws into her skin and changing everything about who she was.

I'd always figured Lydia belonged with Henry the way I belonged with Whistling Ridge. But if that wasn't true . . . where did that leave me?

The journal ended abruptly. At the very end there was a poem—the ballad Aunt Agatha had taught to Elena, the one inscribed on her tombstone.

'Twas years ago in a valley green
That I gave my heart to him
In love and faith we pledged ourselves
Till the light we shared grew dim.

And with him gone, I hollowed was,
A shell of who I'd been
No wish of mine could bring me back
No love enough for him.

Let roses grow where they lay me down,
Let starlight kiss me, too;
Let all the world world feel my broken heart—
How it everlong beat true.

Neither of us said anything after we'd finished. What was there to say?

My eyes drifted to the big sewing room window. Like the one in Aunt Agatha's living room, this window looked out on the front yard. I could see Martha in the driveway from here, the little wren busy tidying its rooftop nest. Beyond it were the orchards—row upon row of trees that, when we'd arrived in Whistling Ridge, had glinted in the sunlight like emeralds.

But today, there was no sunlight to glint off anything. And even if there had been, there would've been nothing to reflect, with all the trees painted over with sooty darkness, like the color had been pulled from them as surely as the happiness had been pulled from Lydia, as surely as the life was being sucked right out of Whistling Ridge.

As soon as Aunt Ruth and I came out of the sewing room, Sophie jumped up from where she'd been watching YouTube videos for science. She put her hands on her hips.

"You have to come on a walk with us," Sophie announced. "Mama said. She says your lungs need the exercise, and you've been spending too much time this week cooped up in here reading and scribbling."

I tucked the diary entries back into my notebook and gave Aunt Ruth a quick hug and whispered thanks. "Okay."

We didn't actually talk about it, but all three of us veered away from the orchard after we'd come to the end of Aunt Agatha's driveway. It was too eerie, too creepy, walking underneath those blackened trees. Instead we walked down the road toward town, staying on the grassy shoulder, away from where cars whizzed by us.

"Do you think Mama and Daddy would be okay with us going this way?" Elena asked, face pinched.

"I don't care," I said at the same time Sophie said, "Don't tell them." The worried look didn't leave Elena's face, but she nodded. Sophie smiled in my direction, and something inside me that had been wound up like a spool of thread loosened a little. Maybe Mama was right, and Sophie and I fought so much because we were alike, not because she was a changeling child from Jupiter.

But that little thread of companionship snapped as soon as Sophie opened her mouth again. "Are you still writing that thing about Lydia?"

My whole body stiffened, until I was as rigid as one of the orchard tree trunks. "Yes."

"You shouldn't," Sophie said.

"Why *not*?"

Sophie and Elena exchanged a glance that made me very, very suspicious.

"I heard what you said to Elena yesterday," Sophie said finally, China-blue eyes wide. "About breaking Martha and stealing more wishes and stuff."

"You WHAT? Little sneak!" Anger roared inside my chest, so strong and hot I could hardly catch my breath.

"You should stop writing the story for the festival. It's making you act weird and mean."

"I don't think it's going to work the way you want it to," Elena added quietly. "I don't think it's going to convince Mama and Daddy to stay here forever."

"Maybe you're wrong," I said. "Maybe they'll change their minds."

Sophie looked as though I'd smacked her. "But— wouldn't you miss Martha? And campfires?"

"What about waking up in the mountains one day and on the beach a week later?" Elena asked.

"And Mama," said Sophie. "With Aunt Agatha and Aunt Ruth not moving around much, Mama has to—"

I put my hands over my ears, like an angry two-year-old. "Stop! Okay, I get the point. Neither of you want to stay. But I don't care," I said, tears pressing at the backs of my eyes. It wasn't even quite the truth. I *did* care; my sisters were both twisted into my soul so deeply that they felt almost like my hair or my fingernails, things I didn't always notice but that I'd definitely miss if they were gone.

"I *need* to stay in Whistling Ridge, okay? And I *know* we can be happy here. We could make real friends, pick apples, help Aunt Agatha. . . ."

Elena and Sophie were silent. Not the *agreeing* kind of silence, though.

"I'm finishing the story," I said stubbornly, trying to ignore the bit of me that flinched away from the idea, the part of me that quailed ("felt fear or apprehension") at the memory of how horrible and hateful Lydia's journal had gotten by the end. "It has to work. It *has* to, okay?"

"Ivy," said Elena. "What if everything that's happened since you took the wishes . . . what if it was trying to tell us something?"

"Like *what*?"

"What if it's trying to tell us that your wish was wrong all along?"

33.

Friday we woke to rain. It pounded at Aunt Agatha's roof, washed down the windows in silvery sheets.

By midmorning, Mama had already yelled at the three of us once for being too loud while playing a math card game, and Daddy had announced that he needed to get some work done and was going to sit in the RV to do it. As he stalked off through the rain toward the camper, I could see the smallest movement on top of Martha's roof: the wren, seeking shelter from the wet underneath one of the solar panels.

"Stupid bird," I muttered. "Hopefully it won't get stuck again."

Why hadn't that bird just stayed away when I'd shooed it off the first time? If it made a nest in the woods, like a *normal* wren, he could have friends. He'd never have to move. He could find a mate and make sure his beautiful nest actually had eggs in it.

"What are you studying, Sophie?" Elena asked, looking at Sophie, who hung upside down from the sofa, reading her astronomy textbook. Even Elena seemed listless, ghosting her way back and forth between a book and her ukulele, which she would pluck restlessly at but never quite *play*, probably because Aunt Agatha was in her bedroom just down the hall and Aunt Ruth was nearby in the kitchen, putting her head together with Mama at the kitchen table.

"More about black holes and planetary nebulae," said Sophie. "It's fascinating. Did you know that black holes break down our existing laws of physics so much that some scientists theorize they could create new universes? And that the gravitational pull of a black hole is so strong it literally warps the space around it? And did you know that black holes don't last forever? They evaporate, though a black hole evaporating is basically like an explosion."

"Nope," said Elena.

I sighed, long and gusty. I felt like a sweet-gum ball today, all prickles and darkness. "Sophie, do you think maybe for one day you could talk like a regular human being?"

"I find typical discourse to be lacking in precision and interest," said Sophie, not looking up from her star book.

"Isn't it a good thing that Sophie is interested in the world around us?" Elena pointed out. The mild reasonableness of her tone made me want to set something on fire. "Sophie likes to share what she learns, but there's nothing wrong with that. It's no different than you reading your stories to us."

"Honestly, girls," Mama called from where she sat at the kitchen table, half-visible through the doorway. She was taking deep breaths through her nose, like it took every ounce of concentration not to murder one of us. "Could the three of you please try to get along? This day already feels like it's lasted for several lifetimes."

"I mean, we *were* playing a game just fine," I said, "before you made us stop."

"You know what?" said Aunt Ruth brightly, standing up and giving Mama a comforting pat on the shoulder, "I'm going to make a fire. And tea. Tea and a fire sounds cozy, doesn't it? Maybe it will help put us all into a better frame of mind."

"I'll help!" Sophie somersaulted off the sofa and scrambled up. "I'll help with the fire, Aunt Ruth."

"Wonderful. Why don't you go ask Aunt Agatha if

she has any old papers for kindling?"

Sophie disappeared down the hallway. I could hear the sounds of rustling and then ripping, and a minute later she emerged again from the direction of Aunt Agatha's bedroom, her arms full of shredded papers.

"I'll put the tea on," said Elena.

I stared out the window while Sophie and Aunt Ruth busied themselves around the fire. A lifetime of camping had made all of us good at fire starting, even Sophie, whose hands were so small she couldn't get the lighter to turn on and always needed help with that part. Outside, the rain poured on the blackened orchard, hammered at the front garden with its beetle-filled flowers. The whole thing looked like something out of a nightmare, or a creepy cartoon movie—black trees, gray rain.

Behind me the lighter clicked and the kindling flared up, filling the room with the familiar sharp scent of burning paper.

"Good job, Sophie, honey," Aunt Ruth murmured appreciatively. As the fire caught, coughing sounded from Aunt Agatha's room at the end of the hall. I flinched.

I'll unravel with it.

I thought of the little dead wren by Lydia's grave.

Why hadn't Mama and Aunt Ruth been able to fix the town by now?

I could tell as soon as I got to the door that led into the guest room my sisters and I shared that something was wrong.

The door was swinging open, but none of us were inside. We *never* left it open; even when Mama had complained that Aunt Agatha's guest room would start to smell musty if we didn't let the air circulate to it, the three of us had agreed that we'd keep the door closed always, because it was the closest thing we could find to privacy in a house filled with seven people. But now the door hung wide, like it had been pushed open in a hurry.

And, I saw immediately, something had happened to my bed. I'd made it that morning before I'd gotten up—making the beds was one of Mama and Daddy's inflexible rules, because it helped keep things looking neater when we were all crammed together in Martha—but now it was all rumpled, the comforter and sheets a tangled mess. Like somebody had been looking for something.

In my bed.

Dread settled over me like water, trickling down my hair, tickling at the nape of my neck.

In three steps, I crossed the room and sank down to my knees by the bed, throwing up the hanging comforter to find the box where I kept Lydia's papers and my writing notebook.

The papers were there.

The notebook was not.

Only the spiral binding and the outer covers were still where they belonged.

All the pages inside had been torn out in a hurry, leaving little bits of paper like confetti, all over the floor underneath my bed.

34.

From the other side of the house I could hear the crackle-pop of the fire, low chatter from the kitchen table as Aunt Ruth and Mama discussed more things they could try to heal the yawning hunger at the Lovelace Homestead.

Like I was in a dream, I replayed the last ten minutes over and over in my mind:

Aunt Ruth, suggesting a fire.

Sophie, tumbling off the couch to help her.

Sophie, coming back into the living room with a handful of ripped-up papers. I'd assumed they were from Aunt Agatha, but . . .

The click of the lighter. The sour scent of burnt kindling.

It still felt like a dream when I barreled out of Aunt Agatha's second guest bedroom and into the living room; still dreamlike when I reached out to Sophie and grabbed a whole handful of that long, beautiful yellow hair.

"Ivy Mae Bloom," Mama barked, standing so quickly her chair tipped over onto the floor. "What are you—"

I almost couldn't talk at all, but when I did, all my words came out like the shrieking of wind on a winter's night.

"HOW COULD YOU? HOW COULD YOU DO THAT?" I didn't know when I'd started crying, but there were tears streaming down my face now. Which was good, because they blurred my vision and made it harder to see the blackened curls of paper in the grate.

What had burned first? The story? The play script I'd been working on this summer, before I'd stolen the wishes and we'd come to Whistling Ridge? My word list? I'd been working on that list for more than a year; I'd never be able to remember everything that had been on it.

Cataclysm ("a large-scale or violent upheaval").

Ruination ("the action of something being ruined").

Rancorous ("characterized by bitterness or resentment").

Or had it been the list of wishes in the back? That was the worst—the thought of my heart on paper, feeding the flames like it didn't mean anything at all.

Sophie's face was blurry as I looked at her, but I could still see the little spark of actual fear that was there. Tears trickled from the corners of her eyes. "I'm sorry, Ivy. I'm sorry! I just didn't know how to get you to stop writing that story! I told you, it's making you act weird and mean! I just wanted to help!"

"LIAR! You don't care about anybody but yourself! You're just a greedy little show-off who can't bear to have anyone pay attention to somebody other than you!"

Mama was looking from Sophie to me and back again, bafflement written plainly in her raised eyebrows, her gaping mouth. "*Girls*," she finally choked out. "What. Is. Going. On?"

I let go of Sophie's hair and she slumped back into the sofa. I was sobbing now, great big huge sobs that made my shoulders shake. For my notebook, for my word list, for my wishes—but also for Whistling Ridge, for Aunt Agatha looking so old and sick. For Aunt Ruth, her heart broken by Uncle Andrew in faraway Montana. Even for Lydia, with all her bitterness and rage.

Sophie raised her chin, like a saint about to be martyred. "I burned Ivy's notebook. When Aunt Ruth asked me to go find kindling, I tore the pages out of Ivy's writing notebook and ripped them up, and that's what I put into the fireplace."

Aunt Ruth and Mama wore their shock identically, blinking at Sophie and me like we each had two heads.

"You *what*?" Mama said finally.

Sophie slumped. "I'm sorry."

"Sophie! Go to your room for the rest of the morning. Ivy—grabbing your sister by the hair and yelling at her is still unacceptable. I understand that you're upset, and I know she doesn't usually seem it, but Sophie is still a very little girl, honey. I'm sure she felt she had a reason to do it, and while you have every right to be hurt, I expect you to make up with her."

"I can't!" My head was beginning to hurt from all the crying. "Mama, I will *never*, ever, *ever* be able to forgive her for that."

Mama hugged me. She smelled like vanilla and a wild, woodsy scent, like starlight. I let myself relax into her, let the warmth of that hug be enough for just a minute.

"Ivy Mae," whispered Mama, "you have always been my little warrior. I know it hurts, but I also know you will have the courage to try, once the hurting starts to fade."

"It *never will*."

Mama stroked my hair. "It will, baby. You just have to give it time."

I drew a deep, trembling breath and pulled away. "I'm going to go for a walk."

"In the rain?"

"I'll go, too," said Elena, jumping up.

Mama glanced out the window. "Well, maybe it will be good for all of us to have a little space from one another for a while. Take an umbrella."

I grabbed an umbrella from our bedroom—and, at the last second, I pulled out the blue crocheted shawl Aunt Agatha had given me the week we'd arrived, too. It was finally cool enough to wear it, and wrapping myself into was a reminder that once upon a time, I hadn't felt like I hated *everyone* in the world. The shawl still smelled like Aunt Agatha—like cinnamon and vanilla and wild starlit magic.

It was windy, the rain flying at us sideways and sneaking its way under the umbrella, as Elena and I set off down Aunt Agatha's driveway. I turned us toward the orchard this time; the depressing gloom of the black-leaved trees pretty well matched my mood.

"Elena Louisa Bloom," I said as soon as we'd gotten past Martha and out of earshot of any adults. "Please tell me you didn't have anything to do with this."

"Of *course* not!" said Elena, looking as though I'd accused her of murdering kittens. "Ivy, how could you think that? I promise I didn't. I mean, yes, I agreed that you shouldn't do all those things you were threatening yesterday, and I think it was a bad idea to steal all those wishes. But I would *never* hurt your notebook. I know how important it is. Was.

"But," said Elena, so quietly I almost couldn't hear her, "I think Sophie was trying to help, Ivy. Honest."

Even in the wet orchard, I swore I could smell the singe of burnt paper.

"Don't ever say that again," I said, my voice dead.

"I know you don't see it, but Sophie *loves* you, Ivy. She wants to be just like you. I think she was worried about you . . . we both were. And—" Elena hesitated. "Ivy, Sophie doesn't want to stay. It's been really hard for her in Whistling Ridge. She doesn't have an easy time making friends like you. Neither of us do. And I think . . . I think we both feel a little bit like you haven't *listened* to us when we told you that."

I marched forward with the umbrella, leaving Elena running to catch up.

"Her burning the notebook wasn't so different from you writing the story," Elena went on. It was more words than she had said all together in a long time, but I couldn't even bring myself to care. My heart was too bruised. "You were both trying to do something to change things."

"Sophie and I are *nothing* alike."

"I know it feels that way. Just . . . wait," said Elena, and stopped walking.

"Oh my gosh. Do you not *get* it? I don't want to talk about this anymore!" The tears were threatening again at the edges of my vision, burning in my throat and stinging at the corners of my eyes.

"No. Not that. Look."

I looked up, following where Elena was pointing. We'd stopped beside an extra-huge apple tree, one that looked like it was older than Mama and Daddy combined. Its branches curled out over the grassy space between the trees, its bark so thick and rough it had to have seen decades of sun and wind.

But that wasn't what Elena was pointing to.

Around us, the black leaves trembled in the rain and the wind, and the bark of the trees was even grayer than it had been three weeks ago when we'd first walked through the orchards of Whistling Ridge and seen how they were losing their color.

But the big one, the one we were standing beside, was different. The barest hint of rosy brown traced its way through the whorls and knots of the tough old bark, and its leaves—they weren't all the way black, like the others. Woven through each of them, almost imperceptible until you were up close, were thin lines of green.

Elena and I stared at the tree for a long minute. Slowly, I put my palm against the trunk, fingers splayed outward into a star shape.

The tree's color deepened, the blush of brown creeping out from where my fingers touched it. It almost felt like the trunk was getting *warmer* under my hand, like I could feel the sap inside it waking up and whispering through, reminding the tree how to be alive.

"Look," Elena whispered. I followed her gaze up, to where the leaves were slowly becoming lighter, greener.

"It's trying so hard," Elena said. "Trying so hard not to give up."

Like all of us. I thought of Mama and Aunt Ruth hovering by Aunt Agatha's bedside.

Was there any hope for this tree, digging its roots deep into the earth to find any hint of magic that hadn't been choked out by the darkness?

Was there any hope for any of us?

35.

The phone in Aunt Agatha's kitchen rang that night. Mama had sent a grumpy Sophie to bed already, but I was hanging around the living room. I couldn't bear to be in the same room as Sophie right now—I'd avoided her all day. Every time I saw her big blue eyes, it was like I could smell all over again the scent of the freshly laid fire, hear the flames crackle around my notebook pages as they burned to ash.

Mama and Daddy hadn't said I needed to go to bed yet, so I had a feeling they knew it would be too much to ask right now.

"Ivy?" Daddy called, a minute after he'd answered the phone. "It's for you."

I turned off the tablet—I'd been trying to distract

myself from the gnawing ache inside me by watching old episodes of *The Great British Bake Off*—and came into the kitchen.

Simon's cheerful voice, on the other end of the line, sent my stomach straight down to my toes.

What was I going to tell him? What was I going to tell Ravi? With my notebook burned, there was no more story, no more project. Maybe Simon and Ravi could enter their cottage model anyway. Maybe they didn't need my words at all; maybe they would always work better together. Maybe I'd been wrong about the rule of three.

Maybe, maybe, maybe.

"Hey, Ivy!" Simon said as soon as I'd muttered a hello into the receiver. "Guess what? My uncle and I finished the plans for the cottage and he said we can start building it this weekend! It's going to be so cool. He even drew a place for little windows and a door! He says we can use scraps of Plexiglas in the windows and put in a door that will really open and close. I was thinking, what if we printed your story out on fancy paper and then rolled it up and put it inside the cottage, so you have to open up the door to get it? Ravi said that will be too hard because maybe people won't open it, but I thought we could put up a sign or something telling them to look.

Maybe something cool and mysterious. Like 'Here be dragons,' except obviously there aren't any dragons, so I guess we'll have to think of something else. . . ."

I could hardly make sense of Simon's run-on sentences, his cheerful chatter. I stood numbly in the kitchen, hardly even listening as he went on about the project, and how excited he was, and how he and Ravi couldn't wait to see it in the festival in a month, and how glad he was that I'd come to Whistling Ridge.

Finally, Simon's monologue trailed off into silence. I wasn't even sure what he'd said.

"So, do you know yet?" he prompted after a minute, when I hadn't responded.

"Sorry. Know what?"

"I asked if you knew how many pages your story was going to be yet. Just to make sure that they'll all fit inside."

"Oh." I closed my eyes, the image of burning papers bright against my eyelids. "Um, no."

"That's okay," said Simon. "I'm sure it will be fine. I hope you let us read more at the park tomorrow!"

"I have to go."

"See you tomorrow!"

"Bye," I said, because I couldn't bear to even think about waking up to another day like this.

* * *

I didn't go to the park the next morning. When Daddy said he was ready to take Sophie and me, I just shook my head. I didn't know if I could open my mouth without crying.

"You sure you don't want to see your friends, honey?" he asked, all Alabama softness. "Maybe it would help, being with them."

"No." I couldn't even handle the idea of talking to Charlie, fielding more questions about Mama and wishes and magic. I wanted to hide my head under a pillow and pretend I didn't know a single thing about fallen stars or wishes or magic, didn't have an aunt down the hall who was getting sicker and sicker, didn't have a mama practically going faint around the edges from failure after failure.

It was easier just to stay home.

I stayed home all weekend, since Aunt Agatha was coughing bad enough Sunday that none of us went down to her church or anywhere else. All the adults had long, lined faces. They didn't have to say it out loud for me to guess that whatever was happening to Aunt Agatha was totally outside the realm of anything that had happened to the star sisters before. I didn't think Mama had ever been sick in her life; even if the rest of us all got a cold and shared it around, Mama stayed perfectly normal.

By Monday, it felt as though I'd become a part of the little white cottage, my toes growing roots and twining themselves into the floorboards.

And, like salt in the wound, Monday a big red tow truck pulled into Aunt Agatha's driveway. The operator hooked Martha's nose right up to the back of the truck, and in less than an hour, he'd driven away in the direction of Al the mechanic, who'd promised to get the RV back in tip-top shape by October 7, one week away. The wren had twittered angrily at the tow truck driver, but when it became clear that the RV was being removed whether the bird liked it or not, it finally retreated to a branch in a nearby tree and sat there glaring beadily at anyone who walked past.

"All right, Ivy Mae," Daddy said a few hours after we'd eaten lunch. He closed up his laptop and tucked it into his computer bag. "You're coming with me. I'm going to go pick up some cough medicine for Aunt Agatha."

"Will that help her?"

Daddy shrugged. "The jury's out. Your mama and the aunts have been arguing about it all weekend. None of them has ever gotten sick like this before, so none of them know what to do. I figure I'll just go buy some while they bicker, and then maybe they'll at least try."

"You go. I want to stay here."

"Nuh-uh. Your mama and I agree it's high time you

picked yourself up and got out of the house." Daddy leaned in and lowered his voice, though it seemed silly to me. Sophie was out in the backyard, swinging on the swing—she'd stayed out of my way since Friday, which was pretty smart, because every time I looked at her I could feel rage bubbling like lava under my skin—and I hadn't seen Elena since lunch. "I'll buy you an ice cream at the pharmacy if you want."

I sighed. "Fine."

I stared out the window as we drove down the hill toward town. It wasn't raining anymore, but the black leaves still waved gently in the wind, and the sky was so cloudy it felt like we were moving through the hazy twilight of a dream.

"Ivy honey, I know you're upset about the notebook," Daddy said as he drove, his eyes on the road in front of him, his hands tight on the steering wheel. "And you have a right to be."

"I don't want to talk about it."

"I know how much that meant to you. And I hope you know, baby, that your mama and I are real proud of you. We're proud of how hard you work—and as one writer to another, your work is getting really good, you know that?"

I didn't say anything.

"I hope you go back to that story. It sounded real nice."

I didn't know if *nice* was exactly the word to describe Lydia, but I muttered a "thank you" anyway. Four days ago, I'd been so disgusted by Lydia's anger and bitterness after she told Henry to go away. What Aunt Ruth had said about anger being easier than sadness had made sense, but it had unsettled me, too. Wasn't Lydia supposed to be the town heroine? Weren't grown-ups like Aunt Ruth supposed to be . . . *better*? Beyond anger, beyond vindictiveness, beyond hurling petty insults at people in your journal?

But today, sitting in the passenger seat of Aunt Agatha's car while Daddy tried to jolly me out of my mood, I wasn't so sure. Right now, I could feel that same black, sticky anger that Lydia had poured into the pages of her diary curling inside my stomach, a tiny dragon whose fire scorched at my insides.

Daddy sighed. "You know, when your aunt Jenny and I were growing up, we didn't always get along."

I rolled my eyes in the direction of the window, where Daddy couldn't see.

"She drove me right up the wall sometimes. I remember once, I had a friend over and told her she wasn't allowed to come into my room to bother us. So instead, she sat outside my bedroom door the whole afternoon, singing 'Ninety-nine Bottles of Beer on the Wall' over and over again, until my friend finally went home because both of us felt like our brains were about to explode."

"*Really?*" I asked, breaking my silence without meaning to. I couldn't picture Aunt Jenny as obnoxious as Sophie. It was hard to think of her and Daddy as ever having been children, especially ones who did things like that.

"Really. It's hard to be the oldest sometimes, Ivy Mae. But what I realized when I grew up was that all Aunt Jenny had ever wanted was for me to pay her attention and love her back. All the antics that seemed like mischief and a drive to be annoying back then—they were her ways of trying to force me to spend time with her, trying to show me how much she loved me as her big brother."

I slouched farther down in my car seat. "What Sophie did was a whole lot worse than singing 'Ninety-nine Bottles of Beer,' Daddy."

"I know. It doesn't compare. And it's okay for you to be upset. I've lost work before, and it hurts something fierce. It's okay to grieve that. But honey, Sophie's still your sister. She's still blood."

"I am *never* going to forgive her. The iron has entered

into my soul." It was a phrase I'd read in *Anne of Green Gables*, and it seemed exceptionally appropriate. Even just thinking about Sophie, her smug little face, made me feel like my insides were full of boiling oil.

Daddy nodded. "I understand. You're hurting right now, and sometimes hurting makes us angry. It's okay to feel that way. But you still have a choice—a choice to work your way past that anger, or to let it swallow you right up."

I itched at a smudgy spot on my knee. Aunt Ruth had said that anger feels safer than sadness. That idea felt like poking at a bruise—a sharp little lance of pain, a wincing away, back to the comfort of the rage.

Had that been how Lydia had felt?

Daddy pulled into a parking space beside Main Street Drugs, and we went inside. It was a narrow cream-colored building with curling letters on the window that advertised the vintage soda fountain. Inside were shelves of Whistling Ridge Christmas ornaments and shot glasses, with a soft-serve ice cream machine in the corner. A white-coated man with black hair and tawny brown skin was behind the pharmacy counter.

"Aha!" he said, looking up as we walked in. "Mr. and Miss Bloom, yes?"

Daddy nodded.

The man—Ravi's dad, I figured—smiled. "My son

has told me so much about you, Ivy. I'm glad to meet you for myself."

The bell over the door jangled as Daddy ran his fingers over the rows of bottles and boxes in the cold medicine aisle.

"Ivy!" an excited voice called, and I could feel my shoulders curling forward, my whole body hunching in the desire not to be seen.

Simon practically skipped into the pharmacy, Ravi trailing behind him. Simon threw himself onto one of the pleather-covered barstools by the ice cream counter and Ravi went over to the soft-serve machine and grabbed three cones.

Simon patted the stool next to him. "Come on! Want some ice cream?"

I shrugged.

"We missed you at Oaktree Park on Saturday," he went on, clearly not noticing my discomfort. "What was up with that? I thought you said you'd be there when I called Friday!"

I slid silently onto the barstool, not looking at either of them.

"Well, anyway, it wasn't as fun without you—right, Ravi?"

Ravi shook his head. I could tell that even if Simon

hadn't noticed the vibes I was giving off, Ravi had; his eyebrows were pulled together just a little, wrinkling the smooth skin of his forehead.

"What kind of ice cream do y'all want?" Ravi asked, poised by the soft-serve machine. "There's regular vanilla and there's my dad's special. Today it's cardamom rose."

"Special!" Simon said before I could even open my mouth. "Seriously, this is the best ice cream you'll ever taste, Ivy. Mr. Amar invents the recipes himself. He's been working on them for years."

"Yeah, sometimes he goes on these experimental kicks where he tweaks his base recipe a bunch of different ways and makes us taste all the options," Ravi said, filling two of the cones with pale pink soft-serve. "It's a hard life."

"I'll try the special," I said, and Ravi filled a third pink cone and handed it to me. The ice cream glistened in the lights from the pharmacy windows.

"You'll have to tell me what you think, Ivy," Mr. Sidana called, leaning out over the pharmacy counter. "This flavor's a new one."

"I've never had ice cream with roses in it," I said, taking a hesitant lick. It was cool and sweet on my tongue; it tasted like sunshine and citrus and the barest hint of warm, intoxicating spice. "It's delicious!"

"Thank you, Ivy," said Mr. Sidana, beaming. "You

clearly have a discerning palette."

Ravi sat down between me and Simon. "When my dad was a kid, his parents would take him and my aunt to India every few years to see my great-grandparents. He always says it was fun to see his grandparents, but the ice cream was the best part. It's called kulfi, and it's served on sticks—like a popsicle, only way better. He can go on for *hours* about kulfi, I swear."

"Maybe if you hang around, you can come to the next ice cream tasting party," Simon said.

The ice cream went sour in my mouth. *Would* there be a next time, with Martha already on the way to Al the mechanic? Getting to the Lovelace Festival, showing Mama and Daddy my story, had felt like my one hope to convince them that Whistling Ridge should be our forever home.

And now, whether we were here at the end of October or not, that hope was gone—nothing but dust and cinders in Aunt Agatha's fireplace.

I took a breath. I was going to have to tell Simon and Ravi about the notebook sometime; I couldn't dodge Simon's questions about my story forever. But if I told, would they even still want to be my friends? It almost felt like when Sophie had thrown my pages into the fire, she'd tossed in my brand-new friendships and all my wishes for Whistling Ridge, too. I didn't know how to say any of that out loud.

But at least if I told them this morning, it would be over and done with.

"I can't do the project anymore," I said, squeezing my ice cream cone hard enough that the waffle cookie splintered under my fingers.

"What?" said Simon, clearly stunned. "But Friday when I called, you—"

"I don't have my notebook anymore," I said, the back of my throat burning even as I took another swallow of Mr. Sidana's ice cream (which really *was* the best I'd ever tasted). "It's gone."

"Gone?" said Simon. "What happened to it?"

"I'm so sorry," said Ravi. "That sounds awful."

"It was." Despite my best efforts to keep it in, a tear slid down my cheek, salt mingling with the sweet on my tongue. "So I can't do the project anymore."

Simon didn't ask what happened again. I couldn't bring myself to say it out loud; I couldn't describe the way the flames had consumed my words, my wishes, the way it felt like they had consumed my heart.

I thought of what Lydia had written about her heart tearing down the middle. And even if I hadn't really understood then . . . I did now.

"I hope you'll still come to the park on Saturday," Ravi said. "And Simon's right. Next time my dad has a tasting party, you're definitely invited."

"Yeah," I said tonelessly, "maybe." I looked over at Daddy where he was leaning against the pharmacy counter, talking to Mr. Sidana. I wanted us to stay— wanted to meet up with Simon and Ravi and Charlie and the others every Saturday, wanted to go to one of Mr. Sidana's tasting parties, wanted to know what it felt like to have *real* friends and a *real* home. I wanted it all so much, the wanting burned like acid on my skin.

Daddy saw my glance and straightened. "You about ready to go, honey?"

"I have to go," I said, licking the last of my ice cream from my fingers and dropping the napkin that had been wrapped around my cone into the trash. "Thanks for the ice cream, Ravi."

"No problem," Ravi said with a smile.

36.

As we left the pharmacy, Daddy draped an arm around my shoulder. "Not even ice cream can cheer you up today, huh?"

I didn't dignify that with a response.

We were getting into the car, Daddy already buckled in and starting the ignition, when I heard my name.

It was Miss Christie, rushing out of the library building across the street and waving her arm in a most un-Miss-Christie-like fashion.

"Wait! Ivy!" she called, holding up some kind of paper.

I got back out of the car.

As soon as she'd made it across the street, Miss Christie was back to her regular straight-backed, prim self, though she still seemed to have a little buzz of energy. She handed me a piece of heavy card stock with a faded black-and-white photo printed on it. It was of a little family: a youngish man, maybe not quite Daddy's age, a woman who sat in front of him, and two little fair-haired girls—one on her lap, one beside her chair. The woman's light hair was pulled into a bun, and even though none of them were smiling, the expression on her face was friendly, the barest beginnings of a dimple visible in one of her cheeks.

"It's Henry Asbury and his wife, Maggie," said Miss Christie with an uncharacteristic grin. "And their two daughters. I couldn't find a record of their names. But I came across this photo while cataloging some old papers the other day and thought of you *immediately*. You can have this copy, if you like."

"Thanks," I said, staring at the photo. *Maggie.* It was such an ordinary, everyday name, and she had such an ordinary, everyday face. She looked like the kind of person who would give good hugs—the kind of person you couldn't help smile at if you passed her on the street. The kind of mama who would sing a lot and tell funny stories to her kids. Nothing at all like the cold, haughty Antoinette I'd written into my story, or the "harpy" Lydia had described.

And Henry—the way his hand was on Maggie's shoulder, the way he leaned into her a little. He loved her, it was obvious. *Really* loved her.

Something icy and uncomfortable snaked its way through my stomach. Hadn't I just barely been sympathizing with Lydia, her anger, the way it curled off the pages in her journal like smoke? Hadn't I felt that same kind of anger coursing through me, acrid and sharp? But this photo—it made everything Lydia had written feel . . . false.

I'd been bothered, reading the sparks and snaps of rage in Lydia's book. But I still hadn't *doubted* that she was ultimately in the right, that she had been hurt in just the way she said she had.

But what if I'd gotten it all wrong? What if Lydia had *written* it all wrong?

What if Henry and Maggie and their two little girls weren't the villains of this story, after all?

The frozen feeling was spreading—like somebody had come up behind me and slid an ice cube down my neck. It was all I could do not to shiver.

All day, all weekend, ever since Sophie had burned that notebook, the righteousness of my anger had felt like a warm coat around me—like something comfortable, something *right*.

But Lydia had felt that way, too, and she'd been wrong.

Could I be like Lydia? Was it possible that Sophie wasn't the bad guy in my life story? The thought was like chewing on rocks—sharp and kind of revolting.

I thought of the ballad Elena had spent weeks singing, the stanza that was carved on Lydia's headstone:

Let roses grow where they lay me down,
Let starlight kiss me, too;
Let all the world world feel my broken heart—
How it everlong beat true.

When I'd first heard Aunt Agatha sing it, I'd thought it was pretty—sweet and sad and perfect for Lydia. After all, Whistling Ridge felt Lydia's broken heart, even if the rest of the world didn't. What was Lydia famous for, if not for the very faithfulness and sorrow that was captured in those lyrics?

Now, it felt like a threat.

37.

Late that night, hours after I'd fallen asleep, I woke to the sound of hurried footsteps and low voices.

"Would calling 911 actually help?" Mama asked from somewhere in the hallway outside our bedroom door.

"Would any doctor know what to do with somebody like us?" Aunt Ruth responded. "It's not like any of us have ever *been* to a doctor."

"We've never needed to!"

"What if they ask questions?" Aunt Ruth said. "What if they run tests and turn up something they don't know how to explain? It's all well and good when people want to barter for a wish—they're willing to suspend disbelief then—but if we show up to an emergency department with Agatha looking the way she does . . ."

"She looks real bad, Marianne," Daddy said. "Don't you think it's at least worth a try?"

From Aunt Agatha's room down the hallway, an even worse constellation of noises: a cough that seemed to shake the rafters, something that sounded like vomiting and made my own stomach twist inside me.

Footsteps pounded down the hallway—but a few minutes later, once the coughing and retching had subsided, the voices were back murmuring again outside my doorway.

"I don't think we can risk it," said Mama, her words tight, like her throat was full of tears. "Did you see her veins? How would we explain *that* at a hospital? The world isn't all that many generations removed from burning women like us as witches. People may come to me for wishes and overlook our eccentricities, but everyone has a limit."

"And who's to say it would even work?" said Aunt Ruth. "We aren't *human*. That cough syrup didn't do much, and I can't imagine morphine or steroids or anything they'd give her at a hospital would be much better."

"What about oxygen?" Daddy asked. "Shouldn't she be on some oxygen?"

"Her fingernails aren't blue," said Mama. "Not like Ivy's when she gets bad."

"The wishes," said Daddy. "You're sure we can't use them?"

"No," said Mama with finality. "Absolutely not. We'd need dozens—hundreds, probably—and even if we had them, that much power and instability would be as capable of killing Aggie as healing her."

"We'll take it in turns tonight to tend her," Aunt Ruth said. "And let's open her windows, let the starlight in. . . ."

"If you're sure," said Daddy heavily. "Tell me what I can do to help, at least."

"Pray," said Mama. "Really, that's all any of us can do."

I lay there while their footsteps receded, pinned to my bed by a weight worse than all the asthma attacks in the world put together. I'd never heard Mama sound like that—so serious, so scared. Like she was a child herself, afraid of what the night might bring.

When I finally fell asleep again, my dreams were haunted by Sophie's black holes, swallowing all the starlight around them with gaping dark maws.

At first when I woke the next morning I thought it was still night—the bedroom was dim, hardly any light filtering through the gauzy curtains at the window. The numbers on the wall clock, though, showed that it was nearly nine a.m.

"What's going on?" Elena asked, rousing right after I did. Sophie was nowhere to be seen, thank goodness. "Why's it so dark?"

I climbed out of bed and padded over to the window, pulling the blinds up to see the sky outside. Behind me, I could hear Elena gasp.

The clouds that had been gathering around Whistling Ridge for the last week had drawn together, covering the whole sky with iron and granite, hiding the sun so thoroughly that it looked like twilight.

Even more chilling, though, was what was underneath the clouds—underneath even the black-leaved trees.

The grass in all of Aunt Agatha's backyard had turned to sepia, like the color had been pulled right out of it.

It was the first day of October, and it felt like September had taken more than just the summer weather with it—like it had taken all the color and light from the whole world when it left.

"We're too late, aren't we?" Elena whispered. "Mama and Aunt Ruth are never going to be able to help Aunt Agatha enough."

"Aunt Agatha," I said, the memory of what I'd overheard in the night crashing back down on me. I flew to the bedroom door and banged it open, dashing through before it had even hit the wall.

Everyone was in the kitchen: Daddy, with his laptop nearby on the table, but closed. Aunt Ruth, squeezing her hands together in her lap. Even Sophie wasn't reading about astrophysics or using hundred-dollar words—she leaned up against Daddy, her skin so pale it looked translucent, seeming for once exactly like the little girl she was.

There was breakfast spread out in front of them, but nobody was eating.

"Where's Mama?" I said as Elena came up behind me.

"Honey," said Daddy, "Aunt Agatha is real sick."

Next to him, Aunt Ruth crumbled the muffin on her plate into dust, her eyes glossy.

Daddy cleared his throat.

"Y'all might want to go in and see her," he said, gentle as Mama catching fireflies at dusk. "We . . . don't know how long it's gonna be."

The words slammed into me, pummeling my chest and wrapping their fingers around my throat. *Don't know how long.* That was what people said about somebody who was . . . dying.

"Mama's in there with her," Daddy went on. "I already took Sophie in. Just, you girls should know—she doesn't . . . look too good."

Elena took my hand, pulling me back down the hall.

Toward Aunt Agatha's bedroom.

The door was half-open. There were lamps lit by Aunt Agatha's bed, and Mama sat in a chair next to it, holding her sister's hand.

Her hand.

Worse than hearing Daddy say *don't know how long*, worse than the colorless grass and the twilight-sky outside the window, was the sight of Aunt Agatha's skin. Just like the Whistling Ridge trees, Aunt Agatha's veins had blackened inside her—tracing rivers of darkness through her hands, her arms, even around the edges of her face.

I thought of what I'd heard Mama say when I'd woken up during the middle of the night:

Did you see her veins?

Elena's hand shook inside mine.

Mama looked up at us with bloodshot eyes and smiled, a wan, ghostly little thing that didn't look anything at all like her regular smile.

"Girls," she said softly. "I'm glad you slept in."

"What's wrong with Aunt Agatha?" Elena whispered.

Hearing her name, Aunt Agatha opened her eyes—the same clear blue as always, reassuring in the middle of those ghastly black veins.

"Ivy," she said, and her voice was so papery-thin I could hardly hear her at all. "Elena." She paused, breathing hard enough I could see the skin at her neck sucking in and releasing, sucking in and releasing. "I've got something for you, Elena, honey."

Aunt Agatha waved at her crochet basket, on the floor beside the bed. Elena crouched down, and when she stood up again she was holding the sage-green shawl Aunt Agatha had made her. It was finished now, a little smaller than mine, but just as warm and cozy-looking.

"Thank you," Elena whispered, starting to cry as she pulled the shawl on.

Tears pricked at my eyes, too, making the bedroom swim around me. I thought of Aunt Agatha in the garden, Aunt Agatha reassuring me that Sophie and I might grow up to be friends, Aunt Agatha presiding over dinner. Aunt Agatha teaching me to crochet. Placing that blue shawl around my shoulders, like a feather-light hug. All the hundreds of moments I'd seen her in over the last few weeks. All the hundreds of moments she'd come to feel like part of me, safe inside my beating heart along with the rest of my family.

Who would finish Sophie's shawl now?

"I'm so sorry, Ivy Mae," said Aunt Agatha, pulling

her hand out of Mama's and reaching out to me, waving me forward with a finger. I stumbled toward the bed and sank down onto my knees so I could rest my head against the mattress. Aunt Agatha's hand, stroking my hair, still *felt* normal.

"I'm so sorry," Aunt Agatha murmured again as my sobs came, shaking my shoulders and making my stomach ache. Through the blur of tears, I saw Elena crawl onto Mama's lap, curling into herself like she was two and not ten.

"No little girls should have to see the things y'all have seen," Mama said, wrapping her arms around Elena. "I wish I could shield you from them."

"Why couldn't you fix the magic?" I asked, the words half-lost in hiccuping. "All three of you . . . for all these weeks . . . and even after Lydia's cottage . . ."

"Things were already too far gone when we got here, Ivy Mae."

"My fault," Aunt Agatha coughed. "I was stubborn. I should've seen it was beyond me sooner."

"Isn't there *anything* else you can do?"

Aunt Agatha shook her head the tiniest bit. "No, honey. It'll be up to your mama and Aunt Ruth to pick up the pieces after I'm gone, to try to make sure this doesn't go too far beyond Whistling Ridge. If it did . . ."

She stopped, gripped by earth-shaking coughing, like I'd heard in the night. In her chair beside the bed, Mama tensed.

"You're just *giving up*?" I pulled my head away from Aunt Agatha's hand and stood up, anger crackling on my arms like lightning. I tried not to think of Aunt Ruth saying that sometimes anger is easier to feel than sadness.

"Ivy!" Mama scolded.

"Let her, Marianne," Aunt Agatha said. "Let her be angry."

Right now, it felt like I might never be anything *but* angry: angry at Mama for shushing me, angry at Daddy for not insisting harder that they call an ambulance for Aunt Agatha in the night, angry at Aunt Ruth for not coming to Whistling Ridge sooner.

Angry at Aunt Agatha for letting herself get so sick, just when she'd become a real part of my life—a part of my family I couldn't stand the thought of losing.

Aunt Agatha coughed again, again, again, the sound thundering all the way into the iron clouds holding Whistling Ridge in their grip.

Mama pushed Elena off her lap and stood up. "Come on out, girls. Aggie needs to rest." She helped Aunt Agatha turn onto her side to ease the coughing, then smoothed the coverlet over her bony shoulders. "I'll send Ruth in, Aggie. Try to get some sleep. We'll think of something."

Aunt Agatha's eyes met mine as Mama pulled Elena and me out of the room, and I didn't need to hear her say it aloud to know what words lay on her tongue:

The time for "thinking of something" was long, long past.

38.

Aunt Agatha held on all that day, though she looked as horrible as ever, and once when I sat in at her bedside I saw her cough into a handkerchief that came away black with poisoned blood. Mama had hurried me back out a second later, but I couldn't get the image out of my head.

Wednesday morning the sight of the almost-empty driveway—only Aunt Agatha's car, no Winnebago—was a spark of pain. By Monday Martha would be back, and one more thing tying us to Whistling Ridge would be gone.

Mama had all three of us girls gather at the kitchen table after breakfast. We usually started our school days together, reading or memorizing poetry or working on a project for history or art. But Mama hadn't made me actually sit down at the table with Sophie for almost a week.

Not since the day she'd thrown my notebook in the fire.

I sat as far from Sophie as I could and didn't look at her.

"I want to make a memory book," said Mama. Her voice was as steady as always, but she looked like she'd aged ten years since we came to North Carolina, and her eyes were deep pools of sorrow and worry. "In a while we'll be leaving Whistling Ridge, but I know this time here has meant a lot to you." She met my eyes. "Let's write down all the moments we want to hold on to when we leave."

"We can't leave when Aunt Agatha's so sick!" I said, thinking of Aunt Ruth in the bedroom at the end of the hall, watching Aunt Agatha as she slept and coughed and struggled. Mama and Aunt Ruth had taken it in turns to sit with her all week.

"Of course not," Mama said. "But eventually, Ruth and I will mend things here, or else . . . if we can't, then we'll be needed twice as much to tend to the magic everywhere else."

Her words were like snakes coiling around me. Was she saying . . .

"You think Aunt Agatha is going to *die*?" I squeaked. Across from me, Elena looked like she'd seen a ghost.

"No! No, of course not," said Mama tiredly. "We're doing everything in our power to help her, Ivy Mae. I still have hope. It's just that your daddy and Aunt Ruth and I are starting to discuss the fact that . . . things may not work out the way we want them to."

"But—" I said, and then couldn't say anything more. Hadn't Aunt Agatha said that if they didn't stop the magic draining from Whistling Ridge, the whole town would unravel, and then the rest of the world after it? Would Whistling Ridge someday be written up in the history books, like all the other disaster-laden places Mama had told me about?

How had it gotten so bad? How, even knowing about Lydia's cottage, had Mama and her sisters been so unable to do the thing that had always been effortless for them?

"It's been hard with Aggie so sick," Mama said, like she was answering my silent question. "My sisters and I . . . we've always been connected by more than just stardust. We've always worked best as a team, even when we were spread across the United States. The way Agatha reacted to the Lovelace Homestead has made it harder for Ruth and me to reach the magic woven under the town. But we're still trying, I promise."

Elena and Sophie and I were all completely silent.

What was there to say? I thought of the notebook Sophie had burned last week. My Lydia Lovelace story had carried me through the last month in Whistling Ridge—at one point, it had felt like the key to everything. Unlocking the mystery of what was stealing the town's magic. Convincing Mama and Daddy that Whistling Ridge was meant to be our forever home. Making all those wishes on my wish list come true. At one point, it had felt like the nine fireflies I'd released in Silverwood at the start of September had led me right to Lydia Lovelace.

But none of that had worked out like I'd thought. Even Lydia's cottage and the connection I'd found there had only led to Aunt Agatha getting even worse.

To Aunt Agatha maybe dying.

"I'm so sorry, girls," said Mama after a moment of silence. "This is a lot, I know. I wish that none of you had to hear or consider any of this. But your daddy and I felt it was best that you be prepared."

I couldn't look at Mama or my sisters, so instead I looked through the kitchen doorway. From where I sat, I had a view of the big living room window and the driveway beyond it. The little brown wren that had been nest-building on top of the RV was flying from the housetop to the branches of the nearest tree and back, over and over again, fluttering its wings and generally acting distressed.

Distressed, but silent. Even from here, I could feel the quiet that wrapped the house, unbroken by any of the usual little chirps or twitters.

"Why isn't it making any noise?"

"Haven't you noticed, Ivy?" Elena said. "It's *all* the birds. They've all stopped making any sound."

When a knock came on the door that afternoon, it sounded like thunder in the silence of Aunt Agatha's house. Elena and Sophie and I had all given up on trying to pay any attention to schoolwork, and Mama and Aunt Ruth hadn't gone anywhere since the day before. It was like we were all afraid to go too far, afraid to make too much noise, in case we missed Aunt Agatha's last breath.

There's no point in going anywhere now, I'd overheard Mama whispering to Aunt Ruth when they thought nobody was close enough to hear, a few hours after she'd broken the news about Aunt Agatha to us. *We might as well wait, and then go back to the Lovelace Homestead and see what we can do . . . after.* When she wasn't at Aunt Agatha's bedside, Aunt Ruth had sat on the couch in the living room with Cream curled on her lap, staring aimlessly at the blackened trees outside the window like they held all the secrets she was trying so hard to find.

Now, the knock made us all jump.

Daddy put his laptop aside and opened the door. I caught a glimpse of familiar curly hair, heard Charlie's soft mountain accent.

"Hi, Mr. Bloom," she said. "I'm Ivy's friend Charlie."

"Oh, come in," said Daddy, opening the door wider. "Ivy's right—"

"Actually," Charlie cut him off, "I wondered if I could talk to Mrs. Bloom for a little while."

"Of course," said Daddy, his voice a little gentler. "I'll go fetch her."

Charlie waited near the front door, her face all nervousness tangled up with hope, as Daddy disappeared into Aunt Agatha's room at the end of the hall. Mama came out a moment later, a smile on her exhausted face.

"Come on back, honey, and we'll talk. I'm down to my last wish, but we'll see what we can do."

I stayed extra still the whole time Charlie and Mama were shut up in the bigger guest room my parents shared. Their voices rose and fell, the only real noise in this whole house. Their conversation felt like the only real noise in all of Whistling Ridge, with the birds silent and Aunt Agatha's sickness freezing us all in place.

As they talked, I couldn't stop seeing the image of the fireflies I'd released in Silverwood spiraling up into the air, their pinpoints of light reflected on the dark mirror of the lake.

If Mama let Charlie walk out of this house with a firefly to wish away her mama's cancer, I hoped she'd end up with a happier ending than my own wishes had.

The phone rang a little while after Charlie left, Mama's very last canning jar clutched in her hands and a hopeful look shining in her eyes. The noise was shrill.

Daddy answered the phone. "Ivy Mae," he called, "it's for you. Your friend Ravi."

Had it really been only Monday that we all sat there at the pharmacy, eating rose-flavored ice cream and talking about taste-test parties? I'd felt so upset then, so mad at Sophie for burning the notebook, at Mama and Daddy for planning to leave Whistling Ridge, that I could hardly talk to Simon.

I hadn't even known what *upset* meant then—hadn't known what it felt like to be wrapped up in bands of steel as surely as the clouds had wrapped up Whistling Ridge. Hadn't known what it felt like for your own heart to be splitting right in two, a little more every time you heard that rattling cough. My anger with Sophie was all wound up with my fear for Aunt Agatha, crowding out everything else, so that I could hardly remember ever feeling differently.

I put the phone to my ear. "Hi, Ravi."

"Hi, Ivy! Simon's here, too. Did you know they

canceled school all week? Something about the weird weather. The district supervisor thinks we might have tornadoes. Simon and I were wondering, do you want to come over for awhile?"

I heard a rustling sound in the background and then Simon's muffled voice saying something I couldn't catch.

"Here, I'm going to put the phone on speakerphone," said Ravi, and a second later Simon's excited chatter burst through.

"Ivy! Wait, why did your dad call you Ivy Mae? Is that your name? It's cool! Maybe you should start going by that. It could be like—"

"I usually just go by Ivy." I was learning that talking on the phone with Simon was like a boxing match: if you didn't cut him off quickly, you'd never get the upper hand. "How long is school canceled?"

"That's the coolest part!" Simon said. "They don't know! There's something wrong with the meteorologists' equipment, so they don't know what to predict right now. They can't even tell exactly what's happening— nobody's ever seen atmospheric pressure affect the way the trees and the grass and stuff look. Isn't that *awesome?* Like living in a mystery!"

"Anyway," Ravi broke in again; I had a feeling he'd probably turned off speakerphone to get a word in edgewise. "You should come over. You could stay for dinner and everything. My mom is making a huge meal—dal, stuffed paratha, I don't even know what all but it smells fantastic."

"Thanks. But I can't." I glanced toward the hallway. "My aunt is really sick. I need to stay here for now."

"Oh." Ravi paused. "I'm sorry. Hang on." Another pause, and muffled conversation I couldn't quite catch. "My mom says she's going to bring dinner over. Like, maybe in an hour or so. That way y'all don't have to worry about cooking."

"Thanks. That would be really nice, actually." Daddy had made pancakes for dinner the night before—burnt on the outside and soggy in the middle. *These taste like distraction*, Sophie had pronounced disdainfully after eating one.

"Well, maybe you can come over another day. I hope Miss Agatha feels better soon."

"Yeah." I thought of the black blood moving through her body—the curse of Whistling Ridge threaded all through her. "Me too."

I bit my lip as I hung up the phone. "Daddy, Simon thinks this is all a barometric pressure thing. How can people be so sure there's a reasonable explanation for something like *this*?"

I looked at the sepia grass outside the window, barely repressing a shiver.

"You'd be amazed what people can justify away, Ivy Mae," Daddy said, following my gaze, his eyebrows drawn together. It was pretty much the same thing Aunt Agatha had said last week, looking at the darkening leaves.

Back when I'd written down the wish to see a whole year of seasons in one place, I'd pictured watching the leaves change in the fall outside my bedroom window. But I'd imagined them turning red and orange and yellow, regular October leaves.

I'd never imagined anything like this.

Later, when Ravi and Mrs. Sidana brought dinner, even *they* seemed subdued. Ravi hung back on the doorstep like the gloom of Aunt Agatha's house was leaking out the front door, sludgy and dark.

"It's nice to meet you, Daniel," Mrs. Sidana said, handing Daddy a tray overflowing with dishes. They *did* smell amazing, just like Ravi had promised. "My name's Priya. Amar said he had a lovely talk with you at the pharmacy earlier this week, and of course Ravi's told us all about Ivy and how wonderful she is."

I couldn't tell for sure in the darkness of the front step, but it seemed like Ravi might be blushing.

"Ravi said you were a writer?" Mrs. Sidana asked, looking at me. "That's terrific. I started writing when I was about your age."

I couldn't quite bring myself to smile—not with the image of my writing notebook charred and curling in the fireplace burned into my mind.

"Thank you, Priya," Daddy said, taking the dishes and passing them through to us girls with instructions to take them to the table. "I can't tell you how much we appreciate it. Honest."

"Harriet Welcher is going to bring dinner tomorrow," Mrs. Sidana said. "We just don't want you to be worried about any more than you have to right now. We're all thinking of Agatha. She's a special part of this town."

You have no idea, I thought, my eyes fixed on the black leaves, the grayed-out grass, the clouds that had stolen all the light from the sky and plunged Whistling Ridge into black and white.

What would happen to the people of Whistling Ridge if Aunt Agatha died and all the town's magic was lost?

What would happen to the world?

39.

By Thursday, nobody was even pretending to do anything but wait. Daddy's laptop stayed closed on the kitchen table. Sophie lay on the living room floor in front of the fire, reading the same page in her astrophysics book over and over, not saying a single thing about black holes or planetary nebulae. Elena sat on the couch, watching the wren, who still hadn't gotten over the loss of Martha's rooftop.

I wandered from my bedroom to the kitchen to the living room and back again, wrapped in the shawl Aunt Agatha had given me. Every room was infused with Aunt Agatha's touch: the gorgeous apple-orchard quilt hung on the living room wall, the handmade lace doily with stars crocheted through it that sat on the kitchen table when it wasn't in use, the wallpaper border in the bedroom my sisters and I shared, patterned with fireflies. It was like the house was an extension of her, like the walls breathed in and out when she did, like the place was a reminder of how bad it was going to hurt when the curse swallowed her whole.

When Mama came out of Aunt Agatha's bedroom late that morning to switch off with Aunt Ruth, her face was drawn and pale; she looked almost as old right now as Aunt Agatha had when we'd arrived.

"It won't be long now," she said in a quiet voice to Aunt Ruth, but we all heard her. Aunt Ruth was sitting in Aunt Agatha's favorite armchair, a blanket drawn about her shoulders like she couldn't shake the chill. "Maybe hours. The light's fading from her. Can you feel it?"

Aunt Ruth put a hand over her face, a dry sob shaking her shoulders. Mama hugged her; silver-white hair from both their heads mingled together in one shining waterfall, but neither of them glowed at all. Like the grief, the weight of carrying Aunt Agatha's sickness with them, had doused their lights, turning them into an ordinary mother, an ordinary aunt.

"How is it doing this, Marianne?" Aunt Ruth said. It was like she and Mama were in their own little world, not even noticing me and Elena on the couch or Sophie stretched across the floor by the fire. Not even trying to keep their conversation private. "How could anything be this . . . this . . . ravenous? It's like it's changing the very rules of the world, like it's warping them somehow. . . ."

Aunt Ruth's words echoed again and again in my ears, zinged across my skin, swirled and pooled somewhere below my rib cage. *Like it's warping them.*

It literally warps the space around it . . .

Sophie.

One week ago.

I closed my eyes, trying to remember exactly what she'd said.

She'd been hanging upside down from the sofa, reading the stupid astrophysics textbook, and Elena had asked what she was studying.

More about black holes, Sophie had said. About how black holes break down the laws of physics. *The gravitational pull of a black hole*, she'd said, *is so strong it literally warps the space around it.*

Warps the space around it.

I shot off the couch, my eyes open again. Everyone looked at me, but all I could see were Mama and Aunt Ruth—golden skin, white hair, moonlight-on-snow eyes.

Nobody in the world looked like my mama and her sisters.

Nobody in the world except the fallen stars I'd heard of, once in a while, in Mama's stories. We'd never met another; falling stars were rare, Mama had explained, and each of them had their own places of magic to tend to. But still, she'd told us stories, like the one about the star who'd used so many wishes that her life became a hollow shell.

"What's wrong, Ivy?" Mama asked.

"There have been others, right?" I said, talking so fast even I could hardly understand what I was trying to say. "Like you. Stars. That fell. There have been other stars that fell to earth and chose to be women?"

Mama and Aunt Ruth traded a glance, then looked back at me. Mama shrugged. "Of course, though I've never personally known any."

"We're spread all over the world," Aunt Ruth added. "There are people like us in most countries, I think. Otherwise, the world's magic would fail. We're all connected by the stardust in our veins, but we usually don't have a reason to meet."

My heart fluttered like the wings of the little wren outside. "And there have *always* been people like you, right? For all of history?"

The star sisters nodded, the question still in their eyes.

"I need to talk to Aunt Agatha," I said, hardly able to breathe.

Mama was shaking her head before I'd even finished talking. "No, Ivy honey. She's too sick—she hasn't even been awake in at least a day. I'll make sure you get a chance to see her, before . . . but not now. She needs to rest."

"It has to be now," I said. "It's important, Mama. I promise."

I took a deep, deep breath, drawing what felt like all the poisoned air in the town—maybe all the air from North Carolina itself—into my lungs.

"I think I know what's stealing the magic from Whistling Ridge."

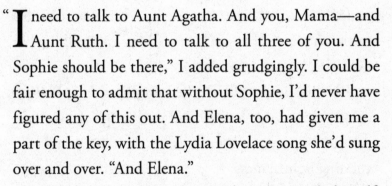

40.

"I need to talk to Aunt Agatha. And you, Mama—and Aunt Ruth. I need to talk to all three of you. And Sophie should be there," I added grudgingly. I could be fair enough to admit that without Sophie, I'd never have figured any of this out. And Elena, too, had given me a part of the key, with the Lydia Lovelace song she'd sung over and over. "And Elena."

Mama and Aunt Ruth stared. "Aggie isn't herself, honey," Mama said finally, all gentleness and questions. "She might not wake up."

"She'll wake up for this."

I didn't know how I knew, but I did, a knowledge that tingled in my fingertips and sang in my heart. Aunt Agatha was connected to the town. To me.

To Lydia.

She'd wake up.

Mama looked at me for a long, long minute, and then finally nodded. "If you're certain."

"Marianne," said Daddy, "are you sure—"

"I trust you, Ivy Mae," said Mama, looking at me and not Daddy, and the words were as much a threat as a compliment. I swallowed.

I waved at my sisters, who were both looking at me with wide, questioning eyes. "Come on."

Mama and Aunt Ruth led the way down the hall. It seemed a hundred miles long right in this moment, like it went on forever, like we kept walking and walking but never reached Aunt Agatha.

When we finally did, the bedroom was dark, like the twilight sky outside had swirled in through the window and filled up every atom of Aunt Agatha's room with brooding lightlessness.

The light's fading from her, Mama had told Aunt Ruth. I'd never realize before just how much light was a *part* of Mama and her sisters, just how much their light affected the world around them.

Not until I saw what it looked like for a star to lose that light.

"Aggie," Aunt Ruth said quietly. "Aggie, can you hear me?"

Aunt Agatha didn't stir. Her eyes were closed, her skin pale and dry; even the blackened veins in her arms and hands seemed less stark, like she was actually fading out of existence before our eyes. Both cats were curled up on the bed with her, like they were protecting her from the world.

Elena and Sophie pressed close on either side of me. Elena took my hand and squeezed, and Sophie rested her head, just for a moment, on my shoulder. They didn't need to speak for me to know what they were trying to say: that they trusted me. Even after everything that had passed between us in the last week, they trusted me. And even if the flame of my anger at Sophie wasn't gone completely, it was like it had retreated to a distant part of my mind, swallowed up by the importance of what she'd helped me realize.

Maybe Sophie and I were never going to be the best of friends. Maybe there would always be a part of me that grieved the words she'd destroyed. But we still belonged together, somehow, just like Mama and her sisters belonged together.

I stepped forward.

"Aunt Agatha," I said, my words dropping like pebbles into the dim silence of the bedroom. "Aunt Agatha, I need you to listen. I need you to wake up."

Had I imagined it, or had Aunt Agatha's papery

eyelids twitched, just a little?

"I know what's wrong with Whistling Ridge," I said, the secret ballooning inside me, filling me up so I could hardly breathe. "It's Lydia Lovelace."

"What?" Aunt Ruth interjected.

"You said there have been other women like you," I said to her and Mama. "Stars that have fallen to earth and become human. I think . . . I'm *sure* Lydia was one of them."

The whole bedroom fell into stunned silence. My sisters and Mama and Aunt Ruth all stared at me like I had grown an extra head.

"Think about it." I went on. "Nobody knows where she came from—she just appeared in town one day. She showed up and wove herself into the fabric of the town. Like . . . like she'd fallen right from the sky."

Mama pursed her lips. "All right, I suppose that could be possible. But what would that have to do with the magic draining out of Whistling Ridge? If she *was* a star, it would have been her job to strengthen it, not to tear it apart."

"Yeah. It was. For a long time. Until she moved to Whistling Ridge and met Henry Asbury."

"Who?" Mama said.

"He was the mayor's son. The one she fell in love

with. She was in love with him, but he broke her heart. She blamed him for it, and somehow, *her* version of the story is what everyone remembers. The story Aunt Agatha told me when we first came to Whistling Ridge was all about how Henry dumped Lydia and she died of a broken heart. That's what Lydia *wanted* people to remember. But it's wrong."

I knew I wasn't imagining it now: Aunt Agatha was stirring, her hands moving light and birdlike over the coverlet. Mama stepped forward and took one of the black-veined hands in her own golden-brown one.

"What do you mean, wrong?" Aunt Ruth prompted.

"Henry didn't turn Lydia away because he was cruel. He just didn't love her the same way she loved him. Henry loved his cousin Maggie. I think maybe he had always loved Maggie, even if it doesn't say so in the journal. Miss Christie gave me a copy of a picture of Henry and Maggie and their kids, and you can *tell*, just from looking at it, how much they loved each other. And I think the more Henry pulled away from Lydia, the harder she pushed him. The more desperate she got to hold on to him. In the diary, Lydia talked about how after Henry first broke her heart, he came back to her, and they were together, but . . . it wasn't like she thought it would be. Elena—sing the second verse of that song?"

Elena looked at me in confusion.

"The ballad of Lydia Lovelace," I said. "The one you've been learning."

"Oh." Elena paled. "In front of everyone?"

"Please?" I asked, squeezing her hand hard, the way she had done to mine a minute ago. One-two-three, our special I-love-you code. *You can do this*, I thought as hard as I could. *Be brave, Elena.*

Finally, Elena nodded. When she started singing, her voice trembled a little at first, but then grew strong and clear.

"And with him gone, I hollowed was,
A shell of who I'd been
No wish of mine could bring me back
No love enough for him."

Aunt Ruth made a soft *oh* sound, like she was beginning to connect the dots, too.

"I think," I said when Elena had finished singing, "that when Henry first told her he was planning to marry Maggie, *Lydia used wishes to get him back*. She wrote a bunch of stuff in her journal about having 'the full weight of her hope' behind her."

"I remember that," said Aunt Ruth. "It was such a

strange way to phrase things."

"And then, after she'd succeeded and gotten Henry back, she started to change. She wrote all these things that made no sense—like that her vision was blurring, and that she wasn't able to care for her roses anymore. She ended up ripping out her favorite rosebush and burning it because it got sick and nothing she did healed it. And she wrote that her relationship with Henry felt like a shell of something real—just like how in the song, it says *Lydia* was a shell of who she'd been. Mama—I think it's like that story you told us. Of the star-woman who used too many wishes and lost herself in the process."

"Oh my," said Aunt Ruth. "That would explain so much."

"I think maybe using the wishes *changed* Lydia. It took all the light and love out of her and left her hollow and dark. And even though she wanted to believe Henry really loved her, she knew deep down he only stayed with her because of the wishes she'd used to keep him there. You read some of the entries, Aunt Ruth. Lydia was so . . . *mean*. She wrote terrible things about Maggie, but as far as I can tell, the only thing Maggie ever did wrong was fall in love with Henry just the way Lydia had."

I could see it in my mind as I spoke—the dusty streets

of Whistling Ridge, Lydia in her rose-ringed cottage, getting angrier and sourer with every day. Until that anger didn't have anywhere to go anymore.

"What *exactly* happens when a star-woman dies, Mama?" I asked. "I know you said before that star-women return to the sky. But what exactly happens when they do that?"

"Her magic folds into the world around her when she becomes a star again," Mama said. "It's not sad in the same way it is for a human; it's more like a homecoming."

"In Sophie's book, it talks about black holes. How when an especially big star dies, it becomes a black hole. It has such a strong center of gravity it pulls everything in toward it—such a strong center of gravity that Sophie says it *warps space* around it. Makes everything act different." I glanced significantly at the window, where black leaves waved in the breeze.

"Oh," said Sophie, the first noise she'd made since we had come into Aunt Agatha's bedroom. The word was half sigh, half revelation. "Oh. You're *right*."

"I think Lydia became a black hole. Or whatever the earthly equivalent would be. I don't think she died of a broken heart—not the way the story goes, anyway. Not tragic and sweet. I think she *chose* to die. I think using all those wishes changed her so much that she was consumed by her anger and bitterness. She *became* that darkness."

Aunt Agatha's eyes fluttered open and closed—like she was trying so, so hard to wake up.

"When Miss Christie took me and Ravi to Lydia's cottage, it was awful," I said. "Creepy. You've felt it. Ravi and Miss Christie were fine, but I—I could tell that whatever was sucking at the magic . . . it was stronger there. And by Lydia's grave—" I shivered. "There was that dead bird. It was like it had had the life—the magic—drained out of it. Every drop."

I paused, took another deep poisoned-air breath. "The ballad Aunt Agatha taught Elena. When I first heard it, I figured somebody had written it *about* Lydia after she died. But it's written at the end of her journal, and one part of it is carved on her headstone, too. Lydia must have shared it, or showed somebody the journal before she ripped the pages out and hid them in her trunk, and eventually it became a song and everyone forgot how it came to be.

"But one of the lines is *Let all the world feel my broken heart.* I think it was meant to be a threat. Like a promise . . . or a curse. I think Lydia Lovelace became a black hole. *She's* what's sucking all the magic from the town."

"But—why now?" Aunt Ruth asked. "Lydia died more than a hundred years ago. Why have we never noticed anything until now?"

Sophie spoke up again. "It's how the gravity of black holes works in space. The more time goes on, the more it swallows, the stronger the black hole's gravity gets. So it becomes more and more powerful, and swallows things faster. *Bigger* things, too. A black hole in space can swallow a whole planet."

Mama paled.

Aunt Ruth sighed.

Aunt Agatha opened her eyes.

41.

"Aggie!" Aunt Ruth said, and for just a minute her voice sounded so young, all tangled up with tears and hope and pain.

I couldn't say anything.

Aunt Agatha looked at me, her blue eyes clear and focused. "Lydia," she said, barely more than a whisper. "All this time."

I nodded. "When you told me the story, I thought it was so romantic. So beautiful. But it wasn't. Not at all."

"Sorrow can be a bitter pill." Aunt Agatha closed her eyes again, like speaking took all the energy she had. "But it's worse to spread it."

Beside me, Aunt Ruth was crying. I thought of what she'd said about Uncle Andrew breaking her heart—thought of her saying *sadness feels startlingly like powerlessness.*

Had she been faced with the same choice as Lydia? Anger or forgiveness? Bitterness or moving on?

I had been so angry with Sophie for so many days for the way she'd thrown my notebook into the fire.

"And—Agatha?" Mama asked, looking from me to Aunt Agatha and back again. "Why would Lydia's curse be affecting her this way?"

Aunt Agatha's eyes fluttered open. "This town . . . is a part of me, Marianne. Like my skin or my bones or my blood."

Behind me, Elena cleared her throat, a timid little sound. She was squeezing Sophie's hand hard enough that both their knuckles were white. Still, her chin was lifted, and she looked resolute. Ever since we'd come to Whistling Ridge, Elena had hung back, even around the aunts.

But now, she looked ready to speak.

"What if," Elena said, her words slow but clear, "Aunt Agatha has poured so much of herself—so much of her own magic—into the town over the years that she's connected to it somehow? So when the magic started draining out of Whistling Ridge . . . it came for Aunt Agatha, too."

Mama's eyes were shiny. "Oh, Aggie."

"I don't think there's a way to stop it," I said, the words thorns in my mouth. "It's not like there's anything that gets rid of black holes in space. Is there?" I was hot and prickly and my throat itched. Some part of me, deep down, had hoped that maybe my big revelation would solve everything—that once things fell into place, Aunt Agatha would climb out of bed, the black fading from her veins, the wrinkles pulled tight and young across her cheekbones again.

But Aunt Agatha still lay there, the breath rattling in and out of her lungs like a fan in need of oiling.

Sophie shrugged. "Some physicists think that black holes evaporate over time and eventually explode. But it would take more than a billion times a billion years. Way longer than our universe has even existed."

"I think," Aunt Ruth said, tears streaming down her face still, "I think if Ivy's right . . . perhaps I may know how to fix it."

The three star sisters traded significant looks, their faces as solemn as I'd ever seen them.

The itchy feeling got worse.

"If there was enough positive energy to counter it . . . ," Mama said, staring at Aunt Ruth.

"It would have to be a significant amount," wheezed Aunt Agatha. "It's been so long, and grown so strong."

"But if there was enough," said Mama, "it could do it.

Stop it all. Make the . . . black hole . . . disappear."

Something squeezed hard around my rib cage.

"What do you mean?" I said, dreading the answer.

What happens when a star-woman dies?

Usually, she returns to the sky.

Mama's eyes were wet now, too.

"If Lydia was one of us," said Aunt Agatha, "if it was her death, steeped in darkness, that has pulled the magic from Whistling Ridge—"

"Then we can fix it," Aunt Ruth finished. "A positive force cancels out a negative one. Any of us could, if we allowed ourselves to fold into the magic of Whistling Ridge. To return to the sky, to what we were before."

"To . . . die?" The words scraped my throat raw.

Aunt Ruth nodded.

"It would need to be both of us," Aunt Agatha rasped. "I'm not strong enough alone anymore. None of us are."

Mama's tears spilled out now, falling down her face like rain, making her look so much younger—as young and scared as I felt.

"You *cannot* be saying what I think you're saying," she said, sniffling.

Aunt Agatha gripped Mama's hand tightly. "You are the best of us, Marianne. You have to be the one to stay. You have your family, your life—your love. I only have Whistling Ridge, and if that goes, I go anyway, in much worse circumstances."

"The life I built in Montana, with Andrew, is over," Aunt Ruth said with a teary smile. "There's too much pain now in the things I used to love. If it hadn't been for the chance to retreat to Whistling Ridge, to spend time with the two of you—and with the girls—I might have gone down the same road as Lydia eventually. Before I came here, I felt near to drowning in the pain."

"I can't do it alone," said Mama, crying harder now. "I can't do any of this alone. Tending to the magic—it will be too much for me on my own."

"If you don't," said Aunt Agatha, "there will be no magic left to tend. No world left to protect. Our corner of it, at least, will fall into darkness."

Mama was quiet for a long time. I stepped back from Aunt Agatha's bedside, until I was between Sophie and Elena again, and I grabbed both of their hands. What would it be like to have to live without my sisters, forever and ever, for as long as a star might remain human? Sophie and I might fight like cats and dogs, and Elena might sometimes send darts of worry through my stomach.

But without them, I didn't know if I'd still be *myself.* Who was I, without the sisters who had slept only a few feet from me for almost as long as I could remember?

Without Aunt Agatha and Aunt Ruth, would Mama

feel like she'd lost two-thirds of her heart?

Finally, Mama nodded and took Aunt Ruth's hand in her free one. Aunt Ruth reached out for Aunt Agatha, until they were all linked up into a circle.

"The cats will need a home," said Aunt Agatha. "And Ivy—the yellow yarn is in my sewing room. It's for you now."

I nodded, unable to speak through the unshed tears caught in my throat. I couldn't imagine crocheting a whole shawl. And for Sophie, of all people.

But for Aunt Agatha, I could learn.

The glow began with their hair.

It shimmered and sparkled, growing brighter and brighter in the twilight of the bedroom.

Their skin was next: glowing warm and golden, until it almost hurt to look at them, and if I squinted my eyes, it really did seem like three stars hung in the bedroom gloom.

When the star sisters had become almost too bright to imagine, something happened that I'd never seen before.

Mama shone brighter and brighter, but Aunt Agatha and Aunt Ruth started to fade.

The light went first, dimming more and more—but in some way I couldn't quite explain, *they* were fading, too. Their edges looked less real, like their skin and bones were dissolving into the air, giving them the look of a photograph that's been left out in the rain to blur and distort.

I gripped my sisters' hands harder than ever and closed my eyes. Beside me, I could feel Elena tremble as she cried.

Please, please, don't go, I thought.

Please, please, stay.

I thought of star-watching with Aunt Ruth in the back garden; of watching Aunt Agatha trim the Lovelace clematis. Of Aunt Agatha's hands, so gentle and soft on mine as she taught me to guide the crochet hook through the yarn. Of how the shawl I wore around my shoulders felt like Aunt Agatha's love and acceptance, like being *seen* for exactly who I was. Of how Aunt Ruth was choosing *not* to be like Lydia—choosing to take her pain and make it something beautiful, not something dark and ugly.

Of how both of them had become part of my life, part of my very own heart, over the last month in Whistling Ridge.

Please, please, don't go.

I'd never wished for anything so hard in my life— not even when I stole the nine wishes in Oklahoma and begged for a forever home.

When I opened my eyes, Mama's light had dimmed, and both the aunts looked more regular, the fuzziness

gone from their outlines. All three star sisters had identical expressions of frustration on their faces.

"Why isn't it working?" Aunt Ruth said, cutting her
eyes to Mama with something that looked almost like
suspicion.

"I swear it isn't me!" Mama protested. "I didn't stop
it." She closed her eyes, a concentrating look on her face.

Once more, all three star sisters brightened, both the
aunts dimmed—and then it stopped. Again.

Aunt Ruth sighed in frustration. "Marianne! You
must let go." She was all teary again. "No parting is forever, little sister."

Mama actually rolled her eyes, looking for the first
time in my life like the youngest sister she was—almost
like Sophie. "It. Isn't. Me. Ruth, I'm sorry. I have no idea
what's holding it back."

Guilt slammed into me. I made a little meeping noise
of embarrassment, thinking of how hard I'd been wishing for Aunt Agatha and Aunt Ruth to stay, for their
magic to fail them.

"Ivy?" Mama asked, one eyebrow up, looking like a
no-nonsense mother again. "Is there something you'd
like to tell us?"

"I'm sorry," I said. "I was wishing they would stay."

"I was thinking about Aunt Agatha saying that

hearing me play my ukulele made her feel less sick," Elena said in a tiny voice.

"I was thinking about how Aunt Ruth and Aunt Agatha never make me feel bad for using big words," said Sophie, sounding her actual age for the first time in a long time. "Besides, studies show that relationships with extended family are—"

"This is probably not the time, Soph," I said under my breath. To her credit, Sophie didn't say another word.

Aunt Ruth frowned. "None of that should . . ."

Mama let go of her sisters' hands, looking intently at me. "Hmm," she said. "Hmm."

She stepped forward and reached her hands out for mine. Her palms were warm and dry and soft; as she held my hands in hers, I could remember every time in my whole life that those hands had held me, comforted me, reassured me that it was going to be okay.

Mama was looking at me so closely she almost seemed to look *through* me—like my skin was transparent, like she could see right past it to the very essence of who I was.

"I think," she said at last, "that there might be something rather unexpected at play."

42.

"How?" Aunt Ruth asked.

"Ivy," Mama said, "have you ever made anything happen that you didn't expect? When you touched something, for instance, did it behave differently than it should have?"

"No," I said immediately, but then paused. Last week, when I'd touched the bark of the cursed apple trees, it had turned browner and stronger beneath my fingers.

I hadn't known how to explain it then. But what if it had been *me*?

"There has been something, hasn't there," Mama said. I nodded.

"Is it possible . . . ?" Aunt Ruth asked.

"It's not as though either of us have had children,"

said Aunt Agatha. "For all we know, it could be."

"And it *is* the first time all three of us have been together in a long, long while," said Aunt Ruth thoughtfully. "Perhaps that sparked something."

"What do you mean?" I asked. I hated when grownups talked that way, like they were speaking in code, their meaning always just barely escaping my comprehension.

"Ivy," said Mama slowly, giving my hands a squeeze, "I think it's possible that you and your sisters have inherited some star magic. I've been wondering, ever since you said you could feel the disturbance at Lydia's cottage when nobody else could."

"But you always said anyone could notice the magic of the world if they knew to look!"

"True. But the way you described it—it sounded like something deeper."

"But—we don't look anything like you, or glow, or—"

"Come here, girls," said Aunt Agatha. Mama let my hands drop and gave me a gentle push toward the bed. Sophie and Elena crowded in beside me. Aunt Agatha reached up and took our hands, one by one. It felt almost as though she had already faded out of being; her hand was so much thinner and more fragile than it had been only a few days ago, like she was halfway to memory.

I expected a lecture—Aunt Agatha explaining to me why they had to go, what Lydia's curse would do to the world if left unchecked. But instead, Aunt Agatha said simply, "It's so, so very hard to let go."

Aunt Ruth moved in closer behind me. I felt her hand gentle on my shoulder, its warmth like a silent message saying, *I love you, I love you.*

My eyes stung. Elena was crying again next to me. Even Sophie, usually the most practical and least emotional of the three of us, was sniffling.

"It's much easier to hold tight," Aunt Ruth said. "To try to force the grief away by sheer willpower."

"You three can do this," Mama said, with enough love in her voice to wrap all the way around me, a blanket on a cold, gray night.

"You will do so much," Aunt Agatha said. "So much, dear ones. The three of you will learn to help your mother. You will learn to move magic through your fingers. Because of you, Whistling Ridge—the whole country—will learn to thrive again."

I caught my breath. If my sisters and I were supposed to be the ones to help Mama tend to the magic after her sisters were gone . . .

That would mean we definitely, absolutely, without question couldn't stay in Whistling Ridge forever.

And with that thought, my tears came for real: streaming down my face, dripping rain-like off my jaw. It felt like I had so many tears inside me that I might never stop crying.

How, *how* could I let go of all the things I'd grown to love so much? Aunt Agatha, with her dry humor and her deep love. Aunt Ruth, with her honesty and friendship. The whole town, with its brown-brick downtown and sprawling apple orchards. Oaktree Park. Charlie, who smiled and waved whenever she saw me. Miss Christie, with her perfect bun and passion for history. *Simon. Ravi.* The rule-of-three friendship I felt I'd waited my whole life for.

How could I *choose* to say goodbye to every one of those people, those places?

Mama put one hand on each of my sister's shoulders, so that together we were held by all three star sisters, surrounded by golden skin and silver-white hair and love on every side. A tangle of sisters: Mama, Aunt Ruth, Aunt Agatha, Elena, Sophie, and me.

Three sisters. Three daughters. And the stardust that flowed through each of our veins.

"It's time," Mama whispered, and I could tell without even looking at her that she was crying, too. "I'm sorry, my loves. This is a very grown-up thing we're asking you to do. But without it . . ." She paused. "It's time."

I nodded, feeling like my body was a million miles away from the rest of me.

"Join hands," Aunt Ruth said, and we did—Aunt Agatha took Elena's hand, who took Mama's, who took Sophie's, who took Ruth's, who took mine. When I took Aunt Agatha's free hand in my own, my whole body felt warm.

"No parting is forever," said Aunt Ruth again.

"When we are gone," said Aunt Agatha, "look up to the night sky and you will feel us there."

I nodded. I couldn't speak through my tears, but I hoped they knew what I wanted to say:

Thank you. Thank you. Thank you.

All three star sisters began to glow again—even brighter and more vibrant than they had a few minutes ago. To my shock, I realized that my own skin was glowing, too—faint but unquestionable, the light pooling on my skin like water.

And to either side of me, Aunt Agatha and Aunt Ruth began to blur into the light. They grew brighter and brighter, until their features began to fade, their hands in mine less and less substantial.

I closed my eyes, still crying, and thought of Lydia: how hard she'd held on to Henry Asbury, how she'd refused to let go even after it was clear he loved some-body other than her. How she'd used wish after wish to make things go the way she'd wanted, and in the process she'd lost herself and poisoned the whole town. How if the star sisters didn't fix it, Lydia's mistake would go on to hurt the whole world.

I couldn't be like Lydia. I needed to be like Aunt Ruth—making the choice to let go, to move on.

Even if it meant letting go of her and Aunt Agatha.

Even if it meant moving on from Whistling Ridge.

Maybe the way I'd been thinking of a forever home had been wrong all this time. Maybe a home wasn't so much one place, or a bathtub, or a pet, or any of the other things on my wish list. Maybe a home was some-thing different—a feeling. A relationship. An idea.

I'd found home here in Whistling Ridge, with Aunt Agatha and Aunt Ruth. But maybe, someday, I'd be able to find home in other places, too.

Beyond my eyelids, the light in Aunt Agatha's room grew and grew and grew, until it was so bright it hurt my eyes even when they were closed. It brightened and brightened and brightened, until I was sure that every-one in Whistling Ridge could see the light from Aunt Agatha's bedroom, and I couldn't have opened my eyes even if I wanted to.

And then, in one tiny, eternal instant, the light winked out.

And when I opened my eyes, my hands were empty.

Nobody lay in Aunt Agatha's bed; only the rumpled bedcovers showed that anyone ever had.

But for one brief moment after my eyes opened, I could see how the bedroom had been transformed. Everywhere I looked were bright gold veins of magic. Brighter than I'd ever seen them when Mama was working alone, shining like a promise.

As I watched, I could see the veins of light spreading, reaching through the walls and patterning themselves across Aunt Agatha's backyard, pushing color back into the grass and then twining up the trees and shaking the blackness from the leaves. Even after the golden light faded, leaving only the afterglow printed on my eyes, the bedroom was lighter than it had been earlier.

The sun, I realized. The sun was shining again over Whistling Ridge.

It was like an explosion. An explosion of light.

As though she were thinking the same thing I was, Sophie leaned over and whispered, "Remember, Ivy? They say black holes end that way. In a burst of light."

I thought of Lydia Lovelace the way she had been at the beginning of her journal. Funny and sweet, writing poetic descriptions of apples and Whistling Ridge that showed how much she loved the town she'd claimed as her own.

Had healing the town somehow healed her, too—whatever lingering essence she'd left behind?

I hoped that it had.

As soon as the magic faded, Mama pulled all three of us into a tight hug. I felt like a baby who needed to be held, protected from the world around me. Coffee and Cream hopped off the bed and twined their way between our legs, mewing unhappily. What on earth would cats make of what had just happened?

We stayed like that, holding each other and crying, until the door opened and Daddy made his tentative way in, joining our hug.

Right there, in the middle of my family—the tangle of arms and shoulders and heads and tears and two irritated cats—I thought of the notebook Sophie had thrown into fire, and the tale that had been growing inside it. Lydia had been the beginning of Whistling Ridge's troubles, and in a strange way, she had been the end of them, too.

I needed to go back to that story. To rewrite it, the way Mama and the aunts and Elena and Sophie and I had just rewritten Lydia's legacy. The way the discovery that my sisters and I had star-magic of our own had rewritten everything I thought I understood about myself. And for the first time since I'd seen my notebook pages curled and blackened in the flames, I knew *exactly* what I wanted to write.

43.

Here are the things that happened in Whistling Ridge, those first days after Aunt Agatha and Aunt Ruth folded themselves back into the magic of the world and returned to the sky:

The sun came out every day, shining as brightly as I'd ever seen it. As though it, too, was grateful to be finally free of the clouds that had been gathering around Whistling Ridge for who knows how long.

The trees, after the black faded from them, were such a beautiful green it almost hurt to look at.

The apples were just apples again—delicious, crispy and sweet, filled with juice—and the chrysanthemums were just chrysanthemums, their reds and yellows and oranges whispering that autumn was really, truly here.

The birds remembered how to sing.

Even the air of Whistling Ridge was different—filled with the scent of cider and sunshine and a musk that promised that soon the leaves would catch fire with color, blazing out in a glorious fall rainbow that would be the furthest thing from the darkness that had been painted across them for so many days.

For four days after Aunt Agatha and Aunt Ruth left (it felt not quite right to say that they had *died*, even though that was certainly how it felt, and Mama was planning a memorial service to which the whole town would be invited), I spent most of my time curled up on the grass in the backyard with a brand-new notebook Daddy had bought me from Mr. Sidana's drugstore. Mama didn't even say anything about doing schoolwork—she just let me write and write and write, like she knew how important it was that I get down all the words that were burning their way to my fingertips.

I was rewriting my Lydia story. The day after everything had happened, I'd used the phone in Aunt Agatha's kitchen to call Simon and Ravi and ask if they still wanted to do the multimedia project with me, and would they mind if we changed some things. They said they were still in, and since there were still three weeks until the Lovelace Festival at the end of October, there would be plenty of time for us to pull it off.

After I got off the phone, I went to Mama and Daddy and told them everything. About how much this project meant to me, and how badly I wanted to see it in the festival in three weeks. About how Whistling Ridge and Lydia's story had become a *part* of me. About how I understood, now, that we couldn't stay here forever . . . but how I still wanted to stay just a *little* while longer.

And they'd said yes. They'd agreed that we could stay until the end of October, which would give Mama time to make sure everything was right with the magic in Whistling Ridge and take care of regular-human things, like what to do with Aunt Agatha's house and finding a new home for Coffee and Cream.

So I was writing my story again. But this time, I was writing it differently. And this time, I knew from the light that hummed and sparked its way through my bloodstream—nothing like the sick, uncomfortable feeling I'd had when reading Lydia's journal—I was doing it *right*.

44.

As far as I could tell, every single person in Whistling Ridge turned out to the memorial service for Aunt Agatha and Aunt Ruth that Sunday afternoon. Mama had spread a story that Aunt Agatha and Aunt Ruth had died in in an accident at the Lovelace Homestead, which had persuaded the town council to put a fence up around the property so that it couldn't be accessed without a key. *Probably there's nothing left there to harm anyone,* Mama had said, *but it's just as well to be sure.*

Mama had requested that nobody wear black to the service—after the nightmare scene that Whistling Ridge had become before we'd found a way to stop Lydia's curse from sucking away all the town's magic, dark, somber colors felt like the last thing either of the star sisters would have wanted. Instead, we wore bright colors: gold and crimson and magenta and teal and violet. Mama wore a dress I'd never seen before that was the same silver-white as her hair, all sewn through with tiny sparkling jewels. All day her hair glowed faintly in response to the dress. She'd never looked so much like exactly what she was—a fallen star.

Since there were no bodies to bury or ashes to scatter, everyone in Whistling Ridge who had a garden had donated a few roses, and Mama had decided that we'd scatter the rose petals around the stone marker she'd used a wish to create, to commemorate Aunt Agatha and Aunt Ruth. The marker said that they *gave all of themselves for the good of Whistling Ridge*, which sounded just like a regular-old-gravestone platitude, but was more true than anyone in town would probably ever know.

Mama called and told Uncle Andrew—Aunt Ruth's ex-boyfriend in faraway Montana—what had happened, and although he'd broken her heart, he still sent a bouquet of white roses and a note that said that even if things had gone wrong between them, he'd always love Aunt Ruth for what they had been to each other once upon a time. It made me think of weeks before, when Aunt Ruth and I had been reading Lydia's journal and she'd said, *There are two sides to every story.*

I hoped that somewhere, up in the sky, Aunt Ruth's pain and sorrow were all gone.

First, though, we met in Aunt Agatha's church building and sang hymns and listened to Mama tell stories about past times with her sisters. A few people from Whistling Ridge—including Miss Christie—got up to say something about what Aunt Agatha had meant to the town. Near the end of her speech, Mama started to cry, the tears glinting silver-bright in the church light.

"If there is one thing that you know, when you're the youngest of three sisters," Mama said, her voice croaking a little, "it is that you are who you are only and entirely because of the sisters who came before you."

On one side of me, Elena leaned her head against my shoulder. On the other side, Sophie snuggled into me, tucking herself under my arm like a baby bird. Elena and I wore the shawls Aunt Agatha had made us. Sophie's shawl was still nothing more than the two rows Aunt Agatha had started before she'd gotten too sick to hold her crochet hook, but that was okay. Mama had promised that we'd find some YouTube videos, and she'd help me learn how to finish it.

And in that moment, right there in the middle of Aunt Agatha's church house, listening to Mama mourn for the sisters she'd lost, I felt the knot of anger and resentment that had been tangled up in my heart since Sophie had burned my notebook nine days ago release.

There might be a part of me that would forever grieve the words that had gone into the fire that day. And I'd never agree that what Sophie had done was *right*, exactly. But she hadn't been wrong that the story I was writing, and the way it had made me act, were not good. And maybe Elena was right, too, and everything Sophie had done had been done out of love, trying to protect us all in the only way she knew how.

After all, she was only eight. Big words and astrophysics aside, she couldn't necessarily be expected to be the smartest or the most mature.

I pulled her closer to me, wrapping my arm tighter around her shoulders, and even laid a feathery kiss on top of her perfect golden hair.

For months and months, I'd been frustrated and angry because I didn't have a forever home of my own. More than anything, I'd wanted a place like Aunt Agatha's cottage, steady and permanent, with walls that held me and an orchard just out the front door. I'd thought *that* was what I needed to be happy.

But Lydia had been sure of what she needed to be happy, too—and chasing after it, using wishes to try to make it true, had killed her and nearly taken all of

Whistling Ridge along with her.

Right now, in the warm sanctuary with the perfume of roses all around me, I wasn't so sure of what I needed anymore. Because maybe I'd been wrong about what it meant to have a forever home after all. Maybe it had less to do with what your walls were made of, and more to do with who lived inside them.

Maybe, just maybe, my *sisters* were my forever home.

After the memorial was finished, Mama and Daddy stood by the headstone for a long time, shaking hands and hugging shoulders and thanking people for coming. Sophie and Elena and I huddled together, like the three of us staying close together could make up for the way that Mama stood all alone, *truly* without her sisters for the first time since the three of them had fallen to earth and become human.

One after another, all the people I'd met in Whistling Ridge came to say hello and tell us they were sorry for our loss. Simon's Mama and Mom, Miss Brenda and Miss Harriet, both hugged me and said how Agatha had always been their favorite neighbor. Simon's little sister, Hannah, the one who had been mean to Sophie on the playground all those weeks ago, even hugged Soph and whispered an apology so squeaky and quiet I wasn't sure anyone could hear it but the dogs of Whistling Ridge. Miss Christie hugged me for a long time; for once, her bun seemed a little less silkily perfect than usual, and her sharp-cheekboned face was streaked with tears.

"Your aunts were special, Ivy," she said to me as she pulled away. "I know you know that, though. And they're lucky to have such a talented writer in the family, to remember them always."

Charlie and her parents came, too. I tried not to stare at Charlie's mama as Charlie introduced her parents to me and her daddy shook my hand. Charlie's mama was just as pretty as Charlie was, but instead of Charlie's wild curls, her mama had a purple turban wrapped around her bald head. She moved slowly and carefully, like she was in pain, and her dark eyes were lined with the kind of wrinkles that showed that a person had been through a lot.

Hadn't the wish fixed her cancer, the way Charlie had hoped it would?

Charlie hung back near me for a minute after her parents had gone on to give their condolences to Mama and Daddy.

"I'm really sorry, Ivy," Charlie said. "I didn't know your aunt Ruth all that well, but I've known Aunt Agatha my whole life, and she was special."

"I know," I said. "Thanks. How . . . how are things with your mama?"

Charlie smiled. "They're good, actually. Really good." She followed my gaze to her mama's purple turban and lowered her voice. "I didn't use the wish the way I expected to. I'd been so sure I would use it to try to give my mom a cure. That's all I've wanted, all year long. But after talking to you at the park all those times . . . and I talked to your mama about it for a long time when I came to bargain for the wish . . . it just didn't feel right."

"So what did you wish for instead?" Mama had a firm rule that we were never to pry into any of her clients' personal business, but surely this was different. After all, Charlie had been the one who had told me about it in the first place.

"Happiness," Charlie said simply. "Everything has been so hard this year. I wished that my whole family would have happiness, and peace, no matter what the outcome of Mama's treatments is."

Something warm and soft bloomed in my chest at Charlie's words. "That sounds perfect."

"It's been good. For the first time in a long time, we've been laughing, going on walks, playing games. My parents don't seem so . . . weighed down. We still don't know what will happen with Mama's cancer, but in a

way I can't explain, it's almost felt okay. Because whatever the result is, we'll get through it together. Anyway,
thanks, Ivy."

Charlie hurried to catch up with her parents, but that
soft, warm feeling inside me didn't leave.

After everyone had finished scattering their rose petals, Simon and Ravi found me. Ravi's hands were in his
pockets; Simon was fidgety, trying so hard to bite his
tongue.

"Sorry, Ivy," said Ravi. "We were all so sad to hear. My
mom cried when we got the phone call. Miss Agatha . . .
she *was* Whistling Ridge."

"Once, when I was eight, I broke my leg climbing in
the orchard," said Simon. "Miss Agatha brought me ice
cream and an apple quilt and a book of one thousand
and one jokes. I didn't even care about my leg after that.
Though I think my moms got kind of sick of the jokes."

I smiled—almost a laugh, but not quite. I would feel
like laughing again sometime, but not today. Not yet.

"That sounds like Aunt Agatha," I said.

"Speaking of ice cream," Ravi said, "my dad's been
experimenting with a new recipe for the soft-serve
machine. He'll probably be doing another tasting party
soon. You know. If you're still around."

A feeling like bird wings fluttered in my chest.

"I'd like that," I said, and as I looked at Ravi's and Simon's faces, at the rose petals scattered all around the headstone Mama had made for her sisters, at the apple orchards that ringed the church's little cemetery, I knew something more clearly than I'd ever known anything in my life.

No matter where we went, no matter how far we traveled, no matter what Mama and I and my sisters had to do to tend to the magic of the world now that my aunts were gone—a piece of my heart would always live here, in the apple trees and cornflower skies of Whistling Ridge, North Carolina.

45.

In the last week of October, on a morning when Whistling Ridge had woken to frost that lined the apple-tree branches with diamonds and set the remaining amber leaves on fire, the Lovelace Festival began.

We'd gotten Martha back—a new transmission that ran, Daddy said, smooth as butter—right after the memorial. The little wren had immediately resumed its rooftop nest building. Daddy had sighed, shaking his head. "I guess I'll tinker around and see if I can't make it a little enclosure for when we're on the road," he said, "if it's gonna insist on nesting up there. Dadgum stubborn bird. How's it going to feel once we stop in, I don't know, North Dakota?"

Mama had come up and put her arm around him,

leaning her head into his shoulder. "Home is a funny thing," she'd said. "I suppose we all find it in the most unlikely of places. Even if those places happen to be constantly on the move. It'll adapt. Maybe North Dakota is exactly where its mate is waiting for it—did you ever think of that?"

Daddy shook his head, but I could see his smile. "Fool bird. Seems like a terrible place to lay eggs."

I watched the little wren flutter around on top of Martha's roof, a curious feeling creeping through me, from my toes all the way up. Maybe I was more like that bird than I had realized. Maybe I could find happiness on the road, just like it was so determined to do.

Home was turning out to be a much more complicated concept than I'd expected, that early-September night when I released nine fireflies by Silverwood Lake.

Now it was the Lovelace Festival, and so much nervous energy was humming through me it felt like lightning might shoot from my fingertips at any moment. Simon and Ravi and their families were waiting for us by the front door to the city hall building—Simon's sister, Hannah, wiggled impatiently, Ravi's brother, Nikhil, was trying to climb up the giant pillars outside the entrance, and their respective parents were deep in conversation and ignoring everyone else. Miss Harriet was laughing when we got there, the kind of booming laugh that gets under your skin so you can't help smiling along, even if you don't know what she's laughing about.

"Ivy!" Simon cried, jumping up from where he'd been waiting on the step. Ravi, next to him, was buried deep in a book. "Happy birthday! Are you ready?"

Technically, my thirteenth birthday had been yesterday, but I nodded anyway. Mama and Daddy had given me a shiny cell phone of my very own, even though it broke their old no-phones-until-high-school rule. *To help you stay in touch with your friends better*, Mama had said, meeting my eyes steadily. *Honey, we know how much these friends mean to you.* She'd promised that they'd set me up so I could text and video-chat with Simon and Ravi and not be dependent on only email.

I still hadn't heard from Ada, but for the first time in months, that empty in-box wasn't haunting me. I'd been too busy thinking about our Lydia project. In fact, I'd realized as I'd programmed Simon's and Ravi's numbers into my new phone, I'd completely forgotten to check my e-mail for a whole week. Ada's silence had gone from being a weight I constantly wore to something I hardly even thought of—and that felt good.

Now, all three of our families filed inside city hall. Projects for the Lovelace Festival had been set up all through the main atrium of the building. There were paintings, things built from modeling clay, even a girl reciting a spoken-word piece about Lydia's great love. Somebody had cut a Lovelace clematis shape into the pages of a half-open book, so that when the book was propped up with its pages spread, the Lovelace clematis popped right out.

Simon, of course, was the first to get to our project. "Here it is!" he said, bouncing on the balls of his feet. "Oh my gosh, it turned out so cool! Come see, guys!"

After that day in the beginning of October when I'd called Simon and Ravi and said we needed to change our project, we'd started right back from square one. Instead of a model of Lydia's cottage, Simon had gone bigger—with his uncle's help, he'd built a model of what we figured Whistling Ridge must have looked like back when Lydia was alive. There was even a tiny plastic horse pulling a carriage Simon had built out of applewood, right in the center of Main Street.

And instead of a backdrop of roses and clematis, Ravi had taken a canvas almost as tall as Sophie and painted a night sky glittering with stars. It was so beautiful it made it hard to breathe for a minute; the painting had *depth*, like you could fall into it. If you looked at it right, the stars seemed almost to wheel and twinkle on the canvas. Sophie had helped him with the early sketches, lending him star charts and explaining which celestial bodies should be brighter or dimmer, which should have a sheen of red or blue.

Faintly, so that you could just barely see them twisting and twining through the starscape, Ravi had painted the words of the ballad of Lydia Lovelace. Elena had helped with that part.

Because when I'd realized that we needed to change our project, I'd realized something else: just like Mama and her sisters and I had needed Elena and Sophie in Aunt Agatha's bedroom on that hard, sad afternoon at the beginning of the month, Ravi and Simon and I needed them, too.

After we'd all had several minutes to ooh and aah over the town and the backdrop, Ravi leaned forward and pushed the play button on the MP3 player Simon had tucked into one of the model houses. There was a speaker in there, too, the smallest one we could find.

A minute later, a gentle ukulele melody filled the room, and then Elena's voice.

It had taken a lot of coaxing to get Elena to read the story I'd written for our recording. It had taken *more* coaxing to convince her to record her ukulele to use as background music. Even though nobody would *see* her performing, she still struggled. But when I promised we could rerecord things as many times as we needed to get it to a point where Elena felt happy with it, she finally agreed.

It felt right, knowing that this project held a part of so many people who made the world feel like *home* to me. Simon and Ravi, who I knew deep down to my toes would be forever friends even after we left Whistling Ridge. And my sisters, who made even an RV and an ever-changing landscape into home.

"It sounds so good," Ravi whispered now, as Elena's soft voice narrated the story I'd written. "She did a really good job. And you did, too, Ivy."

The story started out the way the first version, the one Sophie burned, had: Lydia bumping into Henry outside the blacksmith's shop. And for a little while, it went on the same way, with Lydia falling more and more in love.

But then we got to the part where I'd changed things.

Instead of writing the story like a romance, with Lydia the tragic heroine and Henry the heartless heartbreaker, I'd written Lydia the way she was in the diary. She started out wonderful, but after learning about Henry's engagement, she let her anger and bitterness and her desperate wishing for something she didn't have overtake her. (Mama had forbidden me from including the actual wishes Lydia had used in the story. *Star-women still need their secrets*, she'd said.)

In my story, Lydia tried and tried to make Henry love her, but when he didn't, it hollowed her out, just the way she'd written in her journal.

But right at the end, after Henry and Maggie were married, when Lydia felt lost and hopeless, I'd changed the story.

Sophie had given me the idea on the morning of my aunts' sacrifice. *Remember, Ivy?* she'd said as the sun poured its brightness over Whistling Ridge. *They say black holes end that way. In a burst of light.*

Lydia hadn't gotten that kind of ending while she was alive, not really, though I liked to think that when Mama and the aunts had healed the town, Lydia and her legacy had been changed as well. But in my story, I could give Lydia the ending she didn't have.

So in my story, I gave her a little bird. Like the wren who had made a home on Martha's roof, I wrote about a wounded bird turning up in Lydia's garden. And even though her heart was black with unhappiness, even though she was being swallowed up by her anger, Lydia couldn't bear to see the bird hurt and not do something about it. And as she tended that little bird, watching it grow stronger each day, she began to change again.

Slowly, slowly, the hardness went out of her heart.

The bitterness rolled off her skin.

And when the bird at last was ready to fly again, Lydia felt like *she* was the one who had been healed.

At the end of the story, Lydia left Whistling Ridge. *She was eager to see the world with her new heart*, I'd written, *and to embrace a new adventure.*

It wasn't the way the town legend ended. And it wasn't the way the story of the real Lydia ended, either. But when I'd written it, it had felt *right*. Sometimes stories aren't necessarily fact, but that doesn't mean they aren't *true*.

I liked the thought of Lydia out there, somewhere— maybe only as a memory or an essence, but finally redeemed. Healed by the love of her fellow star-women.

When the narration ended, the whole group of us gathered around the diorama had gone silent—more silent than the day the birds stopped singing. More silent than anything I'd ever experienced. Like all of us were holding our breath, afraid to move or cough. Even Hannah and Nikhil and Sophie were perfectly still, spellbound as the last strains of Elena's ukulele faded.

And then, after a long minute of quiet, all three of our families erupted in applause.

46.

We stayed until the Monday after the Lovelace Festival.

Simon's moms had invited all of us over for a celebratory dinner on Saturday after the festival showcase, along with the Sidanas and Charlie's family. (Mr. Sidana had brought his latest batch of ice cream—this one flavored with almonds and cinnamon—to eat along with the apple pie that Simon, Ravi, and I had won for our display.) Simon and his uncle had carried two big picnic tables out to the orchard, and we'd eaten dinner there, under the orange leaves, the blue sky all around us like a hug. The air smelled like cider and that crisp, indescribable spice of autumn. Like happiness, and excitement . . . and also like change.

"I bet they pull our diorama out every single year for the Lovelace Festival," Ravi said to me after we'd finished the main course, while Miss Brenda passed around steaming slices of our apple pie prize. He was petting Cream absentmindedly while he waited for his pie; the white cat already liked Ravi better than anyone I'd ever seen her with except Aunt Ruth. Coffee, though usually less shy, had been grumpier about moving to the Welchers' house. He still hissed at Hannah every time she got close to him—though privately, I could understand that feeling. Even if she'd apologized, I still wasn't about to forget the way she'd made Sophie cry that day at the park in September.

"I've never seen anything like that, Ivy," said Simon. "It was amazing. Everyone in town is *still* talking about it. I don't know if anyone is ever going to think of Lydia the same way. You heard how much Miss Christie raved about it being 'such an original interpretation of the source material!'"

"I didn't mean to . . . break the story," I said. "I know she means a lot to the town."

"You didn't. At least, I'm pretty sure you didn't." Ravi shrugged. "No more than any change breaks what came before it. Change isn't necessarily a bad thing."

"I guess," I said, thinking of the way Daddy had

driven Martha into town yesterday and made sure her tank was all full of gas, ready to get back on the road tomorrow.

"You'll be back," Ravi said, just like he had read my mind.

And it was true. The day before, Mama and Daddy had sat me down and explained something: that we did have to get back on the road, both because Daddy's editor had threatened to stop buying articles about the Blue Ridge Mountains and because it was time for Mama and my sisters and I to get to work tending the world's magic. *You girls have so much to learn*, Mama had said with a small smile.

And even though I couldn't help the thread of sadness that wove through me at the idea of leaving Whistling Ridge, there was also something different inside me now, too—a thrum of purpose, the tingle of star-magic underneath my fingertips that whispered of all the things I needed to do.

But Mama and Daddy hadn't stopped there. They'd gone on to say that they'd been talking about it ever since Aunt Agatha and Aunt Ruth returned to the sky, and they'd decided to keep Aunt Agatha's house instead of selling it. They'd decided that we'd live part-time in Whistling Ridge, a few months of every year to have four walls around us, to run through the apple orchards and eat soft-serve at Mr. Sidana's pharmacy.

"We know how much this town means to you, Ivy," Mama had said, her hair glowing bright. "And we know how much it meant to Agatha. I don't know if it will ever be the right thing for our family to settle down forever, to put down the kind of roots Aggie did. But for now, at least, we think we could make this plan work."

Remembering that conversation now was like a little spark of happiness laced through the sadness of leaving tomorrow.

"Yeah," I said to Ravi, "I definitely will."

"You know," said Mrs. Sidana from across the table, catching my eye, "many great writers were great travelers, too. And others were immigrants—leaving one home and moving far, far away to create another. I expect someday the world will know your name, Ivy."

Her words were like warm honey, filling me up. "Thanks," I said. "I hope it will."

Dusk fell as we ate our dessert, the apples and cinnamon warm and sweet on my tongue. As the sun sank behind the trees, I caught a glimpse of golden light from the corner of my eye—winking on and off, faster than breath. And then there was another, and another, and another, until all around us there were clouds of blinking fireflies. The fireflies had come back in force after the star sisters had healed the town; Mama said she'd never seen so many this late in the year, not in her whole life. It was like an echo of those wishes I'd set loose two months ago by the lake in Silverwood, Oklahoma.

For so long, it had felt like that wish—the wish for a forever home of my very own—had brought nothing but tragedy and heartbreak.

But right now, in the twilight of the Welchers' orchard, with Ravi on one side of me and Simon on the other and Charlie laughing with her mama nearby and my sisters across the table, with the scent of apple and spice and change in the air—

I wasn't so sure that my wish hadn't come true, after all.

* * *

In stories, the number three is important.

Three princesses.

Three woodcutter's sons.

Three tasks.

My story is the same:

Three sisters—me, Elena, and Sophie, both of whom I'd have been lost without, even if sometimes I was ready to never speak to them again.

Three fallen stars—plus a fourth, who'd been

swallowed by her own wishes and nearly took the whole world with her.

And three disasters.

Mama always says that disasters are like blessings—both of them come in threes.

My wishes had set in motion a chain of events that included a case of pneumonia, Martha's transmission dying, and nearly all the magic being sucked out of Whistling Ridge—but even so, they'd *also* led to the chance to get to know both my aunts better than I ever had before, undo the hurt of Lydia's curse, and discover that my own forever home was something different than I'd ever imagined.

In stories, the number three is important.

This is the story of how I proved that right.

ACKNOWLEDGMENTS

If I'd had access to a collection of firefly wishes when *I* was twelve years old, I would have used them to wish for the chance to publish a book. The knowledge that this is my third book to fly out into the world is the sweetest gift life could have handed me!

As with all books, *The Stars of Whistling Ridge* could not have come into being without the love and labor of many people. There is one person who deserves a mention right up front: My daughter, Kate, who worked hard to be patient on the long days when she was home from first grade due to the COVID-19 pandemic, and I had to bury myself in editing for this book. I could not have met my deadlines without her cooperation, as well as that of my ever-supportive husband, Mahon.

With every book I write, I am more indebted to my incomparable agent, Elizabeth Harding, whose encouragement, enthusiasm, and keen editorial eye are invaluable to me. I'm also grateful for Jazmia Young, Sarah Gerton, and the whole Curtis Brown team.

My work would be only half so good without the incredible expertise of my editor, Alexandra Cooper, who has a remarkable way of discerning exactly what I want my books to become and guiding me there. The Quill Tree Books team put so many hours and so much love into my little star story; I'm especially thankful for Allison Weintraub, Rosemary Brosnan, Nicole Moreno, Valerie Shea, Gwen Morton, Emma Meyer, and Sam Benson. It is a privilege to be a Quill Tree author! Julie McLaughlin, Cat San Juan, and Erin Fitzsimmons created the most stunning cover design I have *ever* seen—I'll never get over how much I love it, and how perfectly it captures Ivy's journey.

There were so many readers and friends who helped shape this book along the way. Special thanks to Shannon Cooley, Amanda Rawson Hill, Ashley Martin, Jamie Pacton, Elaine Vickers, Kit Rosewater, and Jen Petro-Roy, all of whom offered feedback that deepened and strengthened Ivy and her story. *Extra*-special thanks to Kristin Reynolds, who not only gave the book a wonderful critique, but also provided the inspiration for the title!

I would be lost in my publishing journey without the support of my writing community. I'm especially grateful for our Team Mascara Tracks crew—Amanda, Cory, Kit, Karen, Remy, and Stacy—for being with me every step of the way! To every friend I've shared group chats, Zoom calls, or coffeeshop tables with: thank you for being part of my journey.

Throughout my career, I have had the privilege of connecting with so many booksellers, librarians, teachers, and students. To everyone who has read and shared any of my books: I cannot thank you enough.

In the early days of working on this book, I was lucky enough to win a fellowship from the Literary Arts foundation in Portland, Oregon, for *The Stars of Whistling Ridge*. Not only did the fellowship help give me the time, space, and means to write this book, but it was also a wonderful affirmation in a moment when I was battling with self-doubt. To the Literary Arts fellowship committee: Thank you for everything.

I owe a forever debt of gratitude to my family, near and far. My parents, Russ and Cindy Ray, spent hours of my childhood driving us to my grandparents' home in the Blue Ridge Mountains, and Whistling Ridge owes everything to those magical weekends. My relationships with my brothers and sisters—Jason, Josh, Rachel, Jenna, and Jared—shaped me into the person I am today, and this book is my love letter to the importance of those sibling bonds.

And finally, to you, dear reader. I will never get over the thrill of real live people reading my words. I hope that Ivy and her family come to mean as much to you as they do to me.